Johnnycakes, jerk ch
tart.

Alexandra's Dream offers a culinary cruise featuring the heat and spice of Caribbean cooking. Visit our specially designed demo kitchen and meet our celebrity chefs, Ben Cooper and Victoria Fournier. Trained at the Culinary Institute of America, Ben and Tory have planned cooking demonstrations and lectures to tempt both gourmet chefs and those who simply like to eat.

A native of Anguilla, Ben now runs the Café Rendezvous on the island. Who could know the flavours of the Caribbean better? Tory loves the vibrant spices of the islands and explores the waves of immigration that contributed to the region's eclectic cuisine in her recent cookbook, available in our gift shops. Both of our guest chefs will be accompanying shore excursions, including one to the Café Rendezvous, where you'll see why Ben Cooper's restaurant was just awarded its third star.

But before you rush off to the demo kitchen, remember to search your staterooms for the moondrop pendant in our onboard treasure hunt. The last passenger to find it enjoyed special bonuses throughout the cruise and, as promised, the pendant brought her luck in love.

Let's see if it will work its magic this trip!

SARAH MAYBERRY

lives in Melbourne, Australia. She loves food, shoes, sleeping and reading, and most of all her partner of many years, Chris. After researching this book, her new dream is to see firsthand the beautiful islands of the Caribbean that she has read so much about.

Mediterranean NIGHTS™

Sarah Mayberry
ISLAND HEAT

MILLS & BOON®
Pure reading pleasure

*First published in Great Britain 2008
by Harlequin Mills & Boon Limited,
Eton House, 18-24 Paradise Road, Richmond, Surrey TW9 1SR*

© Harlequin Books S.A. 2007
Sarah Mayberry is acknowledged as the author of this work.

ISBN: 978 0 263 86701 5

61-0608

*Harlequin Mills & Boon policy is to use papers that are
natural, renewable and recyclable products and made from
wood grown in sustainable forests. The logging and
manufacturing processes conform to the legal environmental
regulations of the country of origin.*

*Printed and bound in Spain
by Litografia Rosés S.A., Barcelona*

Dear Reader,

Researching this book was about as much fun as a girl can have without a credit card in hand and a bunch of shoe stores at her disposal. First, there are the beaches of the Caribbean. Pure white sand surrounded by lush tropical foliage, blue skies, crystal-clear waters – is it just me, or is that pretty much paradise? The ports and towns of the Caribbean islands are equally beautiful, with their mix of old and new and their exciting, lively blend of cultures – French, English, African, Spanish.

Then there's the food. Fresh, original, full of life – I think I pretty much drooled through the whole researching and writing process. I honestly can't think of a better backdrop to encourage two people to fall in love – or, in the case of Ben and Tory, to realise that they have always been half in love with each other, despite their differences. I hope you enjoy going on the journey with them, and I hope you enjoy the breathtaking setting of the Caribbean as much as I enjoyed writing it.

Until next time,

Sarah Mayberry

A huge thanks to my amazing partner, Chris, for his patience and sense of humour during the writing of this book. We'll never move houses mid-manuscript again, I promise! Thanks also to the amazing Ms W for putting me in the writer's seat on this one, and to Mills & Boon for inviting me to play with a bunch of talented, amazing ladies.

DON'T MISS THE STORIES OF

Mediterranean
NIGHTS™

CHAPTER ONE

TORY FOURNIER UNZIPPED her suitcase and flipped it open. Inside nestled a host of flimsy dresses, swimsuits, flip-flops and sun hats. She frowned at the bright colors and lightweight cottons. Why had she gone crazy and bought hot-pink and aqua? She only ever wore black, beige or white. Suddenly everything in her case looked garish and cheap and even vaguely slutty.

Great.

Pushing a hand through her straight blond hair, Tory started to unpack. She didn't really hate her new tropical wardrobe. Deep inside she knew that. But she was feeling frustrated and oddly depressed. As she hung her sundresses in the closet in the stateroom she'd been assigned, she forced herself to remember that she was on a luxurious cruise ship, about to sail into the Caribbean for ten sun-filled days. There were about a million worse places to be, and not many better.

Back in New York, for example, it was snowing. People were wearing gloves, scarves and hats and tucking their faces into their turned-up collars as they trudged to work. They could see their breath in the air, for Pete's sake.

And she was about to explore sunny, exotic St. Bart's and Grenada and the Bahamas. What was wrong with her?

She didn't have to go far to unearth the source of her downer: her father. At twenty-nine, she should have been used to his unenthusiastic reactions to her good news. It was his way, that was all.

He rarely lavished praise on anything or anyone, and his only daughter was no exception. All her life he'd greeted her successes with a nod of acknowledgment and little more. When she'd been accepted into the prestigious Cuisine Institute of America to do her chef's training, she'd expected champagne corks and back pats from him. She'd been following in his footsteps, after all. But he'd simply reviewed her course selection and told her to avoid working under Monsieur St Pierre. When she'd scored a publishing contract for her collection of Caribbean-inspired recipes, he'd just looked confused and asked why she was dabbling when she should be pursuing her first Michelin star ranking in a prestige restaurant.

And when she'd told him her publicist had organized for her to come on board *Alexandra's Dream* as a guest lecturer to work in conjunction with a local celebrity chef for a special Caribbean-cuisine-themed cruise, he'd shaken his head in disbelief.

"What about this Caribbean-themed restaurant you want to start up?" he'd asked. "That's just going to go on hold, is it? You know I'm not sold on the idea anyway, but you need to show some commitment, Victoria."

He'd slipped into his chef-de-cuisine tone, the one he used to employ when he was castigating a lowly member of his kitchen staff. Perhaps because he was retired now, he used it on her more and more often these days.

"It's ten days, Andre," she'd said. She'd gotten into the habit of calling her father by his name over the long summers she'd helped out in his former restaurant, the critically acclaimed Le Plat. "My real-estate agent is finalizing a list of properties for me, my backers are in place. This isn't going to interfere with my plans."

Her father had just thrown his hands in the air in perfect imitation of her Gallic grandfather.

"No one will ever take you seriously if you flit about like this," he'd said.

Just remembering the conversation made Tory mad all over

again. She wasn't *flitting*. She had a well-thought-out business plan to have her own restaurant fitted out and up and running within the next three months. She'd scouted sites, finalized a menu. She'd even tapped some past colleagues on the shoulder to warn them she would be head-hunting them soon. Ten days in the Caribbean was not going to derail any of that.

She knew that part of her father's attitude could be laid at the door of his retirement. He *hated* being a man of leisure. Practically his entire adult life had been spent in the stress and drama of a commercial kitchen; playing a round of golf in the morning and flicking through industry magazines for the afternoon just did not do it for him. But apart from being patient, there was precious little Tory could do about that. He'd chosen to hang up his apron—going out on a high, he'd called it—so he was going to have to come to terms with this new stage in his life. Unfortunately, it had been two years now and he was still showing no signs of accepting that his career was over.

Of course, she could have told her father her other reasons for wanting to go to the Caribbean, but he wouldn't have understood those, either, just as he didn't understand her passion for island food.

Her fingers brushed against something cool and metallic in her suitcase as she reached in for another stack of clothes, and she pulled a small photo frame from where she'd stowed it safely between two tank tops. Her brother Michael's bright blue eyes smiled out at her, his handsome face tanned and his curly blond hair bleached white from long days in the sun. He looked so happy, so open. The old emptiness echoed inside her as she looked into his beloved face. It had been eight years, but she still missed him every day. Perhaps it was because they had been twins. Perhaps it was because they'd been best friends as well as brother and sister. Or maybe everyone felt the same aching sense of loss when a brother or sister died, as though nothing was ever going to be the same again.

Cleaning the smudged glass on the hem of her T-shirt, Tory placed the photo frame on her bedside unit. She didn't normally travel with a picture of her brother, but this trip was special. Michael was the reason she'd jumped at the unexpected offer when her publicist had called. She wanted to visit the place where her brother had spent the last months of his life, see the islands where he had been so happy. He'd joined the DEA straight out of college, and his first big posting had been to the Caribbean, working with local authorities, using his pilot's skills to best effect in undercover operations. She could still recall the vivid descriptions of the islands in his letters and e-mails home. She wanted to see the Caribbean through his eyes. Maybe it would help her say goodbye to him at last.

Sighing heavily, Tory crossed to the en suite bathroom to stow her toiletries. She caught sight of her reflection in the bathroom mirror—her blue eyes looked troubled, her skin pale after months of winter. She had the same dimpled chin as her brother, but her nose was more snubbed than his. Her shoulder-length blond hair was starting to frizz a little from a day in the Florida humidity, and she smoothed it with her hand. She knew she was generally considered more pretty than beautiful, but she'd never had a problem with her looks—except for her curly hair. Fortunately a few minutes with her straightening iron fixed that every morning.

She tried a smile in the bathroom mirror. She looked tense, uptight.

Unbidden, words from long ago popped into her mind.

So you can *laugh. I thought maybe you were missing a humor chromosome or something.*

She squelched the rogue memory back down where it belonged—in the X files, never to see the light of day.

Stepping back into the cabin, she picked up the information folder she'd been given when she'd reported to the personnel department that afternoon. Flicking past a detailed sailing schedule, information on lifeboat drills and pages of rules and regulations, she found what she was looking for—a detailed plan of the ship. The cuisine arts center, a purpose-built venue unique to the *Dream,* was on the Aphrodite deck, two decks above her cabin. Officially she didn't hold her first onboard lecture until the day after tomorrow, and the bulk of the time she'd be working in tandem with Jacques St. Clair, a high-profile local chef the shipping line had recruited for this specially themed cruise. If she wanted to, she could just kick back and play at being a real passenger for the evening. But Tory had always been a big planner—she didn't do anything by the seat of her pants unless she absolutely had to.

Collecting a notebook and pen, she pocketed her key card and exited into the corridor. It was only when she started walking that she noticed the faint swaying of the ship. She guessed that after a few days she wouldn't even register it. She'd only ever been on smaller yachts and catamarans, but she was pretty confident she wasn't going to spend half the voyage hugging the toilet bowl. Just in case, however, she'd brought some motion-sickness pills. Like a Boy Scout, she was always prepared.

She decided to take the stairs rather than the elevator and was pleased to find she was barely out of breath by the time she'd gained the Aphrodite deck. All those early mornings at the gym had paid off a little, then. The moment she'd agreed to come on board *Alexandra's Dream* she'd gone into bikini-panic mode, booking herself into every body-blasting, fat-pummeling, trimming, toning class her gym had on offer. Since she was so tall— five feet eight inches barefoot—she'd never put on weight easily, but she'd figured she was already going to be feeling pretty self-conscious about her glow-in-the-dark winter-white body, so there was no reason to compound the misery with a spare tire or two around her middle.

The Aphrodite deck seemed to be made up mostly of staterooms, and she made her way along the corridors until she came to two large double doors. A shiny brass plaque announced the

cuisine arts center. Pushing through the doors, she found herself
in a decent-size theater not unlike a movie cinema, only instead
of a movie screen at the front, there was a state-of-the-art demonstration kitchen facing the rows of stadium seating. She noted that
each chair had a small fold-down table similar to a true lecture
theater, but she doubted many of the passengers would be going
to the trouble of making notes.

She turned her attention to the kitchen itself. The countertops
were granite, and there were three deep sinks along the back
wall. The fridge was positioned to one side, a large double-
doored unit, and when she opened it she saw it was already
loaded with many condiments and basic staples like milk and
butter. There were two ovens, both gas, and she noted that a
series of small cameras had been built into the lighting rig above
the countertop. She guessed that they would be fed live to the
big plasma screens at either side of the stage so that everyone in
the audience could see what was going on on the stove top or
countertop.

A smile tugged at the corners of her mouth as she recognized
the pleasant hum of anticipation in her stomach. She loved talking
about food and she was particularly looking forward to working
with Jacques during the cruise. The kitchen was great, the decor
attractive and she was about to visit the spice islands that she'd read
about and researched so much. What was not to love?

The buzz that had eluded her earlier at last arrived. This was
going to be *fun*.

She was running an appreciative hand along the edge of the
European-designed gas stove, complete with eight burners and a
fish cooker, when the double doors swung open and an attractive
dark-haired woman entered the room. The woman's crisp navy
uniform flattered her curvaceous figure, and Tory guessed she
must be in her late thirties.

"You're Victoria Fournier, aren't you?" the woman said, striding forward with her hand extended. "I recognize you from the photo on your book jacket. I'm Patti Kennedy, the cruise director."

Tory shook hands and grimaced comically. "Pleased to meet you, Patti. I'm almost embarrassed you recognize me from that photo— I look like someone just told me I was about to be audited by the IRS."

Patti smiled readily. "I wanted to make sure you were settling in and to let you know it's definitely worth your while getting to know all the little idiosyncrasies of the equipment before you take your first session. We've had some disasters in the past."

"I can imagine, but I never cook in an oven I haven't tested first," Tory assured her. "Several disasters of my own taught me that one."

"I'll leave you to get acquainted with the facilities, then. But before I go, there has been one slight change to the program that you'll need to be aware of," Patti said. "It won't alter anything dramatically, but you might get a few inquiries from our guests if they notice the substitution. We just heard this morning that Jacques St. Clair has broken his leg."

Tory's eyebrows rose toward her hairline.

"I hope he's okay?" she asked, her mind automatically slipping into crisis mode. She had a feeling she knew what Patti was about to ask her—if she felt up to hosting the entire culinary program on her own, delivering lectures *and* providing the cooking demonstrations. She was so busy calculating what sort of preparation time she'd need to reconfigure the syllabus she'd worked up that she almost missed Patti's next words.

"He's going to be fine. And so are we, happily. Thank heaven we have a captain who enjoys five-star cuisine. He's called on the owner of his favorite restaurant in the region to rope us in another top-drawer chef at the last moment. You've probably heard of him, actually—his restaurant won a third Michelin star recently. Ben Cooper, from Café Rendezvous on Anguilla? The captain and Ben have been great friends ever since the captain fell in love with Ben's food several years ago."

Patti cocked her head to one side, waiting for some sign of recognition from Tory.

It took a few seconds for Tory's brain to do anything but resound with shock.

Ben Cooper. Here. On board the ship, working intimately with her, side by side.

Surely not. Surely fate could not be so damned tricky and contrary?

Belatedly she realized Patti was still waiting for her response.

"Um, yes. I know Ben. We…we trained together at the Culinary Institute," Tory heard herself say.

Patti clapped her hands together with delighted satisfaction.

"There you go, then—it will be like old times," she said.

Tory somehow managed to smile and talk semicoherently for the next few minutes until the other woman took her leave. Then she just stood and stared vacantly out into the empty auditorium.

Ben Cooper. It had been a long time since she'd even thought his name. But now she was going to see him—in just three days, in fact, when he came aboard in St. Bart's.

A shiver of something almost like fear raced up her spine.

I'm not afraid of Ben, she assured herself. *He got what was coming to him. So what if he's still angry with me for what I did to him all those years ago? I'm still angry with him for what he did to me. So we're even.*

Problem was, none if it made a difference to the feeling in the pit of her stomach.

Ben Cooper. She just couldn't believe it.

BEN STARED DOWN INTO the perfect, cherubic face of the baby in his arms, his lips curving into a spontaneous, utterly involuntary grin as Eva offered him a slobbery smile. She was so beautiful. Something tightened in his chest, and he fussed with her brightly colored playsuit for a few seconds as hot emotion burned at the back of his eyes.

For six months now he'd nursed this little urchin to sleep, fed her, bathed her, changed her nappies. He'd shared all the responsibilities of raising her with Danique, his ex-girlfriend, just as any decent man would when he learned one of his guys had gotten past the keeper, so to speak, and scored a goal.

He'd expected to be a dutiful father, at best. The kind of guy who handed over the right amount of child maintenance without quibbling, cooed at how cute the baby was at the appropriate moments and kept a miniature portrait in his wallet for appearances' sake.

She'd sneaked up on him, though, this little cutie with her wide-eyed stare and her chubby limbs and her repertoire of gurgles and grunts. Perhaps it was her utter vulnerability, her absolute trust in and reliance on him. Or perhaps it was the young/old wisdom shining from her big brown eyes.

Whatever, he'd fallen hard. He'd become the talk of the small island of Anguilla, with everyone nudging one another with amusement that the last of the Caribbean playboys had fallen, taken out not by a woman but by a baby girl.

It was true. He loved her. Dearly. Fiercely. Irreversibly.

And she wasn't his.

Danique had told him just last week when she'd come to collect Eva from her weekend visitation. His fling with Danique had been all about fun and no tomorrows, and neither of them had ever pretended it was any different. They'd remained friends, though, when the passion had died out, and it had proved a solid basis for their new partnership. Since Danique had had trouble breastfeeding, Eva had been on a bottle since three months, and they'd shared the load between them as much as possible despite the fact that they lived separately and led very different lives.

Last week, Danique had been unusually quiet as she'd gathered up Eva's diaper bag and other baby paraphernalia, and she'd waited until she was ready to go to drop her bomb.

"Ben, there's something you need to know. Before I was seeing you for those few weeks, I had a…thing going with Monty Blackman." Danique's eyes had shifted over Ben's shoulder to focus on the wall behind him.

Ben had frowned; Monty was a well-known local businessman. He was also a very married man with a high-profile, politically astute wife.

"Eva is his," Danique had blurted as though she couldn't hang on to the words any longer. Tears had stood out in her pansy-brown eyes. "I've tried to tell you so many times, but I was scared of how you would react. You've been so great with her, and then there's the money and everything else…."

Ben had shaken his head. "I'm sorry. I just—I don't believe you."

When he held Eva in his arms, his heart ached. How could that be if she wasn't his?

"I had a test done—you can see the results if you like," Danique had said. "And about the money—I'll pay you back, I promise. Every cent."

Ben had sworn pithily. "I don't give a damn about the money." He'd paced agitatedly, then stopped to frown at her. "Why now? What's changed?" he'd asked. Then his frozen brain had swung back into motion and he'd held up a hand to forestall her answering. "Don't tell me, let me guess. Monty's leaving Angela."

Danique had nodded slowly. "I love him, Ben. I've loved him for years and I only broke it off with him because I knew it was hopeless. What you and I had—that was about me trying to feel like a whole person again after waiting all those years for Monty to be honest about us."

"So I was just an insurance policy?" he'd asked bitterly. "A convenient stopgap until the real guy came good?"

"It wasn't like that," Danique had cried.

But it had been, and they both knew it.

Now Ben smoothed a thumb across the silky curve of Eva's

cheek. She smelled of frangipanis and milk, and he didn't know what he was going to do without her in his life. Danique had promised to let him visit, and he was first on the list of babysitters. But it wasn't enough. It never would be.

"I think that's everything," Danique said as she appeared in the living room doorway, two carry bags in hand. She'd come over to collect the last of Eva's baby debris from his home.

"Okay," he said. He had a sudden urge to simply refuse to hand Eva back, but it passed as soon as it registered in his mind. He had no rights in this situation.

"I've got two shifts again next week," Danique said. She was working at the local kindergarten as an assistant. "If you want, I can drop Eva by…"

He shook his head and took one deep lungful of sweet Eva-scented air before he handed her over.

"I'll be away for the next week or so. Nick Pappas called. Jacques was scheduled to run a lecture series on board his new ship, and they need a replacement."

Jacques's restaurant was situated on St. Maarten, a twenty-minute ferry ride away from Anguilla, but despite the distance, the fact that he'd broken his leg trying to climb a coconut tree while blind drunk was common knowledge.

"So you're filling in?" Danique said. "That's nice of you."

Ben shrugged. He wasn't doing it out of kindness. Even the lesser of his two motivations wasn't remotely kind—wanting to be as far from Danique and a smugly self-satisfied Monty as possible. In fact, he'd been on the verge of saying no to Nikolas, a good customer and a personal friend, when the captain of *Alexandra's Dream* had uttered two words that had made Ben's baser self prick up its ears.

Victoria Fournier.

Tory Fournier, as he'd known her.

Well, well.

He could just imagine her face when she learned at the last minute that she'd been paired with him for a whole cruise. It was almost delicious, if you were the kind of person who didn't forgive and forget, even after eight long years.

He guessed he must be that kind of person. To be fair, he argued in his own favor, Tory had humiliated him in a spectacular way. He'd have to be suffering from a severe form of premature dementia to forget it. As for forgiving… He wasn't a saint. Never had been, never would be.

"I'll bring her by when you get back, then," Danique said awkwardly.

Ben gritted his teeth and did what needed to be done. "Look, it's probably not a good idea. You and Monty have got your own thing going on now. And I've got my life."

His gesturing hand took in the comfortable wicker furniture, terra-cotta-tile floors and mishmash of local art hanging on the walls of his hilltop cottage.

"But I know how much she means to you," Danique said, holding Eva close, as though she were the one being asked to give her up.

"No point in perpetuating the situation," Ben said flatly. "How long do you think it's going to take for Monty to get sick of me butting my head in?"

Danique's expression told him Monty's nose was already on the way to being out of joint.

"It's for the best," he said, moving toward the door so she'd have to follow him. He wanted them gone now that he'd said it out loud.

Danique sniffed loudly as she passed him. She was crying. He tried to feel sorry for her but couldn't. Sure, she'd been in a tough situation. But he was the one who'd come out a loser. Him and Angela Blackman.

Ben shut the door firmly behind her, crossing straight to the fridge to grab himself a beer. He was striding out toward the terrace when he heard the sound of Danique's car pulling out of his gravel driveway.

Outside on the terrace, he braced an arm against the railing and took a long swallow of cold, bitter beer. Below him, the hillside swept down toward the beach of Rendezvous Bay, green vegetation standing in stark contrast to the golden perfection of the beach. Beyond that, the crystal-clear waters of the Caribbean stretched off into the distance.

A brisk ocean breeze cooled his overheated emotions, and he dropped down onto one of the weathered timber lounges he kept on the terrace.

Eva was gone. Many of his single buddies would tell him he'd dodged a bullet. He reminded himself of how unhappy he'd been when he'd first learned about Danique's pregnancy, how trapped and angry and hunted he'd felt. He'd gotten lucky. He needed to keep reminding himself of that.

Somehow, the sentiment just didn't ring true.

Squinting out to sea, he saw a slow-moving ship crawling across the horizon, and his thoughts turned to *Alexandra's Dream* and Tory Fournier.

A feral grin twisted his lips as he contemplated the next week or so. He wondered what she looked like now that she was in her late twenties. She'd been slim when he'd known her, with small, high breasts and long, coltish legs. Her delicate heart-shaped face had been deceptively sweet-looking, he recalled, especially with that beguiling chin dimple. She'd suckered him in for weeks after casually letting him down after their one night together. Then she'd sprung her little surprise. They said that revenge was a dish best served cold. He wondered if eight years qualified as being too cold? Perhaps even…petty?

He laughed into the ocean breeze. So maybe he wasn't about to wreak revenge on her. After all, maybe he'd had it coming a little. But he certainly wouldn't be letting her walk all over him with her elegant designer pumps, flashing those pearly whites of hers and flicking that long straight hair over her shoulder. Eight years ago they'd drawn the battle lines between them, and they were still there.

But he was no longer a gauche island boy intimidated by her family pedigree and industry contacts. He'd had his own successes now.

This time they'd meet as equals. He had a feeling it was going to be interesting.

And he needed something interesting right now. Anything, really, to distract him from the empty space where his heart used to be.

TORY SPENT THE FIRST evening on board familiarizing herself with the ship. Since she'd never been hot on Greek mythology at school, she didn't have a chance in hell of remembering many of the deck names, as they were all named after Greek gods, except for the obvious ones that repeated viewings of *Xanadu* had imprinted on her memory. She managed to find the gym, the cinema, the various bars and clubs, the day spa. And all the while her brain was working like a crazed hamster in a wheel, worrying at the problem of Ben Cooper.

She didn't want to see him again. Not because she was scared of how he might react all these years after her revenge. She didn't want to see him because he'd made her feel so foolish. She'd been charmed by him, besotted and bedazzled. She'd said things to him, done things with him that she'd never done with another man. She was no prude and she definitely wasn't ashamed of any of it. But it made her feel so stupid that she'd allowed him to touch her, to know her so intimately, and all along he'd been playing her.

Just remembering made her grind her teeth together. What a jerk! And what a sap she'd been, allowing him to sweet-talk her into a date and then into his bed.

She could never fully regret their one night, however. And it wasn't about the sex—even if she was willing to admit that he'd been one of the best lovers she'd ever had. It was because he was the person who had given her her first taste of island food. She could trace her love affair with all things Caribbean back to the moment when she'd first smelled his unique jerk spices frying in the pan. She could still close her eyes and remember the meal he'd cooked her that night: succulent, spicy jerk chicken, coconut rundown and his own special take on johnnycakes for dessert. The child of a classically trained chef who believed that French cooking was the only true way, Tory had been blown away by the exciting flavors warring for supremacy in her mouth. Then Ben had talked about Anguilla and his family and the shabby beachfront takeaway stand that he one day planned to transform into a prestigious establishment, and the magic had been complete—she'd been utterly enchanted and enslaved by all things Caribbean.

Stupid, stupid girl. Tory shook her head in disgust over her own past naiveté as she made her way back to her cabin. He must have been laughing up his sleeve at how easily he'd gotten beneath her defenses.

She slammed her state room door with a little more verve than was strictly necessary and crossed to the bathroom to brush and floss her teeth and wash her face. Buttoning up the cotton pyjamas she preferred to sleep in, Tory pulled down the covers and crawled into bed. Yawning widely, she flicked the light off, rolled onto her side and slid her hand under the pillow, her habitual sleeping posture. She gave a gasp of surprise and sat bolt upright when something cold and slithery met her fingers. Fumbling for the lamp switch, she flipped her pillow out of the way, then bit her lip on an involuntary laugh when she saw that the object of her fear was a necklace and pendant. Now that she knew it was harmless, she mocked her childish reaction. What had she thought it was— the world's thinnest snake?

Still smiling, she lifted the necklace and weighed the pendant in her hand. Made from silver and shaped like a solid teardrop, it was slightly tarnished and looked like a much-loved, wear-it-every-day kind of necklace. She frowned for a moment, wondering how it gotten in her bed. The sheets were crisp and fresh, so there was no way that it could belong to the previous occupant. Her frown cleared as she guessed what must have happened—the maid had lost her necklace while cleaning Tory's room.

Checking the time, Tory saw it was still early—barely nine. She could notify Lost and Found that she'd located the maid's necklace; no doubt the woman was fretting.

As soon she'd explained the situation to Lost and Found, however, the woman on the other end of the line laughed loudly and asked her to hold. Tory turned the pendant over and over in her hand while she waited for someone else to take her call, and finally a familiar voice came on the line.

"Victoria, it's Patti Kennedy here. How are you doing?"

Tory was a little taken aback that the cruise director would show interest in something as insignificant as a lost necklace.

"Hi, Patti. Sorry, there must be some kind of mistake. I was just reporting a lost necklace in my room…."

Patti laughed. "You obviously haven't read through your orientation material yet. If you open the folder, you'll see a colored glossy flyer with the heading 'Teardrops of the Moon.' The flyer will explain everything, but basically it's a little tradition we've developed on board where we hide the necklace in a stateroom for one of our passengers to find. According to an old legend, the necklace is supposed to bring good luck, especially in love."

"Oh," Tory said, viewing the pendant in an entirely different light now. Good luck she welcomed, but good luck in love? She didn't really have time in her life for love, not with a book to promote and a new restaurant to start up, let alone the more immediate challenge of keeping dozens of cruise passengers informed and titillated on a daily basis—all while working alongside Ben Cooper.

"Maybe you guys should put it in someone else's room. I mean,

I'm not really a guest, am I?" Tory said. She'd been assigned a stateroom because of the short duration of her stay on board and the lack of availability of other crew accommodation. The pendant must have been meant for someone else.

"Don't tell me—a pretty girl like you doesn't need luck in love?" Patti guessed.

"It's not that," Tory said, thinking wryly of how long it had been since she'd even been on a date, let alone gotten lucky. "It's more I kind of feel like a fraud, being here to work and all."

Patti made a dismissive noise. "Forget it. You're a high-profile guest lecturer, not a dishwasher. I think it's terrific you've found it. But if you really don't want it, you can turn it in to us tomorrow and we'll hide it again."

"Okay. Thanks, Patti."

"Read your orientation folder," Patti admonished lightly before ending the call.

Feeling duly chastised, Tory clambered out of bed and grabbed the folder. Propped up against two pillows, she sorted through the folder until she found the flyer Patti had been talking about.

It outlined the legend behind the pendant, detailing how the moon goddess and a handsome shepherd had had to hide their love from the jealous sun god, concealing themselves under an invisible cloak with a diamond clasp. They'd been caught, however, and eventually punished. The moon goddess had been so inconsolable over the loss of her one true love that she'd cried for days and days and days. Her grief was so great and her love so unwavering that her story came to symbolize the power of true love. One of her tears had hardened over the diamond in the lovers cloak and subsequently, tear-shaped pendants became a traditional wedding gift to remind brides of the enduring quality of love.

As Tory read on, she discovered there were more benefits to her wearing the pendant than just being the recipient of good luck in love. Apparently crew members would single her out for special treats and discounts when they noticed her with the pendant, giving her the experience of being a VIP on board. And, of course, she had to hand the pendant back at the end of the cruise in order for the next passenger to play the game all over again.

Tory studied the pendant for a few minutes. She wasn't even sure if she believed in love, let alone true love. She'd been on the planet twenty-nine years and had never really been in love with anyone. Not enough that she had imagined a shared future, babies, the whole shooting match. Maybe she was just going to be one of those women who poured her passion into her work.

It was a peculiarly depressing thought.

Feeling very self-conscious and stupid, she put the necklace on. The pendant slid down her chest to rest heavily at the very top of her cleavage. Switching the light off, Tory rolled onto her stomach and closed her eyes.

Probably she would hand the pendant back to Patti first thing tomorrow.

But maybe she wouldn't.

CHAPTER TWO

"OKAY, PEOPLE, THAT'S enough," Janice called. "We'll break for lunch. I'll see you back here at two."

Like the other dancers around her, Tracy let her shoulders drop and her stomach pop out. Sweat made her leotard stick to her back and chest, and her knee ached from all the high kicks Janice had made them do, over and over. Even though they all knew the routine backward, forward, inside out, their tyrannical leader and choreographer was a stickler for rehearsal and she ensured that they all went over the evening's routines each day before releasing them for their other onboard duties.

"You're not on vacation," Janice said at least once a day to some member or other of the entertainment crew.

Tracy always wanted to respond with a smart-ass quip. They were floating in the middle of the Caribbean on an enormous cruise ship, they lived in crowded crew quarters up to eight berths per cabin and they worked almost constantly. It was highly unlikely that anyone, no matter how optimistic, could kid themselves that this was anything like a vacation. But she never said a word, smart or otherwise. She needed this job. More than ever, she needed this job.

She sighed heavily as she remembered the phone call she'd had from Salvatore last night. He'd let her talk to their son Franco for just a few minutes before getting back on the line.

"He's fine," he'd said in his flat, cold voice. His business voice. They were just business to him now, her and Franco. "Do your job.

Find the pendant—and get it right this time. Then this'll all be over and you'll never see me again."

Amen to that.

Grabbing a hand towel from her bag, Tracy mopped at her shiny face as she made her way to the elevator and down to the administration level of the *Dream,* determined to "get it right" this time, as Salvatore had so charmingly put it.

She'd done everything she could to snatch his damned necklace on the cruise before Christmas, but fate or luck or whatever it was that decided these things had been against her.

This time it would be different, she promised herself. This time she would find the pendant and get Sal out of her life once and for all. She was convinced the pendant was the only reason he still had any contact with her and Franco. He'd been absent from their lives for months before he'd suddenly turned up out of nowhere and explained he'd scored an audition for her on *Alexandra's Dream.* Straightaway she'd known he wasn't doing her a favor out of the kindness of his heart; he'd wanted her on the ship very badly for his own reasons. She'd soon learned what they were—one of Sal's gambling customers, some guy called Giorgio, had run up an enormous debt with Sal's people and planned to pay it off with a precious antique necklace he'd smuggled on board the ship prior to handing it over to Sal. Great plan, except Giorgio had gotten himself arrested for involvement in the high-level smuggling ring that had been busted on the *Dream* during its Mediterranean run. Sal had been left holding the debt, and the only chance of satisfying his bosses and securing his own financial future was to grab the pendant off the cruise ship himself. Which was where Tracy was supposed to come in.

Tracy smiled grimly to herself as she remembered Sal's fury when he'd learned that the pendant had fallen into the hands of the cruise director and the ship's librarian and promptly been turned into a promotional gimmick for passengers. She'd never heard him swear so much or in so many different languages.

The really great thing was that she was the one stuck with the task of unraveling this mess—or risk losing her boy forever.

It was a depressing thought, and Tracy couldn't even muster her plastic polite smile for the male passengers she passed who tried to catch her eye, clearly liking the look of her tight leotard and workout leggings. She'd never been falsely modest about her looks. Men liked her, always had. She had long legs, good boobs, long dark hair—and, best of all, she was a dancer, a former Vegas showgirl who could shake it with the best of them. For some men, she was a fantasy brought to life.

But she never encouraged any of them, no matter how built or wealthy-looking. More likely than not, they were married. And even if they weren't, she wasn't interested. Being interested was what had gotten her into this mess in the first place.

She took a deep breath and stepped into the administration offices, smiling at the receptionist and wandering idly over to the notice board that covered one wall. To her left was the doorway to Patti Kennedy's office. It was slightly open, and Tracy stood staring at the notice board, trying to come up with some excuse to talk to Patti. The cruise director would know where the pendant had been hidden this trip, and if it had been found already. Patti had helped come up with the scheme to use the pendant as part of the onboard entertainment, and she took a personal interest in the person who found it. Tracy just had to get her talking about the damned thing and surely she'd let slip who had it. But as Tracy read the same staff memo over and over, her mind remained resolutely blank as she tried to come up with an opening gambit. Closing her eyes, she swore at herself. This was why she'd left school early—she'd never been good under pressure, and her end-of-year exams had always been a disaster. Her mother used to say her brains were in her feet. Maybe she'd been right, after all.

Checking her watch again, she saw that she'd chewed up ten minutes of her lunch break already. To hell with it—she'd just wing it, pretend she'd come down to ask about the weather or something. Patti would think she was a moron, but no one expected ex-showgirls to be rocket scientists after all.

She almost had a heart attack when she whirled around, all ready to barge into Patti's office, only to find the other woman standing right behind her.

"Oh!" Tracy gasped stupidly, slapping a hand to her chest.

Patti's eyebrows lifted in bemusement. "Sorry, Tracy, I didn't mean to startle you," she said.

"No, you didn't," Tracy said automatically.

Patti's eyebrows arched even higher, and Tracy shrugged ruefully. "I mean, yeah you did, but it wasn't your fault."

"Were you looking for me?" Patti asked pleasantly.

"Um, yeah, I was just talking with the other girls about the special deal we've got going on with the teardrop pendant," Tracy said, her brain just barely keeping two words ahead of her mouth. "We were thinking that it might be cute to kind of incorporate whoever found it this cruise into the end of our routine. You know, pull them out of the audience and make a fuss of them, tell everyone about the legend, that sort of thing."

Patti looked thoughtful. "That's a nice idea, and I'm sure Tory would enjoy being made a fuss of, but it might be a little late to incorporate it into the routine this time around. Maybe next cruise we could think about it, though. Thanks for the thought, Tracy."

Patti smiled, already turning away. Tracy's palms were sweaty with anxiety. She was so close to knowing who'd found the pendant, but a first name wasn't going to get her anywhere. Usually the winner of the pendant was announced to the crew at some point during the cruise, but Tracy had no time to lose—she had Sal breathing down her neck, wanting action pronto. She needed to know *now*.

Patti was about to enter her office. Tracy opened her mouth to speak, but no words came out. She stared at Patti's door as it clicked shut.

Damn it, she'd missed her chance again. Feeling sick and angry with herself, Tracy strode out into the corridor, away from the curious eyes of the receptionist. She was hopeless at this sneaking-around stuff, absolutely hopeless. Lying and flirting and stealing— she hadn't asked for any of it and she wanted it all to be over. Most of all, she wished she'd never met Salvatore Morena and allowed him to con her into his bed.

Instantly she slapped the thought down. No matter how much she hated him, she could never regret what he'd given her— Franco. Her funny, quirky five-year-old son. Even though she was worried sick about him, about what Salvatore might do if she didn't succeed soon and find his stupid pendant for him, she smiled as she remembered what Franco had said to her on the phone last night.

"I've decided I'm going to be an elephant when I grow up," he'd said confidently.

"An elephant?"

She loved that he hadn't quite grasped the concept that people and animals and inanimate objects were different. Until recently, he'd wanted to be a motor-cycle when he grew up.

"An elephant. But I want to sleep in a bed. A nice big bed made from grass and pillows," Franco had said with his habitual lisp.

The smile faded from Tracy's lips as the reality of her situation hit home once again.

If she didn't find Salvatore's necklace, as he wanted, she'd never see her son again. And she'd just blown her one sure-fire chance to find out who had it this cruise. *Alexandra's Dream* could accommodate up to a thousand passengers. She had nine days— and counting—to find a needle in a haystack.

She clenched her jaw and lengthened her stride as her long

legs ate up the corridor. She'd find out who had it. She had to. She had a first name: Tory. And this time nothing was going to stop her from making her son safe.

THE FIRST TWO DAYS OF the cruise were at-sea days with no port visits. Tory spent her first full day on board experimenting in the demonstration kitchen. The oven was a little hot, she now knew, but the stove top was excellent and she'd fallen in love with the high-end mixer and food processor. As usual, she'd brought her own knives with her, and once she got the measure of the oven and the appliances, she spent some time with her sharpening steel and whetstone ensuring that all her blades were at their best.

She told herself it was because she liked to be prepared, that she'd be doing this no matter who she was sharing the podium with, but she wasn't in the habit of self-delusion—she wanted everything to be perfect when Ben arrived. She wanted to have put her indelible stamp on the kitchen, marking it as her territory and identifying him as the stranger, the trespasser in her domain. So she arranged her reference books on the handy shelf near the fridge and she reorganized the spice and herb jars and reordered the various contents of the kitchen drawers. By the end of her first day she was confident she knew the kitchen and where everything she might need could be found.

The next day she delivered her first lecture to a bright-eyed audience of two hundred odd guests, the majority of them women. After introducing herself and explaining a little about her cookbook, Tory began to outline the colorful history of the food of the Caribbean islands.

"The Caribbean offers a unique selection of cuisines evolved from the many cultural influences that have touched the islands over the centuries. Today, we can trace recipes and ingredients back to the Arawak Indians, the original inhabitants, as well as the French, English and African immigrants who have all made their homes here. One of the first things you'll learn is that Caribbean food is party food, because the island people love to party. Even though true Carnival is still a few weeks away, you'll find pre-Carnival costume parades on every island when we dock."

To either side of the kitchen on the plasma screens, images from her digital library flashed on the screen—spice markets, beachside traders, laughing brown-skinned children, colorful Carnival parades.

"Contrary to common belief, not all Caribbean food is hot and spicy," Tory said. "Island food can be infinitely subtle, but it can also punch you in the face with fiery heat. Over the cruise we'll sample a number of famous islander dishes like jerk chicken, john-nycakes, rum cakes and rum punches. I'll show you how to select the best spices and herbs for your cooking, how to store them and mix them and the best cuts of meat for each dish. Island food is casual, family fare, and most of the recipes we'll explore are simple and don't require elaborate preparation or long cooking times. I guarantee that by the time you go home you'll be ready, willing and able to treat your family and friends to a Caribbean feast."

She spent the remainder of her first lecture familiarizing her audience with the individual cuisines of the various islands they would be visiting, focusing particularly on providing a context for their first stop in St. Bart's the following day. Once she was finished, she opened the floor to questions and spent a further ten minutes elaborating on her lecture. She was flattered to learn that many of the guests had read her book—one woman confessed that Tory's recipes had in fact inspired her to take the cruise in the first place—and by the time she'd said goodbye to the last guest and turned off the audio-visual equipment, she was feeling flushed with achievement.

If it hadn't been for the fact that Ben Cooper would arrive tomorrow morning, she would be a happy woman indeed. She caught sight of herself in the tinted glass of the oven door, and the nervous feeling in the pit of her stomach increased tenfold as she frowned at her wildly curling hair. Okay, Ben Cooper *and* her hair—if she could just fix those two things, she'd be over the moon.

Yesterday morning she'd made the unpleasant discovery that she'd left her beloved hair-straightening iron behind in New York. She'd scrabbled through her suitcase, pointlessly tossing around the few items she'd left unpacked as she'd searched in vain for the trusty appliance. She had a very clear picture of it on her bed at home, cord wrapped tightly around the handle, ready to go in her case. Unfortunately it hadn't actually made it in, and now she was faced with the prospect of being a human fuzz-ball for the entire cruise.

Ever since she'd been a teen, Tory had hated her curly hair. In senior high, before she'd discovered the modern wonder of the straightening iron, she'd worn a scarf to bed to try and flatten her unruly head of hair. By the time she was twenty she had managed to tame the fuzz with salon treatments and daily use of a straightening iron and she'd never looked back. Now, however, she was in a bind. There was a hair salon on board, but it was expensive and already overbooked. She had vague ideas of picking up a new straightening iron in St. Bart's when they docked, but she knew she might not have a chance to go ashore since Ben was coming on board and they needed to sit down and talk about the rest of the lecture series. Short of not washing her hair for the entire cruise, she'd quickly realized that in the short term she was going to have to endure the curls.

Shoving a fistful of golden-blond fluff behind her ear, she turned away from her reflection. Perhaps if she just avoided any and all reflective surfaces, she could pretend she looked the way she always did—cool, elegant, in control. For some reason, it felt very important that Ben Cooper see her that way when he came on board tomorrow.

Ready to finish up for the day, she saw that someone had left a newspaper folded on a seat in the front row. Hoping against hope that it was a *New York Times*, Tory veered from her course to the door to pick it up. She saw immediately that it was a local weekly paper, the *Island Gazette,* but decided to read it anyway. It might not be quite the lifeline to the outside world that she'd been looking for, but it would do.

She didn't see the photograph until she'd settled down in the bar with a glass of single-malt scotch on the rocks. She almost swallowed the whole lot in one gulp when she flicked the page over and saw the boy. There were a number of colorful shots making up the double-page spread on recent pre-Carnival parades on various islands. But her gaze flew to the central photograph—a shot of a delighted crowd cheering on a parade.

There, in the front row, his face turned toward the camera, was a small boy with bright blue eyes and dusky skin. Perhaps it was the startling blue of his eyes against his dark complexion or the fact that he was surrounded by dozens of brown-eyed, brown-skinned children or the fact that he seemed to be looking directly down the lens of the camera. Whatever it was, it made the breath catch in the back of her throat, and she sucked in too much whisky as she tried to recover. She coughed till her eyes watered, the paper rattling in her hands, and she brushed the tears away impatiently. It was dark in the Emperor's Club, the very masculine cigar bar she'd chosen to enjoy her drink, and no matter how she angled the paper, she couldn't get enough light on the image. She surged abruptly to her feet and strode out into the corridor, then stopped to stare intently at the photograph under the brighter light.

Blue eyes. A small, neat nose. Dark brown curly hair. A cleft chin. And… She peered closer and a chill stole up her spine. Just visible on the side of the boy's neck was a birthmark.

Her head shot up, and she glanced first left and then right, trying to get her bearings. She was on the sixth deck, one level above her own. Feeling a strange compulsion, she found the nearest staircase and wove her way through the corridors back to her cabin.

The instant she was in her room she booted up her laptop and scrolled through her digital library until she found her folder of family snaps. She'd scanned in a bunch of images from old family albums a while ago, liking the idea of having them easily accessible no matter where she went. The shot she'd been looking for filled the screen as she double-clicked on it. Her heart pounding stupidly against her rib cage, Tory compared the two faces—the little boy from the paper and the little boy on her computer screen. The similarity between the two was uncanny. Same nose. Same chin. Same eyes. Same birthmark.

The boy in the crowd, whoever he was, was the spitting image of her twin brother, Michael, at age seven.

She knew it could just be a coincidence. Lots of people had blue eyes, even among the islanders, where brown was the predominant color. Plenty of people had cleft chins, too, although it was a reasonably rare genetic trait. But the birthmark… Her eyes traveled from the newspaper photograph of the boy to the old shot of her brother. Just visible against the neckline of Michael's T-shirt was the dull red of a port-wine-colored birthmark. The same birthmark that her father had and her grandfather before him and his father before him. It was a Fournier family legacy, that birthmark, passed on from father to son for more generations than anyone could remember.

So what was it doing on the neck of this blue-eyed, smiling boy?

Her gaze dropped to the caption beneath the photograph. *Crowds welcome the arrival of Carnival season,* it read. She felt a ridiculous sense of disappointment. What had she expected, after all—that the boy's name would be there, listed alongside everyone else in the crowd?

Tossing the newspaper onto her bed, Tory ran her fingers through her unruly mop of hair. What she was thinking was crazy. Surely it was. There was no way that boy in the photograph could be her brother's son.

And yet…

She remembered the way her eyes had zeroed in on him right from the start. The jolt of recognition she'd felt when she'd looked into his face. He looked so much like Michael. And that birthmark… What if he *was* Michael's son? What if there was still a piece of her brother alive in the world, a living legacy? Tears burned at the back of her eyes at the thought. Michael's son. It would be amazing. A miracle. A gift.

Suddenly the utter absurdity of what she was contemplating hit her, and she recalled her mother's parting words at the airport: "I hope you can let go of him at last, Tory. You can't carry all that sadness around with you forever."

She scrubbed her face with her hands, then shook her head at her own thoughts.

What she'd been thinking was impossible. Too crazy. Too convenient. An artifact of her inability to move on from the loss of her twin, nothing else. For eight years she'd missed him every single day. But it was time to move on. What had just happened showed her that beyond a doubt.

You're here to say goodbye, not build castles in the air, she reminded herself.

Snatching up the newspaper, she tossed it in the bin. Moment of craziness gone, she assured herself. Never to be seen again.

Except that night she dreamed of Michael.

They were standing on a beach, the sand stretching away on either side of them, endless, limitless, the water in front of them a bright, crystal blue. Michael was crying, a lone tear sliding down his sun-tanned cheek, his arms held before him in bewilderment, as though something had just been taken from him and he couldn't quite believe it.

She ran to his side, threw her arms around him, welcomed him back. But it was as though he couldn't hear or see or feel her. He just kept staring at his outstretched, beseeching arms.

"Where is he? I've lost him," he said, and her heart broke at how shattered he sounded.

"Who have you lost, Michael?" she asked, trying to make him acknowledge her. "Tell me."

But he turned away from her and walked away.

"Where is he?" she heard him yell at the sea, his voice half angry, half fearful.

And then she woke up.

She was damp with perspiration, her face wet with tears. Kicking herself free of her tangled sheets, she staggered into her bathroom and flicked on the light. She looked terrible—puffy-eyed, shaken.

"It's just a stupid dream," she told her reflection.

But the memory of it stayed with her and kept her staring at the ceiling until her alarm went off at seven.

She sat up and saw the chef's whites she'd laid out the night before. Today was the day Ben Cooper came aboard. So much for feeling cool and in control and elegant. She'd had next to no sleep, her hair was a disaster and she was feeling more vulnerable than she'd felt in years.

Great, she thought sourly. *Way to go, Tory.*

He was going to take one look at her with those cocky, all-seeing eyes of his and know he had her whipped before he even started.

BEN SET OUT HAPPILY enough for his one week sojourn aboard *Alexandra's Dream,* flying out of the airport on the neighboring island of St. Maarten early in the morning. His good mood lasted until he spotted Monty Blackman as he disembarked into the airport terminal on St. Bart's. The man stood out like a sore thumb with his garishly bright shirt in hot-pink and lime-green stripes and his baby-blue golf pants. Was the guy color-blind? And where did he find such ridiculous stuff, anyway? Ben figured he'd have to search every island in the Caribbean chain before he could come up with such a bad-taste ensemble.

The last thing he wanted was to talk to the smug, leathery-skinned bastard. Even though Danique was the one who had perpetuated the fraud that Ben was Eva's father, it was Monty he resented the most—Monty with his oily smile and his string of cheap tourist motels and his bad taste in fashion. It seemed impossible that a child as sweet and beautiful as Eva could have been fathered by someone so unworthy. For the first few days after he'd found out Ben had toyed with the idea of demanding a DNA test just in case Eva was really his. But in his gut he'd known Danique was telling the truth.

Turning a shoulder, Ben took pains to keep a huddle of tourists between the two of them as he made his way to the exit.

"Cooper! Just the man I've been meaning to see!"

Ben closed his eyes in frustration as Monty's voice echoed along twenty feet of concourse. Forcing a neutral expression onto his face, he turned.

"Monty," he said, flicking his wrist over to check the time ostentatiously. "Can't really talk right now, sorry—got a boat to catch."

"This won't take a minute. I wanted to talk about Danique and the little one."

Ben ground his teeth together. *Eva*, he wanted to say. *Her name is Eva. Danique and I named her because you were too busy covering your ass to be bothered.*

"I really don't think now's the best time—" he tried again, but Monty just talked overtop him.

"I know you've been helping Danique out with making ends meet, paying for the little one's odds and ends, medical bills, whatever. I just wanted to make things square with you now that things have been sorted out."

Ben was gripped with an icy anger as he saw Monty pull out his checkbook. "Like I told Danique, I don't care about the money," he said, turning away.

"Stop being so bloody noble, Cooper. Everyone cares about money. It's what makes the world go 'round." Monty laughed loudly at his own joke, and Ben was hard put not to knock the other man's too-white teeth down his throat.

"I'm not everyone. Forget about it. I did it for Eva and Danique."

He started to walk off, but Monty stepped in front of him, his smile fading. Suddenly Ben could see the edge that had helped Monty become a multimillionaire by his mid forties.

"I don't like being beholden to anyone," Monty said. "You looked after my girls for me, and I appreciate it, but I want to put an end to it now."

Ben reached for the last shreds of his patience as Monty signed a check with a flourish and tore it free from the book. The check hung in the air between them as Monty offered it and Ben refused to take it. Shaking his head and smiling to himself, Monty folded the check neatly and tucked it into the front pocket of Ben's white linen shirt.

"You young guys crack me up," he said.

Ben walked away without comment. It was either that or give in to the frustration coursing through him and land one on Monty's overtanned face. Not caring if the other man was out of sight or not, he stopped at the nearest garbage can to tear the check into confetti. He didn't want a cent of Monty's money. He wanted his daughter back—and that was never going to happen.

The encounter left him raring for a fight. He didn't consider himself a bad-tempered guy, but the whole situation had left him feeling cheated and angry, and now Monty had pushed all his buttons, offering him money as though that was all it would take to rectify the situation.

By the time he was crossing the gangway onto the *Dream* he was in a foul frame of mind. Suddenly the prospect of seeing Tory Fournier was a lot less amusing than it had seemed a few days ago. He was in no mood for her cool superiority. In fact, if she gave him one hint of attitude, there was every chance he'd let rip with a few home truths. He smiled grimly to himself as he navigated the corridors toward the cuisine arts center. Perhaps a damned good scream-ing match with his old school buddy was just what the doctor ordered.

Then he walked in the door of the cuisine center and stopped in his tracks. He hadn't given it a lot of thought, but somehow he'd figured that time would only have honed Tory's hard, sharp edges. Back in school, she'd been distant, intense, composed. He'd expected more of the same from the twenty-nine-year-old version of Tory.

But the woman jotting down notes at the counter of the dem-onstration kitchen looked anything but sharp or hard. She was wearing a pair of stylish, tailored checked chefs pants with a bright red tank top, and he saw that her hips were more softly curved than he remembered, her breasts fuller. Her hair was shorter, a riot of curls that teased at her neck and jawline. Her face in profile was gentler, prettier than he'd sketched it in his memory.

All in all, she was totally unexpected. He frowned, feeling a dart of unease.

Before he could pinpoint the cause of his discomfort, she lifted her head and caught sight of him.

For just a second they stared at each other, taking stock. Then he saw about a million security cordons clang into place behind her eyes as she straightened and swiveled to face him head-on.

"Ben."

"Tory."

A small muscle flickered in her jaw as he used the shortened version of her name. She'd invited him to call her Tory on their one and only date, and he waited for her to revoke the privilege and instruct him to call her Victoria. He knew the exact moment she decided that there were bigger battles to fight—she broke eye contact with him and her face smoothed into an unreadable mask.

"You're early," she said, reaching for the white chef's jacket lying on the counter nearby.

"Yep," he said.

He was aware of her gaze darting up and down his body once,

very briefly, as she shrugged into her coat and buttoned the quick-release closures with dexterous hands.

"Probably just as well. We've got our first demonstration before lunch. I wasn't sure what you were planning on cooking, but I've prepared a general talk on spices and jerk mixes."

"I'll be demonstrating some local recipes," he said unhelpfully. He wasn't going to make it easy for her. She didn't deserve it.

She crossed her arms over her chest and cocked a hip against the counter. "That's it? You're not going to tell me any more than that?"

"I'll jot down the ingredients for you, if that's what you're after," he said, shrugging.

He slung his toolbox up onto the bench and started to unpack his knives. Out of the corner of his eye he saw her straighten.

"If you have a problem working with me, you shouldn't have said yes," she said crisply.

Trust her to get straight to the heart of the matter. She never had been one to back away from confrontation.

"I said yes because a friend was in a bind. But beyond that, I don't have a problem working with you, Tory. In fact, the way I see it, I owe you a debt of gratitude." He began opening drawers and inspecting their contents.

"I beg your pardon?" she asked, clearly suspicious.

As well she might be.

"If you hadn't sent me on that wild-goose chase to New York, I would never have met Signor D'Sarro. And I wouldn't be where I am today," he said.

That got her. She opened her mouth to ask who Signor D'Sarro was, but she shut it again without saying a word. She hated being behind the eight ball. He remembered that about her very clearly. It was one thing that obviously hadn't changed.

Spotting the rolling pin, he pulled it out of the bottom drawer and transferred it to the top drawer, along with some wooden spoons, the citrus zester and the garlic crusher.

"What are you doing?"

"What does it look like I'm doing? I'm setting the kitchen up so I can work."

She huffed out a breath. "I already had it set up the way I like it," she said stiffly.

"Tough," he said, shrugging again.

She reached out and snatched the rolling pin from the top drawer before he could close it. "A little common courtesy wouldn't go astray," she said. "I *have* been working in this kitchen for two days, you know."

"Who's the guest chef here, you or me?" he asked, turning to face her.

God, he wanted her to fight back, he suddenly realized. He wanted her to say something so incendiary, so provocative that he'd have every excuse in the world to tap into the bellyful of anger that had been growing inside him ever since Danique dropped her bomb.

"We're supposed to work together, share this kitchen," she said, sidestepping his question.

"I repeat, who is the guest chef?" he asked.

She glared at him. He waited for her to pick up the gauntlet that he'd thrown down.

"You always were an arrogant jerk," she said.

He felt a fierce surge of satisfaction. At last, something he could sink his teeth into.

"*I'm* arrogant? That's pretty rich, coming from the Ice Queen," he said.

The hot retort he'd been expecting from her never came. Instead she paled, and he saw that she clenched her hands into fists.

"Don't call me that," she said with quiet intensity, her voice wavering.

It threw him utterly. He wanted to fight, but she'd just thrown him a curveball. He'd been called a lot of things in his time—insensitive, irresponsible, childish—but no one had ever accused him of being deliberately cruel. He had the sudden sense that if he pushed any harder, Tory might burst into tears.

It was so removed from his memories of the self-contained, coolly poised young woman he'd trained with that he was forced to look away.

But it didn't mean he was going to concede the battle. Tory hadn't changed that much; if he gave her an inch, she'd take charge and start throwing her weight around as though she owned the place. Working methodically, he began to rearrange the drawers once again. After a few seconds, Tory made a small disgusted sound in the back of her throat, then she elbowed her way past him and pulled open the bottom drawer, dumping the rolling pin back in it. Shoving the drawer shut with her foot, she crossed her arms over her chest and challenged him with her eyes.

"I'll just move it later," he said.

"Try it."

"Oh, I will," he assured her.

Her eyes narrowed, and her cheeks puffed out as if she were holding in a few choice words of four letters.

He found himself fixating on her mouth, on the full rosebud of her lips. For a long second he couldn't take his eyes off them.

"If I could have, I would have said no to this—you know that," she finally said.

"Then I guess we're both going to have to suck it up."

She turned away without another word, and he stared at her back for a long beat. It hadn't been anything like the first meeting he'd anticipated. He'd expected the conflict but not her vulnerability, and he didn't quite know what to do with it. Frowning, he got down to work.

CHAPTER THREE

THE TERM *BUTT-HEAD* HAD been expressly invented for Ben Cooper, Tory decided as she forced another smile onto her stiff lips. They'd nearly finished their afternoon cooking demonstration, and if she had a voodoo doll made in his image, she'd twist its head off and throw it in the rubbish disposal.

She bristled all over again as she remembered the way he'd walked in as though he owned the place and started rearranging the kitchen. He was exactly the way she'd remembered him, only more so. More confident. More cocky. More charismatic.

God, how she hated admitting that to herself, especially after what he'd said to her. But it was the truth. Age had not wearied him. Age had in fact been damned kind to him. His body was stronger, more muscular, his face more attractive with its laugh lines and the hint of roguish crow's-feet at the corners of his eyes.

The thing that really got her goat—apart from his born-to-rule mentality in their shared kitchen—was that he patently thought he was God's gift to womankind. It was no wonder, of course, given the way the women in the audience responded to him. It almost made her ashamed of her sex. Word had clearly spread since their morning session, and the number of women seated in the theater had doubled for this afternoon's lecture. And it wasn't because they wanted to hear more from Tory. She had no illusions there. They had come to ogle and flirt with Ben—and, worse, he was encouraging it.

For starters, there was his chef's uniform. Every chef she knew wore a white or black jacket with checked pants. It was traditional, professional. Ben, however, wore a pair of dark indigo wrinkled linen trousers paired with a navy singlet worn beneath his open white chef's coat, the ensemble casually revealing his well-sculpted chest and long, strong legs to all comers. She'd stared outright when he'd come back into the cuisine center after changing.

"You're not going to do up your jacket?" she'd asked him incredulously when he'd started preparing food for their demonstration.

"Nope. Cooler this way."

"No doubt, but I would have thought that safety might rate a little higher than your groove factor," she'd said.

Chef's coats were designed to protect the wearer's torso and arms and be easily removed in case of hot spills. She'd escaped many a burn over the years thanks to her chef's whites.

He'd laughed briefly to himself. "Man, you are *so* uptight. I'd forgotten that. I meant it's less hot this way, not more fashionable. And I won't be working with hot oil, so the risk factor is low. Unless you think this coconut salad is going to leap up and attack me?"

She'd ignored him, just as she'd tried to ignore everything else about him, from his low laugh to the deep timbre of his voice to the fresh, crisp aftershave he wore. It was hard to ignore his skill in the kitchen, however.

She'd opened both sessions, talking about spices in general in the first, then jerk mixes more specifically in the second, explaining, among other things, how many of the strong spices in Caribbean foods had originally been employed to cover the lack of refrigeration in the region and that jerk pork had been brought to the islands by the Cormantee slaves from West Africa in the 1600s. Once she'd finished her spiel, Ben had stepped up and immediately upstaged her with his humor, his stupid exposed chest and his show-off cooking skills.

The audience had oohed at his speed with a knife. They'd aahed when he'd dramatically flambéed some bananas in the pan. They'd laughed when he'd juggled mangoes for them.

And she'd stood on the sidelines and known that her own presentation had been about as interesting as a stale bottle of beer by comparison. Now, watching him invite the audience up to taste-test the meals he'd just demonstrated, she thought of her carefully prepared lectures, all her local information, all the images she'd sourced and organized for each lecture. She'd have to stay up late tonight to revamp it all if she wasn't going to wind up looking like a theology lecturer by comparison for the rest of the cruise.

Which brought her back to why Ben Cooper was a butt-head. He was funnier than her. He oozed charisma. And he was sexy. How was she supposed to compete with that?

And it *was* a competition, she had no doubt about that. She'd caught him watching her out of the corners of his eyes a few times, enjoying her growing awareness that his portion of their dual presentation was a hit and that hers was most definitely a flop.

But the worst thing—the absolute very, very worst thing—was that she wasn't immune to his flashy charms, either. She'd tried with every ounce of willpower she possessed to keep her gaze from lingering on the well-defined planes of his chest. She'd ordered herself very specifically not to check out his cute, tight rear end when he bent to pull something from a lower drawer. And she absolutely forbade herself to respond to a single one of his charming jokes, quips or witticisms. To no avail. She'd stared, she'd run greedy eyes over his sexy butt and she'd caught herself smiling more than once at something he'd said.

It made her feel so pathetic. Especially after the fight they'd had when he'd first arrived. She had no illusions about the way he felt about her—he'd made it clear that he wasn't here to make nice. In fact, she'd gotten the distinct feeling earlier that he'd been more than ready and willing to keep battling it out with her until the cows came home. There'd been something intense and almost desperate in his eyes as he'd goaded her. Then he'd called her that old, nasty name from school, and it had taken the wind out of her sails in an instant.

It was stupid to let something so ancient and dusty get to her like that. Before he'd walked in the door this morning, she'd been so sure that she'd come to terms with what had happened between them. But one look into his navy-blue eyes and she'd been awash in memories….

She'd noticed Ben from the first moment she walked into her first class. Along with every other girl, of course. He was tall, dark and handsome, with a cheeky smile and a laconic charm that encompassed everyone and everything—except, it seemed, her. He'd never once given her one of his lazy smiles. And he'd certainly never run his eyes over her in warm appreciation the way he did with the other girls—not until he had an ulterior motive, that is. She'd told herself that she was too busy acing her way through the Cuisine Institute to care. But she'd cared. She'd noticed him and she'd wanted him to notice her back. And then he had, and she'd fallen into his bed as though it was meant to be.

And the next day she'd learned the truth.

"You just going to stand there or are you going to pack up?" Ben asked.

Tory jolted out of her reverie and blinked at him. "Sorry?" She realized too late that the theater had emptied and they were alone again.

He shot her a searching look, and she busied herself disconnecting her notebook computer from the plasma screens and collecting her notes. She could hear the clang and clatter of him tidying the demonstration kitchen, and when she'd finished stowing her own gear, she automatically reached for a bottle of cleaning spray to wipe down the counter.

"You don't have to do that," he said.

"I can't just stand around and watch you work," she said, spraying cleaner across the counter.

He looked thrown, as if she'd surprised him.

"What? I can't help out in the kitchen now? You want to do your own cleaning as well as all the prep and cooking work?" She dropped the spray bottle and held her hands in the air as though he'd told her to stick 'em up.

"No. You don't have to help, that's all," he repeated.

She frowned at him, then her hands found her hips and her frown turned into a glare. "I get it—you think I think I'm too good to clean, is that it?" she asked.

"You *are* Little Miss Haute Cuisine." He shrugged. "Cleaning up is for the apprentices."

She flinched, stung by his comment. Was that what he really thought of her? What he'd always thought of her?

"You have no idea who I am," she said.

He picked up her cookbook, *Island Style,* and waved it under her nose. "You might be slumming it with us islanders for a little while, but you'll be back serving up chateaubriand and *chausson aux framboises* at Le Plat once you've finished playing around."

She was surprised to realize that he didn't know that her father had closed Le Plat on his retirement rather than pass it on to her. She understood why Andre had made that decision, but she doubted Ben would and she wasn't about to give him more ammunition. He'd just take enormous satisfaction from learning that she'd apparently missed out.

She made a grab for her cookbook, but he held on tight and she had to put all her weight behind it to tug it from his grasp.

"You know what, you *can* clean up on your own," she said, tucking her book under her arm and grabbing her computer bag and notes.

She turned for the door but stopped in her tracks when she saw Patti, the cruise director, standing there.

Hot color stained her cheeks as she wondered how much of her and Ben's exchange the other woman had heard. To say they were being unprofessional was a gross understatement. Immature, childish—both descriptions were much more accurate.

"Hi, guys. Welcome aboard, Ben. Nice to be offering you hospitality for a change instead of the other way around." She smiled at Tory, obviously feeling an explanation was in order. "We try to dine at Ben's restaurant every time we pass through. Best food in the islands."

"You're just saying that," Ben said modestly. "But don't stop—I like it."

Patti laughed. "Plus he's charming, but I'm sure you already know that."

Definitely the other woman hadn't overhead their exchange. Tory felt some of the tension leave her shoulders. Somehow she and Ben had to find a way to get through the next few days without sniping at each other. At least not in public, anyway.

"I came to let you know the captain has invited you both to dine with him this evening," Patti said.

"That sounds great," Ben said easily. "Tell Dominique I'll be taking notes on her secret conch sauce."

Tory rolled her eyes. Dominique Charest was the chef de cuisine on *Alexandra's Dream*. Trust Ben to know her personally.

"The captain's dining room is on the Artemis deck, Victoria," Patti said. "I'm sure Ben wouldn't mind showing you the way."

"Of course," Ben said politely.

Tory waited until the other woman had gone before letting her smile fade.

"I have a map," she said shortly as she turned once more for the door. "I can find my own way."

"Good," he said.

She gritted her teeth, a dozen pithy insults tingling on the tip of her tongue. But he'd turned his back, and she found herself measuring his broad, well-muscled shoulders with her eyes.

Confused, annoyed, flustered, she headed for the exit. How on earth could she find anything about this man attractive when he had such a low opinion of her? And then there was her opinion of him—also low. Positively subterranean, in fact. Really, it was an insane situation, and she hoped her stupid hormones would snap out of it soon. The last thing she wanted was to have the hots for Ben Cooper all over again. God forbid.

BEN SAT BACK IN HIS chair and took a sip from his champagne cocktail. Nikolas had opted to open the French doors on his private dining room this evening, and the cool night air almost made up for having to wear a suit. The one downside to eating at the captain's table, he decided as he eased a finger beneath his collar. He couldn't remember the last time he'd been so trussed up. The Caribbean wasn't exactly known for its formal dress code, but he'd suspected the *Dream* might have different standards and was glad now he'd packed his suit.

His eyes automatically flicked to his watch again, and he felt a curl of annoyance at himself. So what if Tory hadn't turned up yet? So what if he suspected she was lost? It was no skin off his nose, after all. She was nothing to him. In fact, if anything, rather than being worried, he should be actively hoping she *was* lost, that she *would* be forced to make an embarrassingly late arrival. It was the kind of social faux pas that he imagined would send Tory and her blue-blood family screaming for the hills.

Despite himself, he was about to make an excuse to go scout around for her when she swanned in the door. He blinked as he took in the dress she was wearing. Made from some clingy, gauzy fabric in hot-pink and aqua florals, it had a halter neck and a plunging neckline. A single row of soft ruffles ran down the front to the full-length hemline, and the clingy fabric outlined every curve of her breasts and hips faithfully. Patti was on hand to introduce her to Nick and his fiancée Helena, and Ben's eyes widened involuntarily as Tory turned and he caught sight of the back of her dress. Or, more accurately, the lack of a back. Bar the bow that dangled down the line of her delicate vertebrae from where the halter tied, her back was deliciously, decadently bare. The skirt of the dress kicked in just short of indecently exposing the perky curves of her butt, also showcased to perfection by the figure-hugging fabric.

"Nice," he heard someone say beside him, and he turned a frown on the blond-haired guy who'd been introduced to him earlier as a travel journalist. The guy shot him a conspiratorial male smile, inviting Ben to comment in return on Tory's figure. Ben just took another slug of his drink.

He didn't want to find Tory attractive, but it was useless to pretend he didn't. He'd been fighting a losing battle against his libido all day. The truth was, he'd always been hot for her. From the first day he'd arrived at the Institute, his gaze had been drawn to her tall, slim figure. There was something about the way she held herself, the beauty of her face combined with her cool composure. His poor-boy's antennae had told him instantly that she came from money, and straight off he'd understood that she belonged at the Institute in a way that he never would. Then he'd learned who her father was and her grandfather, and his already burgeoning sense of inferiority and insecurity had burst into full bloom. He'd spent half his time at the Institute ignoring her or resenting her, suffering from what he now ruefully acknowledged as a bad dose of small-island syndrome.

Belatedly Ben glanced around and registered that there was only one empty seat at the table—and it was beside him. Before he could do more than swear under his breath, Tory was being ushered toward him.

He inhaled a waft of vanilla and musk as she sat beside him and they exchanged unamused looks at their forced proximity.

"Believe me, I know," she said fervently.

"Feel free to ignore me," he said as he drained the last of his cocktail.

"Ditto," she said.

So saying, they both swiveled away from each other to face the person on their other side. Ben eyed the travel journalist with determination. He despised small talk, but the alternative—tense silence while pretending not to notice how good Tory looked and smelled—was not an option.

"So how are you finding the cruise so far?" he asked.

THE CAPTAIN'S PRIVATE dining room was a revelation. Timber floorboards glowed in soft candlelight, and plantation shutters gave the windows an exotic appeal. The table was a superb slab of honey-colored timber, the linen crisp and white, the table settings divine. The captain himself was a handsome, charismatic man, his fiancée equally attractive and vivacious. That they were wildly in love with each other was ridiculously obvious to Tory. The only fly in the ointment was Ben Cooper. But what was new about that? He'd single-handedly turned her tropical jaunt into a war zone—and they were only on the first day of their enforced collaboration.

Fortunately the middle-aged woman on her right turned out to be good company. Recently retired from the military, Lt. Williams had a host of fascinating stories about her postings throughout Asia, and they chatted easily through the starter and main course. Almost it stopped her from being aware of the man seated beside her. Almost she could ignore the low timbre of his voice, the brush of his shoulder against hers, the sound of his laughter. Almost but not quite. She was feeling just a little edgy as they neared the end of the main course—then she tuned in to Ben's conversation with his neighbor, a travel writer who'd been introduced to her as David, and nearly dropped her wineglass. The instant she heard the words *Cuisine Institute* and *petty revenge* her stomach lurched and she jerked upright in her chair.

He wouldn't dare. Surely he wouldn't dare.

"…if it hadn't happened to me, I probably would have thought it was pretty funny, too," Ben was saying as she turned to face him.

His head was angled toward the man on his other side, but she glared at him nonetheless. She simply couldn't believe he was about to do what she suspected he was about to do. Even Ben could not be that brazen. Could he?

"So, what, this guy just turns up at the Institute purporting to be a representative of one of the best, most exclusive restaurants in New York, and you bought it?" David said skeptically.

Tory's whole body tensed.

"He was a brilliant actor. And it was more subtle than that. This classmate of mine—*Victor*—had set it all up beautifully." Ben shot Tory a loaded look before returning his attention to the man on his left. "He started a rumor that a talent scout from Brown's would be coming to put us through our paces, so when this guy called me out of the Institute's restaurant kitchen after the meal and offered me a job once I'd graduated, I thought it was all aboveboard. I thought I was the luckiest bastard under the sun. I rang home and told my folks I wouldn't be coming back to the family business straightaway after graduation, told them this was too good a chance to learn how it was really done to pass up. Then I hocked everything I owned to buy a wreck of a car and get to Manhattan."

"Then you walked in the door at Brown's…" David guessed, leaping ahead to the coup de grâce of Tory's revenge.

"And they'd never heard of me, of course. Every single goddamned person in the kitchen turned around to stare at me when I announced myself, from the pot scrubbers to the chef de cuisine. I could still hear them laughing when I was back out front on the sidewalk."

"So you had to go home with your tail between your legs?" David asked, shaking his head. "Tough luck, man."

"Are you kidding? For starters, I'd lost my nonrefundable flight home when I decided to head to New York. Then there was the fact that I had told my parents I was going to be this big-shot New York haute cuisine chef," Ben explained.

Tory squirmed in her seat as she felt a dull flush running up the back of her neck. She told herself that Ben had deserved every moment of her well-planned and executed revenge, but still her conscience burned.

"So what did you do?"

Tory realized she was holding her breath, wanting to know, too, how Ben had responded.

"I stood out on the street for about ten minutes, putting all the pieces together until I realized Victor had set me up. I swore a bit. Well, a lot, really. Then I finally realized that I had to find some work or starve. Across the road from Brown's was this dinky little Italian place, Signor Mario's, although the owner was actually called Luigi. He had a Help Wanted sign in the window, so I just walked across the street and told him I needed a job."

"From haute cuisine to spaghetti Bolognese in five paces," David said with an appreciative guffaw.

"Best thing that ever happened to me," Ben said firmly. "The way he ran that kitchen, the way he loved and respected the food he cooked, the way he treated his staff, his customers—I couldn't have had a better mentor."

Tory squirmed again, gripped by an odd mixture of guilt, relief and annoyance. How typical—putting Ben on the spot at Brown's might have momentarily fazed him, but, as usual, he'd landed on his feet. If only she'd been able to move on from what he'd done to her so easily.

To her dismay, she could feel Lt. Williams leaning forward on her other side to join in the conversation.

"I couldn't help overhearing—it sounds just like the sort of cruel pranks that cause so many problems in the military academies," she said, her dark eyes flashing with censure.

"Cruel—I guess I hadn't thought of it in that context before,"

Ben said. "But it *was* a pretty cruel thing to do. That's a good word for it, actually."

He didn't so much as glance sideways at her, but Tory bristled nonetheless. He was using their dinner-table conversation to put her on trial. Any minute now he was probably going to reveal that she was the one who'd set him up, and she'd become a social pariah for the rest of the evening.

"You were at this Institute with Ben, I understand?" Lt. Williams asked Tory. "Was this sort of thing common?"

"Not precisely, no," Tory said, hating herself for blushing furiously. She could feel smug satisfaction radiating off Ben in waves. Before she knew it, she was opening her mouth again. "We certainly had our fair share of frat-house bad behavior, though. And some of that was definitely cruel."

It was Ben's turn to stiffen in his seat, and she felt a surge of triumph. See how he liked it when the shoe was on the other foot.

"There was one girl in our year level who, through no fault of her own, had gained the reputation for being standoffish. They called her the Ice Queen, didn't they, Ben?" Tory tilted her head to one side as though she were genuinely asking him to verify her memory of events.

He nodded minutely and avoided her eye. "I believe that was it."

"Anyway, the guys started a book on who could be the first to get the Ice Queen to melt, if you know what I mean," Tory explained.

David smirked, but Lt. Williams frowned.

"How charming," she said. "I hope no one collected."

"Unfortunately she was a little gullible. I understand she wasn't very experienced with men, so when this one student turned on the charm, she was pretty much putty in his hands."

"Let me guess—she found out about the bet, didn't she?" the lieutenant asked, looking really angry now.

"Yes," Tory said. "But not until afterward."

There was a small pause as they all absorbed this.

"How humiliating," the other woman said in sympathy.

"Yes," Tory said again, more quietly this time as she remembered the stinging hurt she'd felt when she'd overheard Ben's friends laughing at her and talking about the bet.

Out of the corner of her eye she saw Ben shift in his chair and open his mouth as though he was about to defend himself. She waited for him to dare try it, but he obviously thought better of the impulse.

"Wow, and I thought the world of journalism was cutthroat," David said.

The arrival of dessert distracted both of their dining companions for the next few minutes, and Tory smoothed her napkin in her lap and absolutely refused to look in Ben's direction. She couldn't believe he'd brought up their personal history like this in front of everybody. And she couldn't quite believe that she'd taken a shot back at him, either. She wondered if anyone realized that they'd both been taking veiled jabs at each other beneath their apparently innocuous anecdotes. She'd tried very hard not to react to what he'd been saying, but she wasn't certain she'd succeeded very well.

At last she risked a sideways glance at Ben. He was looking at her, she realized. They locked eyes for a split second, then broke contact simultaneously.

Concentrating on her dessert, Tory willed the evening to be over.

AFTER DESSERT, COFFEE and liqueurs were served, the captain invited his guests to move away from the formality of the table and take advantage of the couches and occasional chairs nearby. Ben heaved a silent sigh of relief as he at last moved beyond the range of Tory's perfume.

He'd had worse dinners—but not many. The meal itself had been fine—parts of it excellent—but being trapped next to Tory for two hours had been a new and exquisite form of torture. Every time he'd let his guard down and his gaze wander, he'd found himself studying the swanlike line of her elegant neck or the golden curls teasing at her delicate ears. Several times during dinner he'd heard her low, melodious laugh as she'd talked with the woman on her right, and the hairs on his arms had stood on end.

Then there was the little game of tit for tat they'd played. He was still trying to come to terms with the hurt he'd heard in her voice when she'd talked about their date. And that damned stupid bet…

"More coffee, sir?" a waiter asked, and Ben shook off his preoccupation and held out his cup.

He'd never been the kind of person who dwelled on the past. Besides, she'd gotten her own back. More than gotten her own back, in his opinion.

Glancing up, he saw that Nikolas was crossing the room to join him.

"Captain," Ben said with a half-assed attempt at a salute.

"Maître d'. Sorry, no, it's something else, isn't it?" Nikolas pretended to be confused. "Chef de something or other?"

"Close but no cigar," Ben said drily.

Nikolas grinned, his teeth very white against his olive skin. "How did you rate Dominique's efforts tonight?" he asked, his gray eyes intent.

He prided himself on setting a good table, Ben knew.

"Her sauces are excellent. The fish was very fresh and beautifully cooked."

Nikolas made a low sound of agreement. Neither of them mentioned the slightly soggy berries in the dessert.

"And how are you finding working with Ms. Fournier?"

"Tory is also very good at what she does," Ben said easily.

"Helena swears by her cookbook. She's fallen in love with your spicy Caribbean food."

"If Helena is interested in trying real island food, I'll give her some local recipes to try," Ben said.

Ever astute, Nikolas picked up on the reserve in Ben's tone.

"You don't like Ms. Fournier's cookbook?" he asked with the quirk of a dark eyebrow.

"It's fine. It's just not authentic, that's all."

"What do you mean it's not authentic?" an all-too-familiar voice demanded.

Ben turned to see Tory standing behind him, Helena at her side.

"I was bringing Tory over to meet you," Helena said to her fiancée, obviously trying to smooth over the awkward moment.

But Tory wasn't about to let his comment go. "Well? What's not authentic about my book?" she asked again.

Her cheeks had flushed a becoming pink, the color flattering against her creamy skin.

"For starters, have you ever visited half the places you've written about?" Ben asked.

"No. Have you ever visited France?" she countered.

"No."

"Yet I bet you dare to serve a bouillabaisse in your restaurant, right? And I bet there are a host of other recipes cherry-picked from half a dozen other countries around the world on your menu."

He nodded. "That's true."

"I researched my book meticulously and I worked with dozens of expat islanders in New York. I may not have the same beach view you have from your restaurant, but I know what I'm talking about."

"If I'm willing to concede that my bouillabaisse might not hold its own against a local offering in Marseille, will you concede that as a born-and-bred islander I might just have the edge on you?" Ben asked.

Her chin came up and her hand rested her hip. Despite how annoying he found her, a part of him couldn't help admiring her chutzpah. Did this woman never admit defeat?

"Nope. I'd pit my jerk chicken against yours any day," she said proudly.

"Sounds like a challenge." Nikolas was clearly enjoying their sparring.

"Why not?" Tory said.

All eyes turned to Ben. He shrugged nonchalantly. "It'll be like taking candy from a baby, but if that's what the lady wants…" he said provocatively.

Tory didn't rise to the bait. Instead she smiled a secretive, confident smile.

"Done." She agreed. "My jerk chicken versus your jerk chicken. Time and place of your choosing. And when I win, I'll expect a quote for the review pages of my next cookbook."

That nearly made him choke. He'd rather eat her damned cookbook than endorse it. But she was hardly likely to beat him.

"Deal. And if *I* win…" He couldn't think of what to say because the only idea that popped into his head was so inappropriate and never-going-to-happen that it made him want to shake his head to knock the thought loose from his mind. "If I win, you give me your father's famous secret recipe for port wine glaze," he finally said.

"Still haven't worked it out, Ben?" she asked mockingly. "It's very simple, really."

Very aware of Helena and Nikolas watching their interplay like spectators at a tennis match, Ben stuck out his hand. "Are we agreed or not?"

Her hand was warm and firm as it slid into his. "Agreed."

Helena cleared her throat. "Aren't you forgetting something?"

Ben stared at her blankly and was aware of Tory doing the same.

"Such as?" he asked.

"Who is to decide the winner?" Nikolas asked.

"Oh," Tory said.

"Of course, Nikolas and I might be available…." Helena hinted with a glint of mischief in her eyes.

"Perfect," Ben said. "You two are the judges and your decision is final. We'll use the cuisine center as a base. How does two day's time sound, after we've departed Grenada?"

Tory lifted a shoulder in a careless shrug. "If you need two days to get your act together, by all means," she drawled.

Ben looked down at her, at the flush in her cheeks and the challenge in her blue, blue eyes.

"It's a date," he said.

CHAPTER FOUR

TORY TURNED HER FACE into the cool sea breeze and stared up at the navy-blue sky. Why was it that the stars seemed to sparkle so much more brightly out at sea? She told herself there was probably some incredibly rational scientific explanation, like the fact that there was less ambient light from city streetlights to distract the eye, for example. Not quite as romantic and magical an explanation as a woman might hope for but probably more accurate than putting the spectacular sky show down to there being tropical magic in the air.

Of its own accord, her hand found the silver teardrop pendant hanging from her neck. The precious metal was warm from her skin, and she peered down at it wryly. Perhaps this whole true-love-legend thing was starting to rub off on her after all.

Dinner had been a trial. There was no other word for it. Being forced to sit next to Ben all night, rubbing shoulders with him occasionally, inhaling his crisp aftershave… She'd felt on edge and on her guard through the whole meal. Both before and after his childish attempt to make her squirm.

She dropped the pendant as she forced herself to acknowledge that she'd gotten her own back, which probably made her just as childish as him. She frowned at the inky sea. She really should try to rise above it, tell herself that nothing he did or said mattered.

Turning away from the railing, she reluctantly decided that it was time to turn in for the evening. Tucking a stray curl behind her ear, she started back along the deck, looking for the entrance that would lead her to the elevator bank. Her steps slowed, then halted altogether when she spotted the newspaper folded neatly on one of the sun lounges lining the deck. It had been discarded inside out so that the photograph that had so intrigued her last night was staring straight up at her. She wasn't a superstitious person, but she couldn't just ignore it and walk past. She hesitated, then reached for the paper, lifting it to stare into the little boy's eyes again. Just as she had last night, she felt a resonating sense of recognition. She *knew* this boy. She recognized the soul staring out at her from those clear blue eyes.

Her fingers tightened around the paper. Last night she'd told herself she was crazy to even contemplate the idea that this might be her brother's lost son, but tonight she acknowledged that she'd never stopped thinking about this photograph since the moment she'd seen it. Even when she'd been sparring and sniping with Ben today, a part of her mind had been dwelling on this little boy's face.

Just like that, she made her decision. It might be crazy, it might be a sign that she had more issues around her brother's death than she'd yet acknowledged, but she was going to pursue this. She was going to do everything in her power to find this little boy and verify for herself that he was not her brother's son.

Folding the paper more carefully, she turned to head back to her cabin only to almost walk straight into Ben. They both froze, then took a step backward as though being within touching distance might give them cooties or something. He'd taken off his tie and loosened his collar, she noted, and his hair was wind-rumpled. She didn't need to see the thin line of his lips to know that he was as unthrilled to see her as she was to see him. The air practically vibrated with their mutual antipathy.

"Enjoying the ocean breeze?" he asked after the silence had stretched a little too long.

She cocked an eyebrow at him. "Are we making small talk with one another now?"

He shrugged a shoulder. "Just being polite," he said.

She scoffed. He frowned.

"What's that supposed to mean?" he asked.

"A little late for social niceties, isn't it? I can't believe you brought our history up at the dinner table, of all places."

"Why not?" he said. "I didn't cold-bloodedly set someone up to be publicly humiliated in front of one of New York's most prestigious kitchen crews. I've got nothing to be ashamed of."

She almost swallowed her tongue, she was so outraged. "Nothing to be ashamed of? What do you call sleeping with a woman for a bet?"

"At least we both had a good time thanks to my efforts, which is more than you can say about yours."

She flushed with heat, her gaze wavering from his momentarily. She couldn't believe he was throwing her response to him that night back in her face.

"Don't flatter yourself," she said when she'd recovered sufficiently. "For your information, I faked it."

To her everlasting chagrin, he threw back his head and laughed heartily.

"Oh, wow," he said when he could finally talk again. "Thanks, Tory. I haven't had a good laugh for a long time."

She eyed him angrily. "You are such an arrogant jerk. I *could* have faked it, and you'd never have known."

"No. No one fakes a climax like that, babe," he said knowingly.

Tory closed her eyes for a long, embarrassed beat. Why did it have to be this man who had set her world on fire? Why had he been the one to bring her so much pleasure, to make her feel so special, so precious, that she'd had tears coursing down her face when she'd reached her peak?

"If I could take it back, I would," she said.

"You did take it back. The very next day, I believe. Let me see if I can remember your exact words. 'Thanks, Ben, I had a nice time, but I'm awfully busy right now.' Does that sound about right?"

She was surprised to hear the bitterness in his voice. She recovered quickly—as if her rejection had even registered a blip on his emotional radar! The man was a rat.

"Gosh, sorry. Did that seem a little cold to you after *I heard your friends talking about how you'd scored two hundred bucks for sleeping with me?*" Tory's voice rose with emotion as she relived that moment of horrible realization all over again.

Ben had the good grace to look uncomfortable. His gaze shifted over her shoulder and he shuffled his feet. "It wasn't like that," he said. "And I never took the money."

"Really? I just imagined them laughing and talking about me, did I?"

"I didn't sleep with you because of a bet, Tory, and you know it. We were both there that night. We both know how it was."

She blinked at the sudden intensity in his voice.

"No, Ben, I *don't* know why you slept with me, I *don't* know how it was. All I know is that I trusted you, that I went places with you that I had never been with anyone else, and the next day I overheard your friends high-fiving each other over how old Coop had scored with the Ice Queen."

"Will you listen to me?" Ben demanded, taking a step closer to her and grabbing her upper arms in obvious frustration. "I slept with you because I was attracted to you, okay? Because I'd always been interested in you. Because I wanted you."

Tory stared at him. "What?" She couldn't quite believe her ears.

"I thought you were hot. I always thought you were hot."

His confession would have been a lot more flattering if it didn't sound as though it had been dragged out of him under pain of death.

"Then why didn't you ask me out before the bet?" she asked, bewildered.

All those times she'd mooned over him in class. All those nights she'd wondered which girl he was taking out. And all the time he was thinking of *her?*

He looked over her shoulder. "You didn't exactly make it easy for people to get close to you. Always working alone, always acing every class. There was a reason you got that nickname, you know. I wasn't the only one who called you that."

Tory flinched. He was saying she'd been a snob. That she'd deserved that stupid Ice Queen moniker. He had no idea, no concept of the pressure of being Andre Fournier's daughter and following in his footsteps. From the moment she'd picked up her first whisk and joined him at the kitchen counter at home she'd felt the sting of her father's criticism. He'd always been a tough taskmaster. When she'd decided to apply to the Cuisine Institute, he'd sat her down and spoken words that she would remember till her dying day.

"If you are going to do this, Tory, you have to want to be the best, understand? Nothing else. Never settle for less. Never rest until you have achieved perfection. It is the only way. Or it is not worth doing at all. You understand?"

She'd sat there in her father's study and nodded her agreement, watching him sign her application with a thrill of both fear and pride. She was going to prove herself to him. She was going to ace the Institute and make him proud of her in the same way that she was proud of him. His words had dogged her through all her days at the Institute, through every class, every exam, every practical.

Now she glared at Ben and shook his hands off her. "You're right. Of course you are. I should have gone to more kegger parties. I should have screwed my way through my classmates. Hell, maybe I even should have failed a few exams," she said hotly. "That was pretty much what you did, wasn't it? Just cruised your way through, Mr. Too Cool for School. I should have taken a leaf out of your book. That would have really worked for me."

Ben didn't bite back. Instead his mouth quirked wryly. "It was good enough to get me a ranking in the top ten for our year. Number three, I believe. Where did you wind up?"

Tory swallowed a lump of pure fury. "Number two," she said grudgingly.

"I know how much that must have hurt you," Ben said mockingly.

She could still remember the cold hauteur on her father's face when she'd told him she'd missed out on first place. To this day it filled her with shame that she'd let him down. And then Michael had died....

"Look, I was only joking," Ben said.

Belatedly Tory realized she'd let her guard drop. A dangerous thing to do with Ben Cooper looming over her. The last thing she wanted was for him to feel sorry for her.

"It's hard to take anything you do or say seriously, don't worry," she said acidly.

Ben grinned, the concerned expression in his eyes relaxing. "That's better. I like it much more when you come out swinging."

She stared at him sadly. "Do you? You enjoy fighting with me?"

She hated it. She hated knowing that he understood so little about her. When she'd been in his arms that night, she'd felt as though he'd known exactly who she was.

"I can think of better things to do," Ben said.

She met his eyes and was shocked to see desire there. Although why it should surprise her she didn't really know—hadn't her own heart been pounding out of control for the past ten minutes? Weren't her own nerve endings quivering at how close he was standing? Hadn't she been breathing in his scent and responding to the heat of his body and the million other signals he had been semaphoring to her?

"You've got to be kidding," she said, forcing a note of disbelief into her tone even though her knees had just gone weak.

Ben's eyes dropped to her mouth. She felt a sudden overwhelming urge to lick her lips.

"Like I said, there are better ways to resolve differences," he said.

"Make love, not war?" she asked skeptically. Well, she'd been aiming for skeptical, but unfortunately her voice had come out sounding breathless. Maybe even a little hopeful.

"Something like that," Ben murmured, stepping closer and crowding her back against the railing.

"I don't think this is a very good idea," she said faintly as his head lowered toward hers.

"Then don't think," he whispered as she angled her head to meet his and then they came together in a kiss that had been eight years in the making.

Eight years of anger and hurt and rejection on her part and eight years of resentment and damaged pride on his. Somehow, however, all those negatives swiftly became one big, fat positive as their mouths opened and they gave themselves up to the chemistry that burned between them.

Ben's lips were warm and firm against hers, and he tasted like coffee and good port and fresh ocean breezes. His tongue in her mouth was silky and hard and hot, and she made a low, inarticulate, needy sound as his arms wrapped around her and pulled her tightly against his body. Her breasts flattened against the strength of his chest, one of his legs nudged between hers, and his hands spread wide across her bare back as he urged her closer still. Tory grasped at his shoulders and back, pressing her hips instinctively against him and riding his thigh as he lifted her higher still, his hands cupping her butt now. Murmuring something she couldn't quite catch, he deepened their kiss, angling her head back and invading her mouth with even more demanding heat.

She was on fire. The last eight years dissolved as though they'd never existed, and the two of them were once again alone in his dingy apartment, the remains of their meal forgotten as they devoured one another on his badly sprung sofa. Now, as then, she felt dizzy with desire, overwhelmed by her body's reaction to his skilful, hungry touch. She forgot everything—who she was, who he was, what stood between them, why letting this man under her guard again was not a wise or safe thing to do.

His hand slid up her rib cage, and her thighs trembled as she anticipated his touch on her breasts. Last time, he'd kissed and sucked and bitten her there until she'd been begging him to put her out of her misery....

Then she heard the tinkle of feminine laughter and the low bass of a man responding. Someone was coming.

It was the bucket of cold water she desperately needed. She stiffened in his arms, hands coming up to push him away now instead of pulling him close. He took the hint, breaking contact with her and taking a step backward, his hands dropping to hang loosely at his sides.

She didn't dare look at him as she struggled to catch her breath. Her body was tingling from his touch and his kisses, her heartbeat pounding wildly in her ears. With a shaking hand, she smoothed the front of her dress. Then, finally, she made eye contact with him.

"You don't even like me. Why would you want to sleep with me?"

Ben's face was shuttered and unreadable. She waited a long moment for him to say something, anything, but he didn't. Shaking her head at her own folly, she walked away.

Ben Cooper had suckered her in once before with his charisma and his good looks and his charm. But she was older now. Wiser, she hoped. Never again would she look into his eyes and dream gooey girlie dreams.

This time she knew the score. And she refused to be played.

TRACY RUBBED ABSENTLY at her sore feet as she relaxed on a sun lounge on the darkest part of the deck. She felt faintly guilty being up here, but it was well past the time when paying guests would be vying for her seat. Folding her legs beneath her, she took a few deep lungfuls of fresh sea air and tried to clear her mind of the panic that had been rising inside her for the past few days.

She'd spent every spare second, day and night, searching amongst the hundreds of guests for the new owner of the pendant. She'd woven her way through every bar on ship, passed through every restaurant and café, walked miles of deck—and still she had nothing to offer Salvatore. He was due to make contact tomorrow morning, and she dreaded what he would say when she told him she still had no idea where the pendant might be. A single tear slid down her cheek as she thought of how empty and pointless her life would be if he made good on his threat and took Franco to Italy with him. There were times that it had been tough bringing up her little guy on her own, but she wouldn't be without him for the world.

She took in another deep, steadying breath. There had to be some other way to find out who had the pendant. Maybe she could tackle Ariana, the ship librarian. Patti and Ariana had come up with the stupid pendant scheme between them.

Her body softened as her tense muscles relaxed. She had a plan. It wasn't much of a plan, but she wasn't a private detective. She was doing her best in a crappy situation.

Opening her eyes, she uncrossed her legs and stood, sucking in one last gulp of fresh air before descending to the crew accommodation level and the crowded warmth of her cabin. Tomorrow she would have better luck.

Making her way to the elevator bank, she punched the down button just as a tall, elegantly dressed woman joined her, as well as a group of older passengers. Tracy spared an assessing glance for the woman's outfit, admiring the delicate floral pattern in the gauzy fabric of her dress and her stylish heels. Personally, she'd never be able to pull off the bias cut of the long, slim skirt, but she figured she could make a better showing in the cleavage department since the other woman had the sort of slender, willowy figure that didn't lend itself to knockout boobs like Tracy's.

Tracy nearly gasped out loud as her gaze followed her thoughts and she caught sight of the distinctive silver teardrop resting in the low V of the woman's cleavage.

I've found it. She closed her eyes in a brief, thankful prayer, then opened them with a start when the elevator chimed as it came to a stop.

Trying to suppress her excitement, she stepped in first and turned to face the front of the car. Three other people stepped in alongside the woman. Tracy kept her eyes glued to the floor buttons, watching to see what floor the woman would hit. She bit her lip as floor five lit up, praying for her second run of luck for the night.

Please, please let the woman be going back to her cabin....

Tracy's jaw firmed with determination. It didn't matter if she wasn't. Even though Tracy had had an early start and her feet and back ached, she would follow the necklace around all night if it meant getting her boy back.

The elevator eased to a halt on level five, and Tracy followed the woman out into the corridor. Not wanting to appear suspicious, Tracy fell back, pretending to have a problem with her shoe. The tall woman strode purposefully down the corridor, then stopped nearly halfway down to extract a key card from her small evening bag. Tracy picked up her pace, wanting to make sure she didn't mess up the room numbers.

She arrived at the stateroom door just as it was clicking shut. Room 516. Tracy smiled. She had a room number and soon she would have a name.

And before long she would have Salvatore off her back and Franco safe in her arms again.

FIRST CHANCE THE NEXT day, Tory made her way out onto the deck with her cell phone and checked to see that the signal was nice and strong. They'd docked in St. Lucia that morning, and the busy waterfront was spread out before her. Beyond the dock to her right, the white-painted buildings of the town clustered around a half-moon of pure white sand. The breeze smelled of frangipanis and brine, and she itched to go ashore and explore.

But today she had more important matters on her mind than sightseeing. Digging the notes she'd made in her cabin late last night from her pocket, she dialed the number for the *Island Gazette*.

What followed was a frustrating few minutes as she was put through to one department after another. Finally she wound up talking to the editor himself, Charles Gordon, a well-spoken Englishman who sounded as though he was sitting behind his desk in a bowler hat and pin-stripes suit.

"How can I help you, Ms. Sanders?" he asked after she'd introduced herself.

Tory explained that she was trying to find the name of someone featured in a photograph in the paper's current issue. Charles laughed outright at her request.

"I'm afraid that's quite impossible. Unless the image is a head shot, we never take names or get consents for crowd shots," he explained. "I'm sure you understand how impossible that would be."

"But could you at least tell me where the photograph was taken?" Tory asked patiently. She figured a blue-eyed, brown-skinned boy would be sufficiently rare in the Caribbean for someone to notice him. Even a locale would give her a head start.

"I'm terribly sorry, but no. There were an awful lot of pre-Carnival celebrations that weekend. We do like our parties down here, you know." Charles laughed at his own joke.

Tory's heart sank. "What about your photographer?" she asked in desperation. "Maybe I could talk to him or her?"

The editor laughed again. Tory was getting a little tired of being on the wrong side of an in-joke.

"Oh, the man who took those photos isn't *our* photographer. He's staunchly freelance. But you're welcome to try him—if you can get him to answer the phone," Charles added cryptically.

"Matt Striker is located in St. Lucia, near Marigot Bay. That's just south of—"

"I'm in St Lucia right now," Tory interrupted excitedly. "Maybe I could go see him if he won't answer the phone?"

"Well, I guess it's an option," Charles said dubiously. "He has an office in town, but I doubt he'll be there. I'll give you his home address, as well."

Aware that the Englishman was holding something back, Tory nonetheless wrote down Matt Striker's address and phone number.

"Thank you," she said. "This means a lot to me."

"Good luck," Charles said before ending the call. "I have a feeling you'll need it."

Tory stared at the name and address she'd scribbled down. This man might unlock her secret for her. Who knows, he might even know the boy's name.

Her heart was beating a hopeful tattoo as she made her way back to the cuisine center for the morning session. She told herself it was because she had a lead on the little boy and that it had nothing to do with what had happened between her and Ben last night. They'd yet to set eyes on each other post-clinch, and as much as she told herself that their kiss had been an aberration, some weird manifestation of animosity and history, she still felt decidedly nervous as her steps neared the center.

Reminding herself that she'd survived one whole day of working with him already, she squared her shoulders and lifted her chin. She'd more than proved she could take anything he dished out. Roll on the next battle of wills.

BEN WAS RELIEVED TO find the kitchen empty when he arrived for work. Tory's notebook computer and the various open cookbooks and notes lying around told him that she'd already been and gone, but he welcomed the small respite.

He was still frustrated over their skirmish of the previous

evening and he took his mood out on the food, chopping and slicing in an intense round of activity. The familiarity of it all was calming, grounding, and gradually his whirling thoughts and feelings slowed down.

Leaving him with only the clear memory of her words last night, words that had been echoing in his mind ever since she'd uttered them.

You don't even like me. Why would you want to sleep with me?

He frowned down at his work. He was feeling distinctly guilty about not responding to her heartfelt query last night. Like a heel, in fact.

Because the thing was, he didn't dislike her. Not at all. Apart from the fact that she'd always made him horny as hell, there were a lot of things he liked about her. He admired her skill in the kitchen, for one, and her obvious intelligence. He took his hat off to her courage in fighting to the end no matter what, even if they were on opposite sides of the argument more often than not. When it came down to it, he even admired the fact that she'd gone to the trouble of paying him back all those years ago. Any normal woman would have just steamed around to his apartment and screamed at him when she found out about the bet, but Tory never did anything by halves. And last night he'd pinned her to the spot when he'd paraded her prank in front of their dinner companions, and she'd simply come straight back at him with both barrels blazing.

She was also kind. He'd seen how patient she was with the passengers' questions on more than one occasion. It was more than professional politeness—she cared about people. And she was passionate about food in a way he completely understood. He'd heard the ring of devotion in her voice as she described recipes and ingredients—she loved the art of cooking, the joy of feeding others, the pleasure of creating a sensory feast.

No, there was a lot to admire in her. In fact, the only thing he really didn't like about her was her background.

His knife slowed to a halt as he faced an unpalatable truth. He was old enough and ugly enough to understand that resenting the fact that she'd been born wealthy and he'd been born poor was his problem, not hers. The envy he'd felt when he'd watched her unroll her brand new set of Japanese Global stainless-steel knives in their first practical class; the anxiety he'd felt every time his bank account had threatened to at last bottom out; his self-consciousness when he'd clumsily mouthed the many foreign dish names that had been part of the syllabus, always comparing himself to her faultless, lyrical diction and accent—all his problems, not hers. Also the reason he'd never asked her out—until he'd had the perfect excuse to do so.

He winced as he belatedly realized that using his buddies' bet as a pretext for doing what he'd always wanted to do placed him firmly in the pathetic frat-boy-moron camp.

Then there was the way he'd behaved for the past twenty-four hours. He'd come aboard the *Dream* with a lot of angst on his back and he hadn't hesitated in using Tory as a punching bag. Yes, he had some residual feelings from what had happened between them all those years ago, but she hadn't deserved half the attitude he'd been giving her.

The past few weeks had been tough. Perhaps the toughest of his life. He'd lost the baby girl he'd thought was his daughter. And he had no recourse, absolutely none.

But none of that justified what he'd said to her last night or the way he'd let her walk away without a word of reassurance after he'd kissed her. She'd waited for him to correct her, to reassure her that he liked her even if they did have some messy history, even if they did keep butting heads. But he'd been so confused by his stupid, misdirected anger at Monty and Danique that he hadn't said a word.

A single highly appropriate word floated to the top of his mind: *jackass*. He was a big, fat jackass. With bells on.

He was still processing his realizations when Tory entered. She was dressed for work in her crisp checked pants and white coat, her hair a halo of blond curls around her face. Her chin was tilted high in a gesture he was beginning to recognize as her I'll-take-on-the-world look, and her rosebud mouth primmed into a thin line when she saw him.

"You're up," she said, her tone indicating she took this to be a small miracle.

"Good morning," he replied.

She raised an eyebrow as though she begged to differ and began fussing with some handouts she'd prepared.

Ben took a deep breath. He'd never been a big fan of humble pie, but he'd also never held back when he knew he was in the wrong.

"About last night," he said, and Tory instantly held up a hand in the classic traffic cop's "stop" position.

"No," she said firmly.

"Excuse me?"

"No, we are not having this conversation. I don't want to hear what you have to say about last night. It's irrelevant." She concentrated on sorting her handouts into piles.

"You don't know what I'm about to say," Ben said, propping his hip against the bench to watch her. "I might be about to apologize, for example."

A small frown formed between her brows but she didn't look up. "Still irrelevant."

It was Ben's turn to frown. "Me apologizing is irrelevant?" he asked.

"Yep. I don't care."

Ben stared at her for a beat, then shook his head. "Well, you're just going to have to listen," he said. He was determined to get this off his chest. He didn't like being in the wrong. He definitely didn't like her being on the moral high ground.

"I don't have to do anything I don't want to do," Tory said.

Ben threw his hands in the air. He'd tried. He really had. If she didn't want to listen while he tried to make amends, he couldn't possibly be held responsible, right?

"Fine. Forget about it," he said. "The urge to apologize seems to have passed anyway."

The next ten minutes passed in absolute silence, the only sound the click-click of his knife as he continued to prep for their morning session.

Tory placed one of her handouts on each seat in the first six rows of the auditorium, then returned to her notebook computer to fiddle some more. Ben started to rinse out salad greens, using the retractable spray fitting mounted next to the faucet to hose them off.

What happened next was one hundred percent an accident. Afterward, Ben was absolutely certain of it. But with the mood Tory was in, he was behind the eight ball from the start trying to convince her otherwise.

She had finished with the computer and was walking past when he reached out to adjust the pressure on the sprayer. Unfamiliar with the shipboard pressure, he was overgenerous, and a burst of water shot out of the nozzle, ricocheting off the corner of the sink, under his extended arm and straight into Tory's chest and face.

She jumped backward, spluttering, as he flipped the water off altogether.

"God, sorry," he said. "I didn't realize how much juice that thing has."

Tory glared at him, her chef's coat dripping, her mascara running in rivulets down her face, the curls across her forehead plastered to her skull.

"You did that on purpose," she said.

"I didn't," Ben said. "I swear I didn't."

The thing was, though, she looked kind of cute standing there all bedraggled and wet. He couldn't help himself—he grinned. Just a little grin. A grinette, really. But it was enough.

"You smart-ass. How old are you?" she asked, shrugging out of her coat to reveal a supertight white tank top underneath.

The texture of her lacy bra was visible through the fabric, and he had to tear his eyes away.

"It was an accident," he repeated.

She narrowed her eyes at him, then shook her head as though she'd thought better of whatever pithy comment was on the tip of her tongue.

Shouldering past him, she began to set up the ingredients for the johnnycakes he knew she planned to make for today's class. He eyed her for a beat, wondering if he should push the issue on the whole accidental-dousing thing. Her jaw was set, her mouth pressed into a thin, ungenerous line. Probably not.

Returning to the sink to gather the lettuce leaves, he turned to cross to the counter at the same time that Tory was passing with a carton of eggs, and they almost collided. Something hard but wet cracked into his chest, and Ben looked down to see Tory's hand pressed flat against him, a broken egg oozing between her fingers and down his shirt front.

Tory's eyebrows rose in an expression of patently insincere regret. "Oops. Sorry. It was an *accident*." So saying, she wiped her hand down the front of his shirt to dislodge the last of the egg and walked away with a small smile on her lips.

Ben stared down at the egg running down his chest. "It *was* an accident," he said. "With the water, I mean."

"Me, too. With the egg, I mean," Tory said sweetly.

He watched as she began to measure out flour for the johnny-cake batter.

"You are the most stubborn woman I know. Don't you ever give anyone the benefit of the doubt?" he asked her.

"Not when the anyone is you."

Muttering under his breath, Ben crossed to the sink to clean up. It might have ended there if he hadn't heard her snickering behind his back. He frowned for a second, trying to identify the soft, breathy sound coming from behind him—and then he got it. She was laughing at him.

Two could play at that game. Without stopping to think twice, Ben grasped the sink spray in his hand, hauled the retractable hose out as far as it would go, flipped the water lever and stepped to one side.

"Hey, Tory," he said.

She turned around, and he hit her full in the chest with the spray. Water ricocheted everywhere—across the counter, up into her face, even back at him. Mouth open, head jerking backward, Tory instinctively brought her hands up to try to protect herself.

After he'd slowly counted to ten, Ben flipped the water off. "Now that definitely wasn't an accident," he said poker-faced, and then he burst out laughing.

She was soaked from head to toe, her hair coiled in dripping ringlets around her face, her tank top saturated, her checked pants wet down to the knees.

"You—you—" Tory said, shaking her head in outrage. "I can't believe you just did that."

"Seeing is believing—and it looked pretty damned funny from where I was standing," Ben said.

She didn't seem to know what to do for a moment, then she strode past him toward the towel rack alongside the fridge. Still chuckling to himself, Ben threw the tea towel he'd tucked in the waistband of his cargo pants onto the floor to sop up some of the overspray.

"Heads up, Ben," Tory said.

Automatically he glanced up, only to be hit in the face with a spurt of foamy carbonated fluid.

Blinking and swiping at his eyes, he saw that she'd grabbed one of the tall bottles of local beer from the fridge, shaken it, then aimed it straight at him.

Food fights in commercial kitchens were few and far between, but Ben had had some doozies in his time. The childish glee on Tory's face as she sprayed him tapped straight into his own never-far-from-the-surface adolescent love of chaos. His mouth wide with laughter, he reached for the bowl of tomatoes on the counter and launched one straight at Tory's belly.

It hit her with a splotch just as her beer-gun sprayed the last of its ammunition. Her own face creased with laughter now, she lunged for the bag of flour on the counter, grabbing it with one hand and thrusting the other inside it. Realizing she'd just acquired the nuclear weapon of kitchen warfare, Ben lunged forward—just in time to score a fistful of flour in the face as she threw it at him. Coughing and blinking, he groped for her, but she danced beyond his reach and launched another handful of flour at him. This time he kept his eyes closed and bulldozed forward, but she raced around the other side of the counter and gave a shout of triumph.

"Don't get too comfortable," he warned her when he could see again. Pulling open the pantry, he reached for the big bag of corn flour he'd noticed earlier.

"No!" she protested as he faced her with his booty. "Not corn flour."

"I know. It's so fine. It'll be hell to wash out," Ben said with relish as he stalked her around the bench top. She matched him step for step, ensuring she kept the counter between them at all times, her gaze darting between his hand in the flour and his eyes, her own hand in the now only half-full bag of normal flour.

It was a Mexican standoff, and he had no idea who drew first, him or her, but suddenly they were both standing in a cloud of flour, handfuls of the powdery stuff sailing back and forth between them. He caught her full in the face. She caught him in the ear, then got a great shot straight into his hair. For two minutes there was nothing but the sound of their laughter, outraged cries and hoots of triumph as they scored hits with flour, tomatoes and anything else that came to hand. Finally it was too much for Ben. Dropping the flour, he doubled up with laughter and slid down a cupboard door to sit on the tiled floor. Tears streamed down his face as he laughed and laughed, his stomach aching with it. He sensed rather than saw Tory join him on the floor nearby, and it took them both a full five minutes to stop laughing and crying. Even then, Ben had only to glance across at her flour-white face, her eyelashes spiky with the stuff, to burst into guffaws again.

"Stop it! God, I think I'm going to die," Tory wailed as they set each other off again.

"You look like a snow angel. A really demented snow angel," he told her.

"I don't even have a word for how you look," she gasped. "Ready to be deep-fried," she then said, and they doubled over yet again.

Finally they were both so sore that laughter was more pain than pleasure, and the reality of what they'd done sunk in.

"Crap," Tory said as she stared around them. Flour covered every surface as far as the eye could see. Flour mixed with water and beer, a gooey, gelatinous cocktail of goop. And where there wasn't flour there were squashed tomatoes, their pulp oozing everywhere.

"Ben, what time is it?" she demanded suddenly.

He dusted off the face of his wristwatch. "Quarter past ten," he said.

Her eyes went wide with horror. "Oh, my God. We have fifteen minutes till this auditorium is full of passengers," she said. "What are we going to do?"

The panic in her face touched him. She was such a straight-and-narrow, follow-the-letter-of-the-law nerd. Previously he'd found it irritating, but now it struck him as being very endearing. While he knew it wouldn't be the end of the world if they weren't perfectly prepared in fifteen minutes, in Tory's universe it definitely constituted a disaster of epic proportions.

Pushing himself upright, he brushed the seat of his pants off and went to stand in front of her.

Offering her his hand, he helped pull her to her feet. "We work together," he said simply.

CHAPTER FIVE

TORY WASN'T QUITE SURE what had happened. One minute she'd been mad as hell at Ben, and the next she'd been laughing so hard that she'd been in serious danger of losing her breakfast.

They'd destroyed the demonstration kitchen. There was no other way to describe it. They'd had a temporary moment of insanity—a shared one—and now they had to face the consequences. She could just imagine the look on Patti's face when she heard what had happened. *Disappointed* wouldn't begin to describe it.

All the food they'd prepared was ruined. The johnnycake batter, Ben's ingredients for whatever local secret he'd been planning to upstage her with today, even her computer case—all of it was covered in flour.

Standing in the middle of the kitchen, she was filled with despair.

"We are so screwed," she said miserably.

"Here's what we're going to do," Ben said, sliding an arm around her shoulders in what she could only describe as a fraternal fashion. "We spend ten minutes tidying up like crazy, then five minutes cleaning ourselves up. Anything that's left over we explain as a heavy cooking session this morning—everyone will have heard about our jerk chicken challenge by now. We were doing some trial runs. Agreed?"

Tory tilted her head to one side, thinking about it. Ben gave her a little shake.

"You think too much. Trust me. If we just act as though nothing is wrong, they'll buy it. But I'll need your help in the kitchen, since we've lost all the prepped materials."

"Okay," Tory said, shrugging. "I'm in your hands."

Ben shot her a dry look before he released her. "I think that was how we got here in the first place," he said.

They spent the next ten minutes imitating whirling dervishes. After locking the doors to ensure they had no early arrivals, Ben swept the floor briskly, then sluiced a great bucket of water over it, and they both grabbed mops and began working away. After five minutes, she left him to it and started clearing the counter. Within their allotted ten minutes they'd done a respectable job of the floor, and the counter was empty and flourless. There were still telltale flour sprays here and there on various bits of equipment—the stove top was liberally dusted, for example—but Tory decided she could live with that. Some of her urgency left her. Maybe they'd pull this off after all.

"Okay, that's it. Over to the sink," Ben said.

Tory saw that he'd grabbed an armful of tea towels and turned the oven on as high as it would go.

"I've got my chef's jacket in my bag, but I'm figuring you don't have a spare with you?" Ben asked.

"Even I'm not that organized."

He surprised her by flashing a smile at her. A genuine one, if she didn't miss her guess. She didn't quite know what to do with it. The last time he'd been this charming to her was because his friends had bet him he couldn't bed her. Not a great basis for trust.

Ben grabbed her wet chef's coat from where it was hanging on the towel rail near the fridge and draped it over the front of the oven door. Then he turned to her.

"Head in the sink, close your eyes."

She opened her mouth to protest, but time was ticking away. Meek as a lamb, she did as he said, her hands curving over the metal rim of the sink as she felt Ben move up behind her. She could feel the warmth from his body and the firmness of his thighs and belly as he pressed against her. It felt good. Hot. Sexy. She squeezed her eyes shut more tightly and told herself not to be an idiot. Hadn't she learned anything last night?

But something had happened between them just now. They'd been angry, then they'd been laughing. And now they were…cooperating. It felt weird. But it definitely felt better than the bristling alert she'd been on ever since she'd seen him yesterday.

The hiss of water in the sink had her bracing herself, and then warm water was streaming over her downturned head. She stiffened as Ben's fingers brushed through her hair. She could smell his aftershave, feel his hips pressing against her butt. His fingers brushed her neck, combed against her scalp. She tightened her grip on the sink edge, reminding herself of who he was, who she was. Somehow whenever he touched her, she seemed to forget that at about the same time that her thighs went up in flames.

"You'll have to do your face," he said, aiming the stream just to the side of her head.

Continuing her obedient streak, Tory turned her face into the stream and scrubbed at her gummed-up eyelashes with her fingers.

"Okay. My turn," Ben said after the strangest, most disconcerting two minutes of her life.

He dumped a towel onto her hair and she blotted it quickly as they swapped places. Then she was pressing up behind him, leaning over his broad back to aim the water over his head, running her fingers through his hair to dislodge floury paste.

Because he was taller than her, she had to stand much closer. Right up against him, in fact. Her breasts were pressed against his back as she curved over him, and she felt his chest expand with every breath he took. His hair was thick and springy, and she tried to think impersonal thoughts as she ran her fingers through it, chasing blobs of flour away.

"Time for your face," she said, her voice coming out a little too much on the husky side for her pride's liking.

Pull yourself together, Tory, she ordered herself. *Remember last night.*

It was becoming her mantra.

But she couldn't help but watch as Ben turned his head into the spray and scrubbed at his face with his hand. He looked like a little boy with his eyes closed so intently, the water spiking his eyelashes into dark spears.

Judging he was done, Tory flicked the faucet off and handed him a towel.

She was free to register the dampness trickling down her neck now and she used her own towel to blot at her hair again. She didn't dare look at Ben, but she was aware of him doing the same beside her.

"Passable?" Ben asked, and she was forced to glance up at him.

His hair was shiny with moisture and deliciously ruffled, with tiny specks of flour still dotted here and there throughout. But it would pass.

She smiled with relief. She couldn't quite believe it, but they were going to pull this off.

"You're good. How about me?" she asked.

He stared down at her intently, and she flinched as he reached for her face.

"Hold still," he admonished her, and she felt the warm touch of his hand as he tilted her chin higher. "You've got some stuff on your eyelashes. Close your eyes."

She had no choice but to close her eyes again and endure his touch as he brushed gently at her face.

"You're clear. Let's change and open those doors."

He was already turning away from her when she opened her eyes, reaching for his gear bag on the floor.

"We're going to have to cook on the fly here, but what if we whip up some more johnnycake batter, and maybe some codfish fritters and mango chow. How does that sound?"

Tory was speechless. Not because of what he'd just said but because he'd just dragged his shirt off over his head and she was now staring at the best male chest she'd ever seen in real life. Boy had he filled out since she'd last seen him naked. His shoulders were broad and he had a great tan and his pecs were clearly defined, his abdominal muscles also visible as he flexed to slide into his chef's coat. A smattering of crisp dark curls covered the center of his chest, narrowing down to a sexy trail as they traveled south.

"What do you think?" Ben asked, and Tory gave herself a mental slap.

"Um, sure. Sounds doable," she said, tearing her gaze away from him and forcing herself to turn her back and collect her own coat from the oven door. It was warm but damp; she could live with that.

About to shrug into her chef's coat, Tory glanced down at her flour-and-tomato-encrusted top with distaste. She could not stand in front of a hundred people for an hour wearing a top the consistency of cardboard. Ridiculously aware of Ben standing behind her, she closed her eyes and did what had to be done, whipping her top over her head and quickly plunging her arms into her chef's jacket. As luck would have it, she got the arm holes mixed up and had to untangle the jacket before she could pull it on properly and once again be decent. Telling herself he would have seen no more than she'd show on any beach in the world, Tory fastened her jacket, took a deep breath and turned to face him.

"Okay, I'm ready."

She was surprised to see he was fussing with something at the other end of the counter, his back turned to her. Her gaze narrowed as she realized what he was actually doing—respecting her privacy. Of all the things that had happened between them this morning, it blew her away the most. As did the conspiratorial smile he threw her as he crossed to the door.

"Let the games begin," he said, and all of a sudden she had a flash of what it might have been like if they'd been friends at the Cuisine Institute all those years ago instead of distant peers and then estranged lovers. Ben had an ease about him, a playfulness that invited the world to join him in whatever mischief he had afoot. She'd always watched from a distance as he'd drawn fellow students to him, envying both his social confidence and their sheer luck to be part of his inner circle. But today, right now, she was being invited into that circle. And it felt good. Dangerously so.

Ben unlocked the doors with a click, and a stream of passengers began to file in, some of them looking a little confused as to why they'd had to queue up outside rather than be allowed to trickle inside to take a seat as usual.

"Howdy, folks," Ben said cheerily. "Come on in."

He caught her eye over the top of the passengers' heads, and Tory couldn't help but smile.

She was having fun. With Ben Cooper, no less.

She continued to have fun, too. While she talked her way through her half of the presentation, Ben assembled ingredients for the recipes they'd decided to throw together on the fly. By the time she'd wound up, he'd made more johnnycake batter and had prepped almost half the materials he'd need to make the fritters and the mango chow.

When he smoothly took over from her, she began to slice and dice. But Ben didn't just expect her to act as a highly trained kitchen hand. He explained that Tory would be cooking up the codfish fritters and left it to her to describe the best way to form the patties and what flavors complemented them. They worked together to present the various dishes, effortlessly anticipating each other's moves. But best of all, they bantered back and forth, correcting one another occasionally, teasing one another, the patter between them coming easily and naturally.

By the time the session was up, Tory was on a high. No one had noticed the debris from their food fight, and she'd had one of the most enjoyable shared cooking experiences of her career.

The passengers lapped it all up, too, and there was a buzz of conversation and laughter as they filed out into the corridor.

"I think we officially pulled it off," Ben said as the last straggler exited.

Tory snorted her amusement. No one had even mentioned the flour. Or the fact that they'd both had wet hair or that there was a large tomato mark that they'd missed on the wall near the fridge.

"We were lucky."

"We're professionals," Ben said, poker-faced.

She rolled her eyes at him but smiled nonetheless. "*So* professional."

They cleaned up in silence for a few more minutes, but Tory found herself sneaking glances at Ben every now and then. She felt…uncertain.

She didn't know where she stood with him anymore. Those crazy minutes of comical conflict as the flour flew had somehow burned away much of her animosity toward him. Like a primal scream, only with food. But if she wasn't feeling angry with Ben, she suddenly realized she didn't quite know how to deal with him. She already knew that she found him far too attractive for her own peace of mind. Being angry with him had been the perfect protection against her own weakness. Now that option was gone, where did it leave her?

The sound of Ben clearing his throat interrupted her confused thoughts.

"About this jerk-chicken cook-off thing," he said uncomfortably. "Maybe we should call it off."

She'd forgotten about their challenge.

"Does that mean you've changed your mind about my cookbook?" she asked.

They'd used the mango chow recipe from her collection this morning, and Ben had commented on the strong regional flavors in the dish. Maybe he was going to retract the comments he'd made after dinner last night?

"Your cookbook has a lot of strong points," Ben said.

She narrowed her eyes as she studied him. He'd evaded answering her directly, she noted. "Such as?" she asked.

Ben made another pass at the already clean countertop with the sponge. "The photography is great. And you've gone to a lot of trouble to ensure all the classics are in there and to cover something from all the different subregions."

"You still think you're right, don't you?" she said, calling him on his evasiveness.

"Look, Tory, I was born on Anguilla. I grew up with this food flowing through my veins. Is there something so terrible, so wrong about me being more familiar with it than you? Wouldn't it be *more* unnatural if I wasn't more versed in island food?" he asked reasonably.

She knew he was making a good argument. Some people would probably concede he had a point, even. But her cookbook occupied a special place in her heart. It was the first thing she'd done in her cooking career that had been just for herself and not about following in her father's footsteps. In fact, he'd blatantly *disapproved* of her foray into Caribbean cuisine. He'd argued that she'd be dismissed as a dabbler by the cooking establishment if she began experimenting outside of her classical training. Only the fact that she'd still been burning from his decision to shut down Le Plat rather than entrust it to her had made her stick to her guns. Then the book had been a success, and she'd decided to take the next logical step and open her own Caribbean-cuisine-themed restaurant in New York—a move which had only inspired more disapproval from her father.

It was important to her that her cookbook measured up. She'd invested a lot in it, just as she'd invested a lot in her new restaurant start-up. She couldn't just walk away from Ben's dismissal of her work. It was as simple and as stubborn as that.

"I think we should still do the cook-off," she said.

"Tory…" Ben sighed.

"What have you got to lose? If you're so confident you're the best, it's going to be a walk in the park, right?" she asked him.

"I know I'll win. I was thinking more of our relationship."

She stared at him and he frowned.

"Our working relationship, I mean," he amended.

A tension she hadn't even been aware of eased from her shoulders at his words. He *did* feel the new amnesty that seemed to have sprung up between them. And he didn't want to lose it. She tucked that warm little thought away for later contemplation.

"What's wrong, can't you stomach losing to a woman?" Tory asked, carefully keeping her tone light.

Ben eyed her for a moment, then he shook his head ruefully. He'd read her unspoken message—she was going to defend her professional pride, but she didn't want it to be personal between them anymore.

"You are one stubborn lady," he said.

"I'm going to take that as a compliment."

"I meant it as one…I think," Ben said. Then he flashed her a smile that took the sting out of his words. "You going to be a gracious loser tomorrow night, Fournier?"

She blinked at his sudden use of her last name, then remembered that back in his Institute days, Ben had had a habit of calling his friends by their last names or stupid nicknames he'd made up for them. The inner circle, indeed.

"I don't know. You going to cry like a girl when I whip your butt, Cooper?" she fired back.

"If I cry, I'll go one better than endorsing your book—I'll sell it in my restaurant," he said.

She stuck her hand out like a shot. "Deal."

They shook hands. Was it her imagination or did his hand linger on hers for just a fraction longer than absolutely necessary?

"Like taking candy from a baby," Ben said smugly.

"But who's the baby?" Tory countered.

They grinned at each other, and Tory realized that she didn't want their morning together to end. Now *that* was stupid.

LATER THAT DAY, TORY pushed her sunglasses to the top of her head and scowled down at the map in front of her. She'd walked as far as she could along this rutted hillside track the locals called a road, but she'd still found no sign of the distinct house that had been described to her back in town. Part boat, part caravan, part shed, the woman in the general store had said as she'd given Tory directions to the "house" of Matt Striker, the photographer who'd taken the photo she was so interested in. According to the big asterisk the woman had kindly drawn on her map, Tory was supposed to be standing right in front of this architectural freak show right now. She turned in a full circle, eyes straining for any hint of man-made materials. All around her the vegetation was lush and green. Vines climbed trees, palms rustled in the offshore breeze and everywhere she looked there was nothing but nature, nature, nature. Normally she'd think it was idyllic, but sweat was trickling down the column of her spine and between her breasts, and the minutes were ticking away before she had to be back on board the ship.

Why couldn't Matt Striker have been having a rare day at his office in town?

Shrugging with frustration, she scanned her surroundings one last time, only to freeze as she caught sight of something glinting in the bright sunlight. She stared. It was a window, perched high in a wall of vines. Slowly her eyes saw past the disguise that time and the environment had crafted, and she began to make out the outline of something more geometrical than natural beneath the thick foliage.

For the first time she also noticed the faint trace of a track leading away from the road. She rolled her eyes at her city-girl stupidity. Why hadn't she thought of looking for a beaten path before she'd spent ten minutes staring at nothing?

As she stepped deeper into the coolness of the thick tropical foliage, she began to discern the shape of the photographer's extraordinary house. It was a boat, just as the lady in town had said—a land-bound boat canted to one side, its keel now home to a number of plants and small trees, its hull crawling with vines so thick that from the road it had been perfectly camouflaged. The back of the boat seemed to morph into what might once have been a bus, and then into something that might loosely be termed a shed. She didn't bother trying to classify exactly which bits of the strange structure belonged to which school of engineering, she just wanted to find a door to knock on.

"You brought me my stuff, boy?" a voice suddenly boomed from the boat.

Tory started with surprise, then pressed a hand to her thundering heart and took a deep breath to steady herself. Then she looked down at her yellow top and her white skirt. She wasn't the most curvaceous of women, she knew, but it had been a long time since she'd been mistaken for a boy.

"Um…Mr. Striker, my name is Tory Fournier. I came to ask you a question. The *Island Gazette* gave me your details. I've been trying to call you…."

She gave a yelp of surprise and skipped backward as something came flying out of the boat and landed at her feet, the well-covered ground cushioning its impact.

An empty gin bottle. She stared at it for a long beat. She had a disheartening feeling she knew why Charles Gordon had wished her luck this morning.

For a moment she was filled with despair. What was she even doing here? She was chasing a phantom, indulging herself in the worst possible way. No doubt this whole stupid search was going to be one big goose chase, at the end of which she'd be left feeling just as empty and bereft as she'd been when she started.

Rattled, she pulled the folded newspaper from her shoulder bag and stared down into the little boy's face. Her eyes traced the too-familiar features—the chin, those eyes, that birthmark. Her head came up. She had to know.

"Mr. Striker, I'm coming in," she said.

She found the doorway as she rounded the prow of the ship— a rough opening in the hull with a step leading up to it made from rows of rusted coffee cans with a plank of wood resting on top of them.

Arms extended for balance, she stepped up into the dank darkness of the hull.

The first thing that hit her was the smell—mold and damp wood and alcohol and body odor. She blinked to help her eyes adjust to the gloom.

"Mr. Striker?"

Her answer was a loud, resounding belch. She grimaced and turned toward the sound. He was lying in a rope hammock that had been strung up between the walls of the hull as it narrowed toward the prow. He looked to be in his midfifties, his face puffy from years of drink and furry with two or three days' worth of beard. His once-white business shirt was stained yellow under his arms, and the fly on his mission-brown shorts was open, revealing a flash of pale belly and a square of what she fervently hoped were his underpants.

"Mr. Striker, I need to ask you about a photograph you took two weeks ago during the pre-Carnival costume parades. I was hoping you might be able to tell me who it is in the picture or at least where it was taken."

He just stared at her out of bloodshot eyes.

"Who are you?" he asked.

"Just a tourist," she said. "My name's Tory Fournier. I saw this wonderful photograph you'd taken and I thought I recognized the little boy in it."

Technically it was the truth, and she figured he wasn't up to a full explanation. She offered him the folded newspaper, but he refused to take it. Instead he closed his eyes and waved a hand at her.

"Can't think till I've had a drink," he said grumpily.

Tory opened her mouth to try again, then shut it with a click. Clearly she was not going to get any info out of this man right now. He could barely hold his head up, let alone think straight. Delving into her shoulder bag, she found a pen. She glanced around for something to lean on while she wrote a note, but every surface was covered with rubbish or stacks of photos and magazines. Bending her knee, she rested the newspaper on her thigh and wrote a short, clear note in the margin, circling the boy in the picture and leaving her e-mail address as a contact point.

Dropping the pen back into her bag, she looked around again, this time trying to find somewhere to leave the newspaper where he would be sure to find it when he sobered up.

A pair of well-worn sandals were near the door. They were the only pair of shoes in sight, and even though a glance at the photographer's dirty, heavily calloused feet didn't offer much hope that he actually wore them much, she didn't have many other options. Stooping, she tucked the newspaper page inside his shoe, recoiling a little from the ripe odor of sweat-soaked leather.

"Okay, well, thanks for your time," she said politely as she stood.

Matt Striker's mouth dropped open as his head flopped to one side. A loud snore filled the room.

"Right. See you later, then," she said drily.

It was a relief to step out into the sunshine. As she walked back down the hill, she spared a thought for the man she'd left behind. Somewhere in the world Matt Striker had a mother and father, possibly brothers and sisters. For all she knew, he might even have a wife and children. What had gone so wrong in his life to lead him to a rotting boat and the bottom of a gin bottle in the Caribbean islands? She knew a lot of people came to the islands thinking they were escaping their pasts, only to find that, inevitably, their pasts came with them. It was something her brother had talked about a lot in his e-mails and phone conversations— how the islands were dotted with lost souls looking to escape from themselves.

Reentering the port town of Castries offered a sharp contrast to Matt Striker's rotting, gin-soaked existence. Brightly dressed locals teemed the streets, mixing with tourists, and the sound of tin drums echoed from the nearby market. Everywhere Tory looked there were smiling faces, despite the obvious poverty of some of the islanders and the run-down nature of several of the buildings.

She still had time to spare before being due back on board to prepare for her afternoon lecture. Hoisting her bag higher on her shoulder, she followed the drums to the market. Situated on the corner of two streets in the modern part of town, it was made up of row upon row of locals under brightly colored umbrellas, their goods and wares displayed on sarongs spread on the ground. She saw dasheen, yam, sweet potato, breadfruit, green plantain and bananas on offer, as well as bags of spices, both whole and ground, and locally made baskets and bright batiks. She inhaled the scent of fresh spices and morning-caught fish and she smiled at the locals and bought trinkets here and there for friends back home.

And all the while she told herself that there had never been much hope of finding the little boy anyway. She knew from her research that there were more than seven thousand islands on the Caribbean plate—the thought that she could find one little boy when there were so many places to look was absurd. And, clearly, relying on the photographer would be a gross act of self-delusion. Which meant her search was over.

Head down, she wound her way through the market.

BEN WATCHED TORY FROM a distance, troubled by the haunted expression on her face. He had no idea what could cause her to look so forlorn, and it bugged him.

All that had really mattered to him back at the Institute were the two most obvious things about her—that he wanted her and that she was the daughter of the acclaimed Andre Fournier. Now he wanted to know more—why she looked so sad when she thought no one was watching being at the top of his list.

He watched as she talked with a stall holder selling the local specialty, banana ketchup. She laughed at something the man said, then handed over money for two bottles.

The smile slowly faded from her face as she moved on to the spice stall next door. She looked as though she'd lost something— or someone—he decided. Worse than that, she looked heartbroken. Instinctively he found himself lengthening his stride to draw abreast of her. No matter what had happened between them in the past, he couldn't stand to see her so pensive.

"You know, buying fresh spices from the market is a real art form," he said as he came alongside her.

She gave a little jerk of surprise at his sudden appearance.

"I take it you're a master of the art form?" she asked after a short beat.

"Of course," he said modestly, pretending to buff his fingernails on his shirt lapel.

"Let me see if I can guess what we're looking for," she said, putting on a thoughtful look. "Good aroma. Deep color. Whole spice, preferably, so I can grind it myself to release the flavors. But if I must have ground spice, it should be fine and even." She tilted her head to one side. "How am I doing?"

He glanced down into her face. What was it about this woman that intrigued him so much?

"You're doing okay," he said grudgingly.

She laughed. He felt an absurd sense of achievement at having chased the sadness away from her eyes, even if it was only for a few seconds.

"How do you like Castries?" he asked as they started walking again.

Her gaze skittered off to the side evasively.

"I haven't seen that much. But what I have seen is lovely. Hard to go wrong, really—blue skies, tropical vegetation, clean sand."

"Yeah. Kind of beats the hell out of Coney Island."

She gave him a mock fierce look.

"Hey, don't pick on Coney Island. It's not its fault it's under snow for two months of the year."

The sun gilded her hair, making a golden halo of her curls. He couldn't resist reaching out to wrap one around his finger. Her face filled with caution, and he felt obliged to explain himself.

"I like your hair like this—it suits you," he said, dropping his hand self-consciously.

After last night, he should have learned to keep his hands to himself.

"Left my straightening iron at home." She shrugged a shoulder awkwardly.

"You mean it was like this all those years ago and you *straightened* it?" he asked incredulously.

Her smooth, perfect hair was the first thing he thought of when he recalled their time together at the Cuisine Institute.

"Did you think this was a perm?" Tory asked, clearly insulted.

He was amused to realize she was indignant on her hair's behalf.

"Let me make sure I've got this right—you hate your hair so much you iron it into submission every day, yet you're offended when I suggest your curls might not be natural?"

She looked embarrassed, as though he'd caught her out in a secret conceit. Then a hopeful light sprang into her eyes.

"I could buy a new iron! There must be someplace that sells electrical goods around here," she said, already looking around.

"No."

"No?" She sounded confused. "There's no electrical place?"

"No, you're not buying another torture contraption for your hair."

She gave him a dry look. "Now you're a hairdresser, is that it? A rights worker for heat-stressed coiffures?"

"Just a connoisseur. Trust me, your hair suits you this way." He started to lead her away from the market.

"A connoisseur? Of *hair?*" she asked incredulously.

"No. Of beautiful women," he said matter-of-factly.

She'd been about to argue further, but his words took the wind right out of her sails. He felt the tension in her as he led her through the cobbled streets of the old part of town.

"Where are we going?" she asked after a long beat.

"You can't come to Castries and miss out on seeing the cathedral."

They turned into Bourbon Street and she gasped in awe as she saw the weather-worn Church of the Immaculate Conception rising above its surrounds.

"Wow. It's like a little piece of Paris in the middle of the Caribbean," she said.

Ben put on his best cheesy tour guide voice.

"Italianate in design, the cathedral was built in 1897," he said self-importantly. "Made from local stone, it features some of the finest trompe l'oeil work in the Caribbean."

"It's gorgeous. It looks so out of place but also kind of perfect," she said, craning her neck to admire the bell tower.

"Wait till you see inside," he said.

He didn't want her to miss out on anything. There were so many beautiful places for her to visit in the islands, so many markets, so many interesting buildings....

"I'll draw you up a list of places you have to see at each port," he said out loud.

She shot him a surprised look and he shrugged.

"It's your first visit, right? You don't want to waste your time on the usual tourist traps," he said casually.

But he was frowning as they pushed through the enormous scarred wooden doors at the entrance to the church. One food fight, and suddenly he was leaping and panting around her like an overeager puppy. What was up with that?

"Oh, it's stunning," Tory whispered as they walked past the statues flanking the entrance and into the church.

Ben glanced up at the high, vaulted timber ceiling, then around at the many frescoes lining the walls. He loved this place. He wasn't a religious man, but he always tried to visit the cathedral when he was on St. Lucia. The frantic hustle and bustle of the streets was left outside, and inside there was only the almost in-audible susurrus of locals and visitors praying softly and the quiet shuffle of feet as people admired the architecture and iconography. Today there were several bowed heads in the pews, and neither he nor Tory spoke as they walked around the perimeter of the church.

He enjoyed the way Tory's face lit up when she saw the first of the frescoes up close and took in the fact that many of the saints were black, in deference to the local culture. Some of the frescoes were old and faded, but a larger number had been restored recently and were as brilliantly colorful as the day they were created.

He fell back as Tory moved farther along, clearly enthralled. Leaning against a pillar, he tried not to follow her progress.

It was a losing battle. He couldn't take his eyes off her. Which inspired a pretty fundamental question: what the hell did he think he was doing?

Their ridiculous fight this morning had cleared the air between them, it was true, but he had no idea what had led him to hook up with her in the market just now. She'd looked a little wistful, but so what? His life wasn't exactly a ball of laughs at the moment, either. Making Tory happy wasn't one of the driving forces in his life. Far from it. At best, she was a colleague, albeit one that he was slowly beginning to respect. But that was it. Definitely that was it.

Ben pushed himself away from the pillar. There was something about lying to himself in a church that made him feel doubly stupid.

Just admit it—you want her, he told himself. *Get it out in the open, deal with it. Because it's never going to happen.*

Even though he was already utterly convinced, Ben outlined all his arguments to himself anyway. For starters, the cruise only went for a handful of days, and he was disembarking in the Bahamas before the ship docked back in Fort Lauderdale. He might not know Tory as well as he should after going to class with her every day for three years and spending one amazing night with her, but he knew she wasn't a holiday-fling kind of woman. Which meant she was off-limits. No escape clauses. No get out-of-jail-free cards. No excuses, no matter how much he wanted to run his hands over her body again. Sex with Tory would only buy him trouble.

In the interest of removing himself from temptation, Ben joined Tory where she was studying one of the stations of the cross.

"Listen, I'll see you back on board," he said quietly, not quite meeting her eye. He could tell she was surprised at his abrupt departure. "I've got some errands to run," he fudged.

"Sure. Thanks for bringing me here," she said. "I appreciate it."

Even though he told himself to just turn around and walk away, he couldn't resist making eye contact with her one last time. They stared at each other for a long, tense moment, then Ben took a step backward and waved a hand awkwardly.

His footsteps beat a rapid tattoo on the stone-flagged floor as he headed for the door and sanity. Tory Fournier was off-limits. He had to get that through his thick skull.

Problem was, he'd never been very good at self-denial.

CHAPTER SIX

TRACY'S SHOULDERS WERE stiff with tension as she walked down the corridor toward Victoria Fournier's stateroom. She now knew everything there was to know about the woman who had found the pendant—her full name, her date of birth and passport number, her role as guest lecturer on the cruise, even her home contact details.

Her concierge friend had been very obliging in allowing her to use his access terminal to verify a guest's details. She'd pretended that she'd met Tory in one of the bars and that the other woman had left her evening wrap behind. Her concierge friend had offered to have the wrap returned to Tory's room, but Tracy had spun a line about her and Tory really hitting it off and wanting to catch up with her again.

It had been too easy to get what she wanted, mostly because her friends and colleagues trusted her. Ever since she'd fallen into this mess she'd come to understand how easy it was for Salvatore and others like him to slip beneath the radar and sneak their way into people's lives. Ordinary people didn't suspect the motives of others. Ordinary people relied on common humanity and decency to keep them safe, making the mistake of believing that everyone shared their values. It was why she'd married Salvatore, for Pete's sake. She'd believe the bull he'd spun her. And now she was lying and stealing and setting people up because he had her in the palm of his hand.

Stopping in front of room 516, Tracy glanced over her shoulder before swiping the master key card she'd "borrowed" from her friend in housekeeping. Twisting the handle quietly, she cracked the door a fraction, then rapped on the door frame sharply.

"Housekeeping," she said, ears straining for any sound from within the stateroom.

When silence greeted her, she pushed the door fully open and entered the room. The bed had already been made up, she saw, and she quickly stepped left and ducked her head into the en suite to confirm she was definitely alone.

She saw nothing but her own pale reflection in the bathroom mirror and she told herself to calm down. But despite the fact that she'd concocted what she hoped was a believable story if she was busted in the room, her heart was still beating fit to burst and she had a ridiculous urge to go to the bathroom. Rolling her eyes at her body's stupid fight-or-flight reaction—how was needing to go to the toilet supposed to help her in a crisis?—she began to search the room.

There was no sign of the pendant on top of the bedside stands, so she unzipped the suitcase stowed against the wall. It was empty, but Tracy wasn't surprised—most people unpacked as soon as they arrived since space was at a premium in the cabins. Dragging the built-in drawers open one by one, she flicked through a pile of expensive underwear, then through a stack of tanks and pyjamas and workout gear.

Nothing. Her heartbeat picked up even further as her anxiety slid up a notch. She'd banked so much on the pendant being here.

Swearing under her breath, Tracy slammed the last drawer shut.

It was that stupid damned true-love legend. No doubt this Victoria Fournier person thought she had a good chance of scoring if she kept the lucky charm around her neck twenty-four hours a day.

Hope fading, Tracy nonetheless did a quick check of the en suite to ensure the pendant wasn't stored among Victoria's toiletries or on the vanity somewhere. Again nothing.

Damn.

Salvatore had told her he'd have a guy meet her tomorrow in Grenada once she lifted the pendant. She had no way of contacting Salvatore until then and now she was going to have to tell whoever it was that she didn't have it. She knew what would happen then—Salvatore would get mean. Which probably meant she wouldn't get to talk to Franco for the rest of the cruise.

Angry tears pricked the back of her eyes, and Tracy swiped a hand across her face. What good were tears to her? They weren't going to fix anything or make her feel better. They were about as helpful as needing to go to the bathroom when something stressful was going down—in other words, useless and pointless.

Unable to give up just yet, she dropped to her knees and lifted the skirt on the bed, just on the off chance that the catch had failed on the pendant and it had landed on the floor or something. She found two dust bunnies and the wrapper off a stick of gum but no pendant.

Giving up, she scanned the room to ensure everything looked the way she'd found it, then cracked the door and used the narrow opening to ensure no one was coming along the corridor to her right. It was impossible to check the other direction without opening the door fully, so she squared her shoulders, lifted her chin and did her best to look like she could afford to stay in a luxury stateroom. Then she sailed out the door, pulling it shut behind her as though she were the Queen of Sheba.

An older man was letting himself into his room two doors up, but Tracy ignored him. She didn't slow her pace until she'd gained the elevator bank.

The adrenaline was draining from her system by then and she felt a little sick and shaky. She was the unluckiest woman on the planet. Why couldn't the pendant have been in the room?

She thought briefly of Bob, the passenger who'd gotten involved with the pendant on the cruise before Christmas. Even though he'd pretty much been a sleazy jerk, she still felt sick when she remembered his injuries after Salvatore had arranged for his thugs to attack him, trying to regain the pendant. She would hate for something like that to happen again. But she knew that if Salvatore thought it was the only way to get what he wanted, he would do whatever it took.

A chill raced up her spine and she rubbed her bare arms. She just wanted this all to be over.

TORY FELT STRANGELY alone after Ben left her in the cathedral. Perhaps not so strange, since she essentially *was* alone, despite the other visitors in the church. But even though she'd been surprised by his approach in the market and even more surprised when he'd led her to the church, she'd also been warmed by his obvious desire to show her *his* St. Lucia. She'd felt special, as though her happiness and enjoyment mattered to Ben. And then he'd bailed on her with no explanation, leaving her feeling distinctly abandoned.

Inevitably her thoughts turned to Michael as she reflected that feeling abandoned had been more or less a constant state since his death. As a twin, she'd never really been alone. She had always had someone to play with, someone to fight with, someone to offer her sympathy or a kick up the rear when she needed it. Even when they weren't physically together, she'd always known that she was part of a whole, half of Michael and Victoria, the daring duo, the troublesome twins. Then Michael's plane had gone down off the coast of Barbados and she'd become a solo act….

She tried to shake off her melancholy mood, but for some reason she was feeling her aloneness more acutely than ever today.

Blinking in the bright sunlight as she emerged from the church, Tory checked her watch. She still had a half hour up her sleeve before she absolutely had to be back on board the ship and she frowned at her shoes for a long moment, aware that a big part of her wanted to rush back to the ship because that was where she was most likely to bump into Ben again. It was the Cuisine Institute all over again—except she was twenty-nine now instead of twenty-one.

Forcing her steps away from the docks, she meandered her way back through the streets, stopping to admire some of the pretty colonial architecture along the way. A sign caught her eye as she neared the market again, and an idea that had been bubbling in the back of her mind suddenly floated to the surface of her consciousness.

Why send a postcard when you can call home anytime? the sign read above an advertisement for international calling cards. Tory stared at it, then scrambled in her bag for her cell phone. She punched in the number for her parents' home without hesitation.

Michael had sent her a stack of postcards, letters and e-mails when he'd been stationed in the Caribbean with the DEA, working with local authorities to intercept drug runners. For twelve months he'd taunted her with tales of brilliant sunny days and clear blue water and local sights while she'd toiled and strived in her classes at the Institute. He'd also talked about the people he met, the places he loved, how at peace he'd felt down here. It had been so long since she'd read any of them she really couldn't remember the details, just the overriding sense of his enjoyment of his posting, but now it suddenly struck her that hidden among them might be some clue as to who the little boy was. If he *was* Michael's son, it meant her brother had grown close to a woman down here. Close enough to bring new life into the world. Close enough that he may have mentioned her name or where he'd met her in one of his letters.

She wasn't naive where her brother was concerned. He'd been a good-looking young guy with a rangy body kept strong by lots of diving and water sports. He'd never suffered from a shortage of female attention. She'd often envied his confident ease with the opposite sex. She'd always been the worrier, and he'd always been the rule-breaker—and girls had liked that about him. When they were together, they'd balanced each other out perfectly. But when they were on their own, each of them had reverted to type. It was

Michael's love of adventure and excitement that had led him to sign on with the DEA. She'd understood that it suited him much more than the career in the kitchen that Andre had envisioned for his only son, but her father had never reconciled himself with Michael's choice. Just another reason why she'd tried so hard at the Institute—she'd been trying to make it up to her father for the dream he'd lost when his son had chosen not to follow in his footsteps.

The phone rang three times, and she was about to resign herself to leaving a message when her mother picked up.

"Mom, it's me," Tory said. "How are things back home?"

"Tory! I was just thinking about you. Where are you? Is it beautiful? It's so cold outside I can't even think about sticking my nose out the door," Kendra Fournier said from her Long Island home, her voice warm with pleasure.

"It's lovely. I'm on St, Lucia, just south of Martinique. It's balmy and there's a nice offshore breeze," Tory said.

She described the island briefly to her mother, touching on the cathedral and the market. Then her mother wanted a full description of her work on board the *Dream*. Leaving out the unimportant bits—like her squabbling with Ben and their consequent food fight—she gave her mother a quick rundown on her duties to date.

"It's hardly onerous," she said drily. "I feel like I should be paying them, really."

"And how is Jacques St. Clair to work with? Your father seems to think they did some training together many years ago. I gather he wasn't very impressed," Kendra said.

Tory wasn't surprised. Her father was rarely impressed with anyone. "Jacques broke his leg and couldn't make it. I'm working with Ben Cooper."

"Ben Cooper? I don't believe we know him," Kendra mused. "Oh, wait a minute—I was reading a write-up in one of your father's magazines just the other day. He recently won another Michelin star, correct?"

"Yes. He's very good," Tory said. "Great with the passengers. Accessible, fun. I'm learning a lot, actually."

She surprised herself when she said it, but it was true—she *was* learning from Ben. His energetic, exciting way with food was different from anyone she'd ever worked with.

Her mother made a vague noise of agreement, but Tory could tell Kendra wasn't convinced. Andre had always said that arrogance went hand in hand with great cuisine, and her father had followed his own dictate religiously. Her mother was his greatest fan, and consequently there were only a handful of chefs de cuisine in the world that they both wholeheartedly approved of.

Her mother began to talk about a new restaurant opening she'd been invited to, and Tory had a vision of her cell phone bill spiraling out of control as the minutes ticked by. Before her mother could launch into a full catalog of the restaurant's failings, she interrupted.

"Mom, I'm sorry, but I need to get back on board the ship. I actually called to ask a favor. Do you still have that box of Michael's letters and postcards from the Caribbean?"

Tory had put them in her brother's old bedroom with his other belongings after the funeral.

"I suppose so. I've been meaning to clean out the room for a while now, but I haven't got around to it yet."

Kendra had been threatening to turn Michael's room into a home gym for nearly five years. Tory never failed to feel a pang of hurt and grief at the thought of erasing her brother's memory so completely, but she knew better than to say anything. It inevitably led to the same conversation about how Tory had to learn to accept her brother's loss and move on, and what she was about to ask was going to ring enough alarm bells as it was. The last thing she wanted was another lecture from her mother on dealing with her grief—especially given what she was pursuing down here in the Caribbean.

"I was wondering if you could just bundle all that stuff up and FedEx it down to me care of the port in Grenada. We dock there tomorrow, so if you overnight it, it should get here in time," she said lightly, trying to sound as though it meant less than nothing to her.

Her mother was nobody's fool, however.

"Tory…" Kendra started to say, and Tory spoke over top of her.

"It's okay, Mom, I just want to find a reference Michael made to a beach down here. It was his favorite place, and I really wanted to say goodbye to him there."

Who knows, it might well be the truth if she couldn't think of some other way of tracing the little boy.

There was a long pause as her mother tossed up the relative merits of denying Tory or supporting her in her apparent quest for closure.

"It will cost a fortune," she grumbled.

Tory scrambled for her purse. "I'll pay, of course. I'll give you my credit card number."

Five minutes later, she ended the call feeling as though she'd achieved something, no matter how small. Somewhere in Michael's correspondence might be a clue, some hint of where she should go next. All was not lost. Not just yet, anyway.

She returned to the ship with a light step, heading straight for her room to change before her afternoon lecture. She'd brought several sets of whites and checked pants with her and she threw her handbag on the bed before turning to the wardrobe.

She pulled out her spare set of checked pants, but instead of easing them from the hanger, she studied them critically. They just looked so…starchy. And traditional and androgynous all of a sudden. She had a flash of the wrinkled linen pants Ben cooked in. He was much more in keeping with the relaxed island atmosphere of the cruise. Before she could think it over too much, she pulled on a pair of bright aqua slim-line cropped pants and slid her feet into some hot-pink-and-white wedge-heeled espadrilles she'd picked up especially for the trip. A hot-pink tank completed her ensemble, and she scooped up her white chef's coat and notebook computer on her way out the door. She felt breezy and relaxed, much more in keeping with her tropical surroundings. Plus, she and Ben would look more of a matched pair if she was dressed as casually as he was.

She stopped in her tracks as it occurred to her that she'd just dressed to please Ben. When she'd looked at her checked pants, it was *his* opinion she'd been thinking about when she saw them as stiff and unsexy. Frowning, she almost turned to go back and change again, but at the last minute she caught herself. So what if she did want Ben to think she was attractive. Was that such a bad thing?

There were about a million reasons why the correct answer to her question was *yes*. But she still didn't go back and change.

Fingering the pendant around her neck, Tory smiled faintly. It had been a long time since she'd had as much fun as she'd had that morning with Ben. And even longer since she'd been as attracted to anyone as she was to him. Was there really any harm in seeing where their attraction might go? What was the worst thing that could happen, after all, as long as she went into anything with her eyes wide open?

BEN TOOK ONE LOOK AT Tory in her tight aqua pants and felt all his good resolutions fly out the window. The moment she walked in the door, his eyes found her long, lean legs and stayed glued to them like fluff on Velcro. He wasn't a saint. He wasn't even a particularly good man most of the time. And he was definitely, definitely horny. It was something he'd only realized in the last few days. For six months Eva had been his focus. He hadn't had time or room in his life for anyone or anything else, and his personal life had necessarily fallen by the wayside.

Was it any wonder that he was hot for Tory? She was undeniably a sexy lady. And they had history. Bad history, some of it, but a whole long, steamy night of good history, too. He had only to close his eyes and he could remember the feel of those lean, firm thighs clenched around his hips. Or the sound of her crying out with passion. Or the way her nipples had puckered into his hands as he'd caressed her.

He was only human. Human, horny and, thanks to her sexy little pants, very turned on.

Moving behind the counter, he did his best to will his arousal away. They had another show to put on in under half an hour, after all.

"You cleaned up," she said, wide eyes racing over the newly pristine surfaces of the demonstration kitchen.

He shrugged an acknowledgment. "It was no big deal."

"I thought we would do it together, after the session," she said.

"I didn't mind," he said.

"Well, thanks," she said sincerely. "I appreciate it."

She flashed him a smile before starting to unpack her equipment. Watching her bend to plug in her computer cable, he had to shove his hands in his pockets to stop himself reaching for her ripe aqua butt.

He knew there were reasons why sleeping with her was a bad idea. He'd gone over them earlier today in the church. He'd also acknowledged to himself that he was bad at self-denial. Score one for team self-indulgence, but he wanted what he wanted. And belatedly it occurred to him that Tory wearing those pants might be a signal that she wanted it, too.

Keen to test his theory, Ben moved closer to where she stood at the end of the counter flicking through her notes. His eyes dropped to the swell of her breasts where they pushed up toward the neckline of her tank top. She had small coral-pink nipples, he remembered. Incredibly responsive and sweet in his mouth.

"You got anything planned for tonight?" he asked, just in case she'd dressed like that for some other lucky bastard.

Her cheeks went a little pink and she shook her head, not taking her eyes off her notes. "No."

Interesting. The pants were definitely for him, then. Hallelujah.

He inhaled her perfume, a heady mix of rich musk and sugary vanilla.

"We should get together, then, talk about the next few sessions," he heard himself say.

Now she looked up. There was caution in her eyes, as well as something else. Interest? Excitement? Or was he just imagining what he wanted to see because his trousers were feeling distinctly snug in the crotch?

"Okay. If you think we should," she said slowly.

"I definitely think we should," Ben said.

Her gaze flickered down toward the countertop again, and he saw that she'd spread her palms flat against the surface.

"Where do you want to meet up?" she asked.

"How about La Belle Epoque, the champagne bar? That's on the Bacchus level."

"Bacchus, huh? I guess that's appropriate for a champagne bar."

"Oh, yeah. Bacchus had all the fun. Wine, women, song."

"Now why does that remind me of someone?" she said, cocking her head to one side and pretending to ponder the matter.

He stared at her mouth. All of a sudden, he needed to kiss her more than he needed oxygen. Where had this hunger for her sprung from? It was almost as though all their previous encounters to date had just been an elaborate form of foreplay. And he was *so* ready for the main event.

He followed the plump curve of her lower lip with his eyes. If he lowered his head a few inches, he'd be kissing her. He could slide his tongue inside her mouth and uncover all her secrets. He could lick her and suck her until she begged him to do the same everywhere else on her body….

"We should…it's nearly time for the session," Tory said. Her voice was low, husky. Ben saw that her breasts were rising and falling rapidly, as though she'd just tackled a flight of stairs.

Or as though she was turned on. He looked up at her face, and what he saw made him reach for her.

"Tory," he said, but she stepped backward.

"They'll all be here any second."

She moved toward the other end of the counter, and he watched with frustration as she pulled on her chef's coat. It was probably just as well, given his current state of physical arousal, but it didn't stop him from fiercely resenting the fact that they had to put on a dog and pony show for the ship's passengers when he and Tory had some serious unfinished business to take care of.

Sighing heavily, he ran a hand through his hair. Patience was a virtue, apparently, but as well as sucking at self-denial, he'd never been great with virtue, either.

"Okay, let's do this thing," he said.

TORY SPENT THE WHOLE of their presentation quietly freaking out. On the surface, she did all the right things. She worked her way through her notes for her talk on local fruit and vegetables, explaining the many different and unusual varieties and comparing them to more familiar offerings to give her audience an idea of tastes and textures. She made jokes. She even bantered back and forth with Ben when he took over for his half of the session. But inside, she was a mess.

When she'd admitted to herself that she'd dressed to make herself more attractive to Ben, she hadn't expected to inspire such instant results. But Ben had practically eaten her up with his eyes the moment she'd walked in the door. And then he'd asked her out. And then he'd looked at her as though he really was going to eat her alive…and she'd been absolutely terrified by how much she wanted him to. In fact, she'd been so shaken by the surge of desire that had risen up inside her that she'd frozen. And now she couldn't stop herself from analyzing the situation from every angle and worrying at all the things that could go horribly wrong if she took Ben up on the blatant invitation in his deep blue eyes.

What if she wanted Ben too much, for example? Was it possible for a woman to climax prematurely? Like, before a man even got her clothes off? Because she was afraid that was exactly what might happen if she and Ben wound up alone. Worse, what if she cried again as she had the last time when she came? Her toes curled in her shoes at the very thought. The thing was, she'd always been so powerfully attracted to Ben, and the events of the last few days proved that that attraction was alive and well and ready to roar. She knew that once she was in his arms she'd be on a roller-coaster ride of lust and desire and there would be no telling where she might end up.

By the end of their session she'd worried herself into a headache. God, she was such a geek. Here she was, on a cruise ship in the middle of the Caribbean with a sexy, gorgeous man sending signals that he wanted to have sex with her, a damned love charm around her neck, for Pete's sake, and all she could think about was what might go wrong.

When had her life become so small and scared?

She started packing away her computer as soon as the passengers began filing out. She had the audio-visual equipment sorted in no time and she held her computer case to her chest as she finally turned to face Ben. The look in his eyes was gently questioning.

"Well, I guess that's it until tomorrow," she said, edging toward the door.

Ben cocked a hip against the counter.

"What about tonight? Did you still want to meet up?" he asked.

She stared at him. He stared back. Her brain went blank as the familiar tidal wave of lust rose up inside her.

"Okay," she heard herself say. She even nodded for good measure.

Ben looked both pleased and relieved.

"Why don't we say seven, then?" he suggested.

"Okay," she said again stupidly.

He smiled at her, and she hugged the computer case a little more tightly as she backed toward the door.

"I'll see you then," she said, feeling incredibly awkward and self-aware and gawky.

"Yep."

He almost let her get out the door before he spoke again.

"Tory?"

She froze and looked back over her shoulder.

"Nice pants, by the way," he said. "Great color. Great…fit."

The look he shot her was so damned sexy she almost melted on the spot. Her whole body went hot, then cold.

"Okay," she squeaked yet again and then she escaped into the corridor.

She was so flustered she walked straight past the elevator bank, and it wasn't until she saw a flight of stairs that she realized how far she'd wandered. Shaking her head at her own idiocy, Tory walked down to the Bacchus deck.

She had to pull herself together. She was a grown woman. A sophisticated grown woman who'd had several lovers since her one-night fling with Ben all those years ago. So what if none of them had burned their way into her memory and her senses the way Ben had? It didn't mean she had to give up any pretense of personal pride and dissolve into a puddle of need at Ben's sexy feet, did it?

It was useless to try and deny the excitement threading along her nerve endings, however. In a vain attempt to try to bring some order to her thoughts, Tory turned into the Internet café located near the library on the Bacchus deck.

Swiping her room card at one of the free computers, she sat down and tapped at the keyboard until she'd connected to her e-mail account. Predictably, her in-box was filled with spam, and she spent thirty seconds deleting offerings of penis enhancement, diet pills, Viagra and special stock tips before she unearthed anything legitimate. The first message was from her real-estate broker. He'd located two possible locations for her, both of which he would have lined up for inspection when Tory returned from the Caribbean. She almost deleted the second and most important e-mail, however, because she wasn't familiar with the sender's name. It was only as her mouse hovered over the delete key that her frazzled brain kicked in.

The e-mail was from Matt Striker. She jerked upright in her seat and fumbled the mouse in her excitement to click the message open. Holding her breath, she scanned Matt Striker's note with dawning hope.

Ms Fournier, I am afraid I am unable to help you with ascertaining the identity of the boy in the photograph. I was able to source the original image from my files, however, and the uncropped image is attached. You will see from the store signs in the background that the photograph was clearly taken on St. Maarten. I hope this helps you in your search. Yours, Mathew Striker.

St. Maarten. She sat back in her chair and smiled. They docked in St. Maarten the day after tomorrow!

Quickly she sent off a note of thanks to the photographer, carefully following his lead and not referring to their earlier meeting in any way. Frankly she was astonished that the man she'd seen passed out earlier that day had been capable of putting together such a lucid document given the short recovery time between then and now, but she thanked her lucky stars nonetheless.

Her step was a hundred times lighter as she headed back to her room. She was well and truly back on the trail. And she was meeting Ben tonight. Suddenly her world seemed filled with possibilities instead of pitfalls.

CHAPTER SEVEN

BEN ADJUSTED THE COLLAR on his shirt. He felt…*nervous* was the only word he could come up with to describe the tension in his body. Which was just plain stupid. It wasn't as if this was some big date or anything. Hell, he'd even slept with Tory before—there wasn't the thrill of the unknown to put him on edge. So why was his foot tapping the ground in a constant tattoo and why was he darting glances toward the door of La Belle Epoque every thirty seconds?

They were having a drink. That was all. Obviously parts of his anatomy would be doing the happy dance if it turned into anything more than that, but either way, there was nothing to be nervous about.

For the tenth time in five minutes he shot a glance toward the door—and this time she was there. He was on his feet before he could stop himself. She looked amazing in a knee-length floral sundress in muted shades of lemon and peach. He eyed the sway of her willowy body as she strode toward him—and then he saw the notebook in her hand.

She'd brought a notebook to have drinks with him.

His mouth quirked up into a smile as he remembered the pretext he'd used to ask her out tonight. *We should get together, talk about the next few sessions,* he'd said. So she'd brought her notebook.

A few days ago, that notebook would have made him roll his eyes and call her uptight and prissy. Now he was charmed. For some reason, he found it very endearing that she'd dressed to impress in a sexy little dress but covered her ass by bringing her notebook just in case he'd meant what he'd said about talking work tonight.

"You made it," he said when she stopped in front of him.

"Yes."

He gestured toward the chair opposite, and when she sank into it her skirt flared briefly around her knees.

He tore his eyes from her long, long legs and reminded himself that he wasn't a caveman. Or that for tonight, at least, he was pretending he wasn't.

"What would you like to drink?" he asked.

"Scotch, please. Single-malt, if possible."

His surprise must have shown, because she arched an eyebrow at him when he'd finished giving their orders to the waitress.

"You were expecting me to order a champagne cocktail, weren't you?" she asked.

"Actually, I had you pegged as a cosmopolitan kind of woman," he admitted.

She wrinkled her nose. "Cosmos are *so* last decade. Have you been trapped on a tropical island for the past eight years or something, Ben?"

He laughed and reached across to pluck the notebook from her hand. "You won't be needing this," he said, tossing it onto the table.

"I thought you wanted to talk about our sessions?" she asked, her eyelashes sweeping down to mask her eyes.

"Did you really?" He waited for her to make eye contact again. Finally she did. Her gaze was searching.

"No."

"Well, then." He allowed himself one quick scan of her body. Her skin looked silky smooth, and he reached for his drink to stop himself from taking something that hadn't been offered. Yet.

Their drinks arrived, and Ben watched as Tory took an appreciative mouthful of her whisky.

"Acceptable?" he asked.

"Very nice." She sat back in her chair a little more and crossed her legs.

"So you're going to be starting up your own place soon," he said by way of a conversation starter. What he really wanted to ask was if she remembered how good they'd been together all those years ago. Whether she was as turned on as he was just thinking about holding her body close to his again.

"Yep. We haven't picked a location yet. I'm aiming for midtown Manhattan, somewhere interesting rather than austere."

"Don't take this the wrong way, but I'm kind of amazed that you're not taking over Le Plat. Most chefs would kill for a chance to just walk into the kitchen of that place."

"My father closed Le Plat when he retired," she said casually.

"What? When did that happen?" Ben asked. Anguilla wasn't exactly a thriving metropolis, but they weren't that far off the beaten track.

"About two years ago now. He kept it pretty quiet, just held one last dinner for friends, then shut the doors. He'd made his mark on New York and he didn't want to hand his pride and joy over to strangers, so it seemed like the logical thing to do...."

She shrugged her shoulders as if closing one of New York's most critically acclaimed restaurants was the only logical decision Andre Fournier could have made.

Ben stared at her as he processed her words. "But what about you? Didn't you want it?" he asked.

"At the time. I realize now he made the right decision. It was his place, his reputation. He didn't want to have people reporting back to him that things had changed or to open the paper on the weekend and find a bad review. I can understand that."

She looked supremely at peace with her father's decision—except for the white-knuckle grip she had on her whisky tumbler.

Ben was so offended on her behalf that he forgot to be diplomatic. "Nice vote of confidence. Does your old man even know what you can do in the kitchen?"

She shrugged again. "He's always had very high standards. He can afford to—he's at the top of his game."

Ben frowned. What she was saying, in a roundabout kind of way, was that her father didn't believe in her. And that she accepted that as a matter of course. He had a sudden flash of what her childhood must have been like with an egomaniacally arrogant father breathing down her neck every time she dared pick up a knife.

He thought of his own parents in the kitchen of the small takeaway shack that once stood where Café Rendezvous now sprawled over the sand. His father had shared his skill with humor and patience, his mother with passion and a full-figured woman's love of taste and texture. Cooking had always been a pleasure in his family, not a make-or-break test of skill.

"Your father is an idiot," he said gruffly, angry on Tory's behalf.

Predictably, she bristled.

"If you'd seen Le Plat, if you'd eaten there, you'd understand. He spent his life building its reputation," she said defensively.

"But you're his daughter. He spent a lifetime building you, too," he countered.

She stared at him, and in the depths of her eyes he saw the pain she was fighting to deny. Of course it hurt that her father had cast a very public vote of no confidence when he'd closed his restaurant. Of course she felt the rejection, the sting of his disapproval.

But she would never admit as much to herself or anyone else. Ben understood where she was coming from. There were aspects of his own life that didn't bear up under close scrutiny, either. Particularly lately.

The background music had edged up a notch, and Ben saw that a corner of the bar had been turned over to dancing. Within the hour they were going to be yelling over music, he guessed.

"Have you been up to the observation deck yet?" he asked.

She shook her head no. She looked tense, withdrawn. The opposite of how she'd looked when he'd almost kissed her this afternoon. He'd made a bad misstep with the Le Plat talk, he knew.

"Come on. It's pretty spectacular up there." He stood and held out his hand to help haul her to her feet.

She reached for her notepad instead and stood under her own steam.

That'll teach me to pick on Daddy, Ben thought wryly. No matter how arrogant an ass Andre Fournier obviously was, Tory clearly worshipped him.

Flipping open his wallet, he found his room card so he could settle the drink tab. Beside him, he felt Tory stiffen.

"You have children?" she asked incredulously.

Ben realized she was staring at the photo of Eva in the photo sleeve of his wallet. His chest tightened painfully.

"She's not mine. She's…just a friend's. I don't even know why I've got that thing in there."

To prove his words to both Tory and himself, he tugged the photo free and tucked it behind his credit card.

He could feel her gaze on him, but he didn't want to talk about Eva. Talking wasn't going to change what had happened or make him feel any more reconciled to losing her.

"Let's go," he said.

WHAT AM I DOING? TORY asked herself for the tenth time that night as she followed Ben up to the observation deck. It had seemed so clear in her mind when she'd been getting ready earlier.

She and Ben were attracted to each other. She could *feel* it, even if neither of them had said anything or made a move yet. She wasn't the babe in the woods that she'd been all those years ago. She knew when a man was interested in her these days. And Ben was interested, definitely.

So she'd shaved and moisturized, then zipped herself into the sexiest, flirtiest little dress she'd brought with her. Last-minute doubts had prompted her to accessorize with her notebook, but Ben had reassured her so instantly and so charmingly when she'd first arrived that she'd felt a welcome surge of confidence.

Then he'd brought up Le Plat. And it had been downhill from there.

Maybe they were just too different. Maybe they were destined to be great in bed but bad everywhere else.

"Almost there," Ben said as they negotiated a last short flight of stairs toward a glass door. She could see the night sky through the glass and she sucked in a shocked breath as Ben shouldered the door open and the cool night air hit her bare arms and legs.

"Too cold?" Ben asked solicitously, picking up on her reaction.

"It was just the shock of it, I think," Tory said, already bewitched by the sea breeze tickling its way through her hair.

It was never truly cold in the Tropics, but tonight the air was definitely cool. Tory followed Ben to the very front of the observation deck. They weren't the only passengers with the same idea; the deck was dotted with couples taking in the fresh sea air. Ben found them a secluded position on the rail and began to decipher the glowing dots on the horizon for her.

"Obviously that's St. Lucia off behind us now. To our left, that very faint glow is Barbados."

Tory tensed as she realized that she was looking across the very stretch of water where Michael's plane had gone down. Her fingers gripped the railing tightly as she stared out at the night-dark sea.

She'd always fretted over the last minutes of Michael's life. Had he known he was going to die? Had he been fighting to the end? Knowing her brother, she suspected he had gone out doing his utmost to save himself and his two passengers. The cause of the crash was officially unknown, but she had flown with Michael many times and knew how careful and exacting he'd been as a pilot. More than anything, she hoped that the end had been mercifully quick, that he hadn't been afraid for too long and, most of all, that he hadn't been in pain.

"You're cold," Ben said when a shiver worked its way down her spine. "Do you want to go in?"

"No, I'm fine," she said, trying to regain her equilibrium.

Ben stepped behind her, his arms reaching forward to grasp the rail on either side of her, bracketing her with his body. Instantly she was enveloped in his scent—crisp and clean and lemony—and she could feel the warmth of his body against her back.

"How's that?" he asked.

His breath tickled the back of her neck.

"Um, good. Thanks." In truth, her thoughts had scattered, her pulse had gone through the roof and she was unbearably aware of every inch of his body pressed up against hers.

"So. Looking to the right—or starboard, as Captain Nikolas would no doubt say—you can see a hazy glow on the horizon. That's St. Vincent and the Grenadines."

"And Grenada's right at the bottom?" she asked, trying to cudgel her suddenly sluggish brain into coherency.

Despite the fact that they were standing at the prow of the ship, a breeze washing over them, the sea spread wide before them, the world seemed to shrink to just the few feet that involved her and him and the sizzling awareness that lay between them.

"Yeah. It's a great place," Ben said. "Make sure you visit the spice markets tomorrow. Grenada is the home of nutmeg, you know."

He'd moved closer. His lips hovered just to the left of her ear now, while his hips formed a cradle for her backside. His arms brushed her upper arms, his thighs the back of her legs.

Tory realized she was trembling with need and desire. More than anything, she wanted to lean back into Ben's embrace, to feel his lips on the sensitive skin of her neck, to revel in his touch on her body again.

It was one thing to flirt and fantasize and remember how it had been last time they were together, but taking the next step would commit her to a night in Ben's arms. Was she ready to go there again?

It's just sex, she told herself, her pulse hammering in her ears. *Live for the moment for once in your life.* But sex had never been something she could isolate out from intimacy and commitment. She wasn't built for one-night stands.

For long seconds she teetered on the brink of indecision, but finally she could resist her own desire no longer. Tilting her hips, she pressed herself back into Ben's embrace, issuing a wordless invitation. She felt him suck in a sudden breath, then his arms left the rail and wrapped around her as he pulled her closer still.

She could feel the heat of his hands as he spread them flat on her belly and she let her head drop back to allow him access to her neck and shoulders. He didn't need to be asked twice. She bit her lip as he pressed a kiss below her ear before nuzzling more intimately into the curve of her shoulder.

Of their own volition, her hands reached behind her to slide down the sides of his torso and onto his hips. He felt so firm and strong. Memories from last time washed over her, and she bit back a low moan as Ben's hands swept up her rib cage to rest just beneath her breasts. More than anything, she wanted him to touch her there. She shimmied her hips in invitation against him, reveling in the press of his arousal against her butt.

He groaned deep in his throat, the sound vibrating through her own body, they were pressed so close.

"Tory, you're killing me here," he murmured as he nibbled on the lobe of her ear.

"Then let's go," she said. Before she could let herself think, she broke away from him and held out her hand. "Let's go back to my stateroom."

Ben's eyes were very dark in the romantic lighting on the observation deck. He didn't bother with a verbal response, he just took her hand and led her back inside.

"What floor are you on?" he asked.

"Five. Room 516," she said a little breathlessly.

He set the pace after that, navigating their way to the nearest elevator, her hand tucked in his, his body close to hers, his eyes undressing her with every hot glance.

As they walked up the corridor toward her room, Tory's heart began to beat a fierce tattoo against her breastbone. She felt a little light-headed as her body burned with the memory of their last time together—how powerful Ben had been, how firm and strong, how sexy and desirable he'd made her feel. She was so turned on and distracted she didn't quite understand what Ben was asking for when he extended his hand and raised his eyebrows once they'd reached her door.

"The key card," he said, his gaze dropping to explore the neckline of her dress.

Her breath hitched in her throat as she realized that in just a few seconds he'd be touching her breasts, not just looking at them, and she fumbled the card as she slid it from her small evening bag.

He flashed her a quick knowing smile, then he swiped the card and ushered her inside.

They were both too urgent, too full of need to exercise self-restraint or finesse. The door was still swinging shut as they came together, arms snaking around bodies, mouths opening in a heady kiss that made Tory's knees tremble.

Ben speared his hands up into her hair and cradled her head in his palms, his mouth devouring hers with such intensity that he literally took her breath away.

"You taste amazing," he whispered against her neck as he licked and sucked his way down to her cleavage, and she had to hang on tight to his shoulders as his mouth found one of her already-jutting nipples through the fabric of her dress.

"Oh!" she cried as she registered the hot, wet feel of his mouth closing over her.

His shoulders were so broad and firm under her hands, his arousal so demanding against her belly, his mouth so perfect on her breasts. Suddenly she couldn't wait a moment longer to feel her skin against his, to experience the sensual slide of his body inside hers.

"Ben," she gasped, trying to convey her need to him.

"Definitely," he agreed, and they tore at each other's clothes, covering each newly exposed expanse of skin with kisses, murmuring their mutual approval as they stripped down to lace and satin and cotton and then finally nothing.

She'd already seen his chest once when he'd changed after their food fight this morning, but the sight of Ben in all his naked glory was enough to make her fan herself with pure lust. He was perfect, utterly perfect. Broad shoulders, narrow hips, thighs that made her lick her lips and so aroused and ready for her that she was panting before he even started backing her toward the bed.

He was devouring her with equal avidity, his navy gaze sliding from the pebbled peak of one breast to the other, down toward the thatch of curls at the apex of her thighs, then down the length of her legs.

"This body," he groaned reverently as he cupped her breasts, lifting them even as he lowered his mouth to tongue first one nipple and then the other.

"Ditto," she said breathlessly, her palms gliding over the muscled planes of his chest.

Then they were on the bed and she was welcoming his weight into the cradle of her thighs, tilting her hips to invite him closer still. He paused only to protect them both, and then she gave an inarticulate, needy cry as he slid inside her.

After that she was reduced to pure sensation. The glide of him inside her. The rasp of his stubble across her breasts. The slick of his tongue on her skin. The glorious contrast between her soft curves and his hard muscles.

He knew just what she needed. When to go hard. When to back off. When to tease, when to give her everything. He made her beg. He made her moan. He stroked and cajoled and teased and enticed her to the edge of climax—and then he sent her over.

She was still shuddering with aftershocks when he found his own release, and they lay panting and sweaty on the bed for a full five minutes afterward, trying to recover. Remembering last time, she brushed a surreptitious hand over her face, and her toes curled with self-awareness when her fingers came away wet with tears. She'd cried again. *Damn it.* What was it about Ben Cooper that made her feel so intensely? Trying to be subtle about it, she turned her head away from him and swiped at her cheek with a shaking hand.

She thought she'd gotten away with it until Ben spoke.

"Don't," he said.

Just the one word. But when she looked into his eyes, she saw so much more. He looked shocked. Dazed. Confused. Moved. Raw. All the things that she felt. Something inside her uncoiled, relaxed.

He reached out and touched her face, capturing a stray tear on the tip of his finger.

"That was incredible," he said quietly. "Let's not pretend it was anything different."

All the wariness, all the hard-won tricks of the more experienced woman she'd become since she'd last slept with him melted away just like that. She felt twenty-one again, new and malleable and open to anything.

"Come here," he said, eyes still locked with hers.

He tugged her toward him, and she slid on top of him, her body perfectly matched to his, face to face, shoulder to shoulder, hip to hip.

Sliding a hand up onto the nape of her neck, he pulled her head down for a long, drugging kiss. Slowly they made love again, every caress an ode, each kiss a promise. Tory had never felt more desired, more valued, more precious.

Somewhere in the small hours after they'd made love for the

third time, they fell asleep in each other's arms, and Tory's last thought was that for the first time in a long time she felt complete.

BEN WOKE WITH A NUMB arm and the nagging sense that he'd forgotten to do something. He didn't have to look far for the cause of the numb arm—Tory had fallen asleep with her head on his chest, his arm wrapped around her shoulders. Lifting his head, he stared down into her sleeping face. She had a faint smile on her lips, and her curls formed appealing curlicues along her forehead. His gaze tracked down the rest of her body, gravitating to her small pink-tipped breasts, her flat belly, the length of her legs. He grew hard remembering how it had felt to be inside her again after all these years. *Perfect* was the only word he could come up with. Like coming home after too long away.

Tory moved in her sleep, rubbing her cheek against his chest, and he automatically lifted a hand to soothe the soft skin of her shoulder. She felt like silk and velvet, precious and rare. A warm, expansive feeling burgeoned in his chest as he studied her face. She was gorgeous—flushed and at peace and utterly vulnerable. His arms tightened as he felt a fierce, primitive urge to protect her from the harsh realities of life.

Ben frowned as his well-honed bachelor instincts belatedly kicked in and he consciously registered his own thoughts. Being with Tory was *perfect,* like *coming home?* He sounded like a bad poem in a greeting card. Worse, he realized with a dart of unease, he'd actually said some of those things out loud to Tory last night. And now he was lying here, staring into her face and thinking *about protecting her from the world?*

Suddenly overwhelmed by panicky claustrophobia, he fought the urge to push her away. He needed to get some space, get his head together.

His body stiff with tension, he wriggled his shoulder and lifted his torso a fraction to encourage Tory to roll in the other direction.

She frowned in her sleep and muttered something under her breath but she didn't budge. Holding his breath, Ben reached across and slid his free hand under her head. Supporting her weight, he slid his numb arm out from under her and slipped a pillow beneath her head to take up the slack.

She frowned and burrowed into the pillow. Only when it became clear that he hadn't woken her did he let his breath hiss out between his teeth.

He dressed in haste, dragging his shirt on, stuffing his feet into his shoes without bothering with socks, snatching up his own key card on his way to the door.

Briefly he hovered on the threshold, staring back at the bed. She looked small and very alone curled up on her side, the sheets tangled around her. He considered leaving her a note, but the urge to run was too strong. Anyway, what would he write? Thanks? See you later? Please disregard anything said in the heat of the moment?

Easing out the door, he clicked it shut quietly behind him and sagged with relief. Except the tight feeling in his chest didn't abate one bit, even though he'd won his freedom. If anything, he felt more tense, more edgy. Walking briskly, he headed back to his penthouse suite on the Aphrodite deck. There were precious few people out and about in the wee hours of the morning, but he still passed a handful of crew members, some of whom smirked at his obviously bed-rumpled appearance.

Once he'd gained his suite, he shucked his clothes and stepped into the shower. Bracing his arms against the tiled wall, he hung his head and let the water stream down his back.

He shouldn't have slept with her. It had been amazing, but it had been a mistake. Of that he was absolutely certain, regardless of whatever crazy things he'd been thinking and feeling when he'd first woken.

He might be committed to his family, his restaurant and his staff, but he'd never been committed to a woman in his life. It

wasn't that he was actively against monogamy and marriage—
throughout his twenties he'd waited for the commitment bug to bite
with one of his girlfriends, but it had never happened. No matter
how much he liked a woman, something always got in the way—
the hours he worked at the restaurant, his need for personal space,
the sheer monotony of going through the motions of everyday life
with another person. Slowly he'd settled into his bachelorhood,
and, at thirty-one, he'd solidified into the role. Commitment, he'd
concluded, wasn't for everyone. It worked for his folks, for his
brother and sister, but not for him.

Thinking of the string of beautiful women he'd dallied with
over the past few years, Ben felt reassured. He worked hard and
he played hard, taking his pleasure where he found it with like-
minded women who understood the rules of engagement. His life
was good. Full. Rich. Exciting.

So why had he broken his cardinal rule and slept with a woman
who screamed commitment, monogamy, long-term? Not just slept
with her—that was too tame a phrase for the night he'd shared with
Tory. He'd made long, slow, intense love to her. And she'd cried
afterward, and he'd kissed her tears away and fallen asleep with
her in his arms....

Briefly he remembered the flood of protective feeling he'd experienced when he'd woken with her in his arms.

He straightened abruptly, taking the full force of the shower in
the face. The only explanation he could come up with was that six
months without sex had turned him into a sappy, sentimental slob.
And God only knew what Tory would be expecting from him
when she woke up. Hadn't he decided to back off for exactly this
reason when he'd realized how much he was fixating on her in the
cathedral at St. Lucia this afternoon? Hadn't he decided that he
would be asking for trouble if he let his hormones and nether
regions call the shots where she was concerned?

Flicking the water off, he stepped out of the shower and grabbed a towel. Padding back into the bedroom, he dried himself roughly before sitting on the edge of the bed and cradling his head in his hands.

Belatedly it occurred to him that it wasn't just Tory's expectations he'd have to wrangle come dawn. As if that wasn't a thorny enough issue, there was also the fact that he'd just had hands down the best sex of his life. Her scent, the taste of her skin, the feel of her legs around him, her tongue on his body—there was no way he could pretend none of that had happened. So now he was in the unenviable position of being painfully attracted to a woman who was going to be white-hot angry with him once he let her down—and he was stuck on a cruise ship with her.

He pressed his fingers against his eyes. In a perfect world, Tory Fournier would wake in a few hours, thank him for a great night and propose that they spend the remainder of the cruise exploring the sensational chemistry between them, no strings attached.

Ben snorted disbelievingly in the silence of his stateroom. He was certifiable if he thought he had even a chance of something like that happening. Tory was going to be hurt when he made it clear that last night was not the beginning of something between them. He had no doubt about that. Just imagining her face when she woke up and found him missing made him feel sick. He liked her. He respected her. He even cared for her, in his stunted bachelor's way.

So why hadn't he listened to his better instincts and kept his hands off her?

Groaning, he crawled beneath the sheets and flicked off the light. It was those stupid, sexy, tight aqua pants. As he'd admitted to himself earlier today, he'd never been great at self-denial. Now he had to face the consequences of his self-indulgence.

IT TOOK A FEW SECONDS for full memory to return when Tory woke a few hours later. Pushing the hair from her face, she registered first that she was naked beneath the sheets, then that her body felt languorous and heavy. Memory came back to her in a hot, sticky rush—Ben's mouth on her breasts; Ben stroking her with his fingers and, later, with his mouth; Ben staring into her eyes as she lost her mind again and again and again.

She smiled. If she were a cat, she'd be purring. In fact, she might give it a go anyway—she felt fantastic. Absolutely sated. Supremely sexy. Last night had been...amazing. She'd felt so connected to Ben, and it had been obvious to her that the feeling had been mutual. She'd always believed that great sex was about a meeting of minds as well as bodies, and last night had more than proved it to her.

Smiling, she rolled over to confirm that all her hot, steamy memories hadn't just been a figment of her imagination.

Only to find that the other side of the bed was empty.

Her stomach lurched with uncertainty and her whole body was instantly stiff with tension. Surely he hadn't...?

"Ben?" she called toward the bathroom.

A profound silence was her only response. She flopped back onto her pillows and closed her eyes for a long beat as reality sank in at last.

The best night of her life. The most intense, connected lovemaking she'd ever known. And her partner in crime had fled.

On the scale of things, it wasn't as bad as hearing Ben's buddies yuk it up over him sleeping with her for a bet, but it was right up there.

"Oh, God, no," she groaned, suddenly remembering her stupid climactic tears.

Why, oh, why had she made herself so vulnerable to him again?

She was such a glutton for punishment. Hadn't she learned her lesson where Ben Cooper was concerned? For some reason, she was ridiculously responsive to his particular brand of charisma. All he had to do was touch her and she was halfway to heaven. But it didn't mean anything. It hadn't eight years ago and it didn't now. She was opening herself up to a world of rejection if she believed any differently.

She groaned again as she recalled the syrupy-sweet thoughts that had been ballet dancing their way across her mind when she'd woken. So much for feeling *connected* to Ben. So much for a *meeting of minds*.

Rolling out of bed, she wrapped her arms around her torso and paced. She had to get her head straight if she was going to escape this situation with her dignity intact.

As tempting as it was to wallow in the enormity of her naiveté, it was useless to regret or wish back anything that had happened last night. The past was the past. Today, this morning, was all about damage control and pride preservation. So she'd clung to Ben as if he was her lifeline and sobbed her ecstasy into his shoulder every time she came last night? Big deal. For all he knew, she broke into tears every time she had an orgasm. She might just be one of those highly emotional women who lost it completely when they found release. He knew next to nothing about her, after all. In fact, the only way he'd know for sure that she'd read anything into their one night together would be if she rolled into the demonstration kitchen this morning looking and acting like a kicked puppy.

Her spine stiffened more with every passing moment. Her chin came up as she eyed her reflection in the bathroom mirror.

She had to walk into that kitchen, look him in the eye and thank him like a sophisticated woman of the world for a great night. She had to make a couple of coolly urbane jokes about her response to his lovemaking—something self-effacing but witty that she'd work out between now and then—and then she had to carry on as though they'd done nothing more personal last night than, say, play checkers or discuss global warming.

She nodded decisively at her reflection.

It was a plan. A good plan, even. More importantly, it was a plan she was reasonably confident she could pull off.

Stepping in the shower, she turned the water on and reached for the soap, racking her brain for something pithy, earthy and apparently off-the-cuff to say to him about her stupid postcoital waterworks.

Ducking her head to wet her hair, she froze as she caught sight of the small red love bite on the side of her left breast. It was shaped, absurdly, like a heart, and she had a sudden flash from last night of Ben suckling on her breasts while his big hands held her close. She could remember every detail—the rapt expression on his face, the tug of desire between her thighs, the intensity of the attraction between them.

She sucked in a mouthful of air and let her shoulders sag. She could go up to the kitchen and act her butt off for Ben, but it was useless to try to lie to herself, as well. Last night *had* meant something to her. It had moved her, touched her. And now she felt cheated, as though Ben had offered her something profound, something life-changing, only to snatch it away when she'd reached for it.

"Stupid," she said.

What had she thought was going to happen when they woke this morning? Even if Ben hadn't hightailed it out of her room like Steve McQueen in *The Great Escape,* they were on a cruise ship in the middle of the Caribbean. In a few days' time, Ben would be flying back to Café Rendezvous on Anguilla, and she would be winging her way home to New York to start up her own restaurant. There had never been any chance that their time together was just the beginning rather than the sum total of their relationship, no matter what fantasies she'd spun last night as Ben held her in his arms.

Time to give it up, girl, she told herself as she at last acknowledged the sad truth. All those years ago, she'd thought Ben was special. Time, distance and old misunderstandings had not dimmed that belief one iota, it seemed. All she'd had to do was scratch the surface and her old crush had been lurking, waiting to be resuscitated. But it was time to put childish things away.

They'd had a one-night stand. No more, no less.

Shoulders squared, she prepared herself for the performance of a lifetime.

CHAPTER EIGHT

BEN BRACED HIMSELF AS Tory swung through the double doors into the cuisine arts center. He'd had a couple of hours to ready himself to face her disappointment, hurt and anger. The last thing he wanted to do was upset her, but he would only hurt her more if he let her believe that last night had been anything more than great sex.

He took a deep breath—and got his first surprise when she flashed a warm smile his way.

"Good morning," she said.

She was wearing a short little wraparound skirt in bright yellow, paired with a navy-and-white-striped tank top. Her legs seemed to go on forever, and he had to wrench his attention back to her face.

"Uh, yeah," he said uncertainly.

"I slept like a log after you left," she said breezily as she set up for the day. "Must have been all that sea air."

She shot him a wicked look, her mouth quirked in a wry little grin.

Ben blinked again. "Right," he said stupidly.

Perhaps because he'd spent so long thinking over what he was going to say to let her down gently, he found himself launching into his prepared speech despite the fact that she wasn't looking remotely wounded, let down or expectant.

"I thought perhaps we should talk about last night," he said in his best sensitive-new-age-guy tone.

To his everlasting surprise, Tory made a frustrated noise and rolled her eyes.

"Don't tell me you're one of those guys who likes to rehash everything and analyze it to death?" Propping her hip against the counter, she crossed her arms over her breasts and raised an eyebrow at him. "Go on, then," she said when he continued to stare at her. "If you feel you have to get it off your chest, off you go."

She sounded indulgent. As if she was humoring him.

Not quite the scenario he'd imagined when he'd gone over and over this scene in his head in the early hours of the morning.

"It, uh, just occurred to me that we hadn't really discussed the...status of what happened between us last night," he said stiffly.

Tory frowned. "The status?" she repeated, clearly confused.

"What it might mean. For us. In the future," he clarified. Then he winced, realizing that she might misconstrue what he was saying as a declaration rather than a clarification.

He needn't have worried.

Tory threw back her head and laughed. A full-bodied belly laugh that made her breasts jiggle invitingly.

"God, Ben, you're the last man I'd have expected this from," she said. "Surely you're not going all gooey and sentimental on me?"

"No," he said, suddenly feeling defensive for some reason. "We didn't really talk last night, that's all. I wanted to make sure that neither of us had different...expectations about what happened."

"This is because I cried, isn't it?" she asked, eyes sparkling with humor. "Think of it as a compliment, the seal of authenticity that we had a good time."

Then she leaned across and pressed a brief kiss to his lips.

"Thanks for the trip down memory lane—I had a great night," she said, patting his arm dismissively.

Ben stared at her back as she turned away and began organizing her presentation.

He'd totally misread her. She was completely cool with their one-night stand.

Unless he was missing something. Maybe she was pissed with

him for leaving her room the way he had, and this was about punishing him? The Tory he used to know would never be so cavalier about sex.

Tory turned in profile to him, and he saw a small, soft smile curving her lips. She looked utterly at peace with the world and herself. As though she did this sort of thing every day. Hell, she'd even thanked him for a "great night." If she'd capped her reaction by suggesting they do it all over again tonight, he'd have been convinced he was fantasizing the whole scenario.

The bottom line was that he was off the hook. No awkwardness. No misunderstandings or morning-after tension. No problems whatsoever, in fact.

So why was he feeling so damned disgruntled?

TORY FUMBLED THE REMOTE control for the digital projector, clumsy with reaction after her Oscar-worthy scene with Ben. Out of the corners of her eyes she watched as he resumed his prep work near the stove top.

He'd bought the whole blasé *Sex and the City* routine hook, line and sinker. She'd pulled it off despite how weak her knees had gone the moment she'd walked in the room and seen him again.

Why was she still hot for him after hours in his arms last night? Surely her body had had its fill of his skillful caresses? She was disturbed to realize that it didn't seem to matter what Ben did or said, she continued to find him compellingly attractive. Last night had shown her that the eight years she'd told herself she hated him had been one big, fat lie, and now she understood that even the knowledge that Ben was supremely uninterested in her as anything other than a one-off bed partner still wasn't enough to dim her attraction for him.

She was officially a hopeless case.

Exasperated with her own twisted psyche, she made a frustrated growling sound under her breath, and Ben's head shot up.

"Did you say something?" he asked. He sounded almost hopeful, as though he wanted to continue their discussion.

"Gas," she improvised, wincing and thumping her chest. "Too much orange juice at breakfast."

He went back to his work, and she shoved the power lead viciously into the electrical outlet.

Just a few more days and it's all over, she reminded herself. *And you'll never have to look into his handsome face again.*

It was a measure of how messed up she was that she didn't feel any relief at the prospect, just a dull kind of resignation.

"Hi. I hope I'm not interrupting?"

Tory looked up to see an attractive dark-haired woman standing in the doorway. Dressed in a neat white skirt and white polo shirt with the shipping line logo on it, she was clearly a member of the crew.

"Of course not. How can we help?" Tory asked, glad of the distraction.

"My name's Tracy. I'm on the entertainment staff, and I just wanted to ask if you'd mind me sitting in on your sessions. I love your cookbook so much, and my friend has offered to cover my morning shifts so I can attend, if that's okay with you?" The woman spoke in a rush.

It was only when Tory felt her heart lift at Tracy's compliment that she realized how much of a beating her self-esteem had taken over the last few hours.

"I'm glad you like the book. And of course you're welcome to sit in," Tory said.

Tracy smiled brilliantly, looking hugely relieved. "Thank you! I can't tell you how much this means to me. Is there anything I can do to help? I feel guilty not pulling my weight."

"I've seen how hard you guys work," Tory said. "You should take a break while you can."

Tracy shrugged dismissively. "What about those recipe flyers? Do you want me to hand them out for you?"

Tory looked at the stack of photocopies beside her computer.

"I was going to put one on every seat...." she said, and Tracy stepped forward eagerly.

"Let me do it." She flashed Tory a bright smile, scooping up the photocopies.

"Thanks," Tory said, turning back to the projector just in time to catch the assessing look Ben sent up and down the other woman's body.

Jealousy stabbed at her. Unable to help herself, she glanced over her shoulder to study Tracy again, trying to see what Ben might see when he looked at her.

The other woman was tall, with full breasts, sexy curves and attractive features. She looked fit and athletic and she carried herself with a self-confidence that Tory would never possess. All in all, she was hot, Tory acknowledged reluctantly.

"What do you do on the entertainment staff, Tracy?" Tory asked before she could stop herself.

Tracy was working her way along the stadium seating. "I'm a dancer. Have you seen any of the big shows in the main ballroom?"

Tory didn't need to look over at Ben to feel his interest sharpen. Great. Now Tracy was built, sexy, confident *and* flexible.

"Um, no, but I've been meaning to," Tory said, her jealousy creeping up a notch.

"I saw you guys the other night—you were really good," Ben said. "I'm Ben, by the way. I haven't written a cookbook, but Tory lets me cook with her anyway."

"Hi, Ben," Tracy said, smiling at his self-effacing comment.

From then on in, Tracy and Ben kept up a steady stream of chatter until the first of the passengers arrived, and more than once Tory had to bite down on the urge to tell them to get a room. Especially when Tracy revealed she was an ex-Vegas showgirl and Ben peppered her with a series of humorous questions. Sophisticated women of the world didn't get jealous when their casual lay horned in on another woman in front of them. She'd made her bed and now she had no choice but to suck it up, no matter how hard that was.

Because life was cruel and perverse, the morning session seemed to last forever. After working through her own presentation, Tory stood to one side and watched Ben wow the crowd yet again. Every move he made reminded her of their night together: the dexterous way he peeled an orange, the way he closed his eyes with pleasure when he demonstrated to the audience how decadent his mango sauce was, the small sounds of appreciation he made as he inhaled the sharp scent of freshly ground spices.

Shifting her weight from one foot to the other, Tory forced her gaze away from him and out into the audience. She locked eyes with Tracy, and realized that the other woman was staring at her intently, her face set like stone. A quick smile soon curved Tracy's mouth, however, and Tory smiled back warily. She knew it wasn't the dancer's fault that Ben had been flirting with her, but Tory couldn't help wishing she didn't have to witness it firsthand. No doubt Ben would seek Tracy out tonight and add another notch to his bedpost, just above the one he'd carved for Tory last night. The thought made Tory feel distinctly queasy.

She got through the rest of the session by speculating on what she might find in her brother's letters and postcards when she collected them from the port's administration offices this afternoon. Of course, there was a reasonable chance the package might not even have arrived, island time being what it was, but she decided to be optimistic. Something had to go right today, after all.

She managed to escape the cuisine center in record time, her notebook computer banging against her leg as she strode up the corridor. She almost didn't hear Tracy calling after her.

"Victoria! Wait up a minute," Tracy called.

Desperate for some time alone to try and reassemble her composure, Tory forced herself to stop and smile patiently.

"I was just wondering—have you been to Grenada before?" Tracy asked as she drew alongside.

"No, I haven't," Tory said, her heart sinking as she anticipated what the other woman was about to suggest.

"I know the island really well. If you like, I could show you around. There's a great beach if you wanted to catch some sun…?"

Tracy looked so hopeful and expectant that Tory didn't have it in her to say no.

"That sounds great. And anyone who isn't my mother calls me Tory," she added.

"Tory. Okay," Tracy said, smiling brightly. "When do you want to head off?"

"Let me just drop off my computer. And I need to stop by the port authority's offices to pick something up."

"I know where they are, too," Tracy said confidently.

Tory managed a smile. "Let's go, then."

TRACY HAD TO WORK overtime not to stare at the silver pendant hanging around Tory's neck as they made their way across the gangway and onto the dock. If only she could just reach out and yank the silver teardrop loose, all her problems would be over. Sal would hand Franco back, and she would never have to set foot on a cruise ship again in her life.

"Oh! I didn't realize it was so beautiful," Tory said beside her, stopping in her tracks as she took in the full vista of the horseshoe-shaped harbor of St. George's.

Tracy had seen it many times, but she could see how it might take a person's breath away. Pastel-tinted warehouses marched along the edge of the docks, quickly giving way to the red-tiled roofs of traditional villas and shops. Buildings were whitewashed and charming, the sky was a brilliant blue and the streets bustled with colorful locals.

"St. George's has the reputation of being the most beautiful town in the Caribbean," Tracy said. "They say that if the wind is in the right direction, you can smell ginger, nutmeg, cinnamon and vanilla all at once."

"That's a big ask, and I think all the islands are beautiful," Tory said, shading her eyes and squinting into the sun. "I'd hate to have to choose between them."

"The port authority is this way," Tracy said, indicating the modern building to the left side of the docks.

Shortening her step a little, Tracy let the other woman pull slightly ahead. A satisfied smile curved her mouth as she spotted what she'd been looking for—just visible above the neckline of Tory's top was the bow of her bikini tie. Which meant that if Tracy played her cards right, she could get Tory down to Grand Anse Beach and into the water. The surf was safe there, but Tracy figured there would be ample opportunities for someone to lose a piece of jewelry out in the water. Especially if they had a helping hand.

"I guess you must have always wanted to be a dancer, huh?" Tory surprised her by asking, glancing back over her shoulder.

Tracy answered without thinking. "I was too stupid to do anything else. It's the only thing I've ever been good at."

She saw the surprise in Tory's face at her honesty and tried to backtrack.

"Whoa—talk about too much information. Let me try that again. Sometimes dancing is great. Sometimes it's a drag. It's my job, you know." Tracy shrugged.

Tory surprised her again by reaching out to give her arm a squeeze.

"I know," she said, her tone rich with understanding.

For the first time all day, Tracy let herself relax a little. Maybe forcing herself on a complete stranger for the day wouldn't be such an ordeal after all.

BEN POWERED HIS WAY through the surf, enjoying the sting of salt water against his skin, pushing himself to go harder, faster. For a few blissful moments his mind was free and clear of everything except the here and now. Eva, Danique, Monty, Tory—he let them all wash away as his lungs burned and his shoulders ached with effort.

By the time he'd had his fill he was feeling calmer than he had in a long time. Turning toward shore, he waited until his feet hit sand before surging to his feet, water sluicing down his body.

His hard-won calm deserted him on the spot as he strode up the sand toward his towel and saw her tugging her tank top over her head.

He stopped dead in his tracks, even though she was a good forty feet away and completely unaware of him.

He'd had Tory in his arms all night. He'd caressed her curves again and again, but he was still struck dumb by how sexy she was as she stripped down to a simple red bikini. Her legs, her ass, the gentle curve of her waist, her perky breasts—she was hands down the most attractive woman he'd ever seen.

Tracy was stripping down beside Tory, her fuller, more buxom figure shown to advantage in a black thong bikini. Ben spared her a single appreciative glance before allowing his gaze to feast on Tory again.

As he watched, she laughed at something Tracy said and began smoothing sunscreen into her legs. He was rooted to the spot as she lazily rubbed the lotion in. His mouth felt dry, and he realized his jaw had dropped open a little.

Suddenly he realized what he was doing—staring and salivating like one of Pavlov's dogs. An unfamiliar emotion swamped him as Tory tilted back her head and laughed again. She looked utterly carefree. As though she didn't have a problem in the world.

He identified the unfamiliar emotion with a frown: resentment. He resented her easy-breezy attitude to their night together. He resented that she'd just blown him off this morning when he'd tried to talk to her about what had happened. And he definitely resented the powerful attraction he still felt for her—especially since she appeared to be completely unaffected, judging by her current behavior.

Disgruntled, confused, frustrated, he pivoted on his heel and strode back into the surf.

"YOU WANT TO GO IN?" Tracy asked as Tory relaxed back onto her towel and propped herself up on her elbows.

The silver pendant stood out in stark relief against the woman's flawless skin, and again Tracy was hard-pressed not to stare at it. If she kept it up, Tory would be convinced that Tracy was a big old lesbian about to make a pass at her.

"Water's warm and the surf's real safe," Tracy cajoled, flicking her hair over her shoulder.

Tory let her sunglasses slide down her nose a little as she scanned the water. Something—or someone—caught her eye, and she stiffened.

"I might just catch some rays for a while," she said.

Tracy followed Tory's sightline toward the water's edge, where a broad-shouldered, dark-haired man was striding into the surf.

"Is that Ben?" she asked shrewdly.

Tory shrugged as though she didn't really know. Tracy toyed with the idea of pushing the swimming thing but decided to play it cool. Forcing herself to be patient, she sank back onto her own towel. Tory had been tense ever since they'd stopped by the port authority offices and discovered the parcel she was expecting hadn't arrived yet. Tracy could tell the other woman was fretting over the situation, but there was precious little either of them could do to hurry FedEx along.

"You and Ben are old friends?" Tracy asked, scooping up a handful of sand and letting the grains sift through her fingers.

"Did he tell you that?" Tory asked.

"No. You guys just have that comfortable thing going that people get when they've known each other longer than a few days."

"Yeah?" Tory didn't exactly sound convinced.

"Sorry. I didn't mean to touch on a sore subject," Tracy said.

"It's okay. We studied together, that's all. Apart from that, we hardly know each other."

Right. Except for the way Tory kept glancing down the beach to where Ben was swimming strongly through the surf.

As if she was more than aware of her own preoccupation, Tory flipped onto her belly. The action sent the pendant swinging forward on its chain to dangle in midair above her breasts.

Tracy couldn't help herself—she stared, thinking of the diamond hidden beneath the tarnished silver and of her son and what it would feel like to have him home safe again.

"I told Patti I didn't want it," Tory said.

Tracy blinked and forced her brain into gear. "Sorry?"

"The lucky-charm pendant," Tory said, touching the teardrop with her forefinger. "I told her she should give it to a proper passenger, but she insisted I keep it."

"You know it's supposed to bring you luck in love," Tracy said, mentally slapping herself for getting busted staring. Couldn't she get one simple thing right?

Tory snorted inelegantly. "It's not doing a very good job," she said wryly.

"Maybe you have to want it to happen, too," Tracy suggested. "True love is the last thing I'm looking for, let me tell you. Caused nothing but trouble in my life."

She felt Tory's gaze flicker to her wedding ring. She only kept it on because it helped ward off some of the more hopeful male passengers.

"We're separated, and he's a jerk," Tracy explained. "My mom told me I was an idiot for marrying him, and I guess she was right."

"Your mom should meet my father. Sounds like they'd get on great," Tory said drily.

"Yeah? He break your balls, too?" Tracy shifted up onto one elbow, genuinely interested. She remembered the look Tory had given her earlier, when Tracy had blurted out that comment about being too stupid to do anything but dance.

Tory laughed. "If I *had* balls, yeah, he'd break them. He's got some pretty strong opinions."

Tracy could see the exact moment Tory felt guilty for saying anything bad about her old man; the smile faded from her eyes and she dug her fingers into the sand.

"He just has high standards, that's all," she finally said, as though the beach were bugged and her words were going to get back to her father somehow.

Tracy had reconciled herself to her mother's disapproval a long time ago, but she knew the symptoms of someone who still figured they could somehow do that one magical thing that would earn their parent's unconditional love.

"The thing with my mom is that nothing I do will ever be enough," Tracy said. "I realized that a long time ago. It's like her whole life depends on her being better than me—smarter with money, a better mom than me, a better cook. I sometimes think that if she gave ground on any little thing, she'd just shrivel up like the Wicked Witch of the West and die."

"You have children?" Tory asked, surprised.

Tracy saw the other woman's glance go to her flat abdomen. Tracy patted her belly proudly. "Three hundred sit-ups a day. I snapped back like a rubber band after Franco was born. One good thing about moving for a living."

"How old is he?"

"Five."

Tory frowned. "This is probably a stupid question, but is he on board with you?"

Tracy pushed her sunglasses closer to her face. "My ex has him for the moment," she said. Her voice came out flat, emotionless.

"You must miss him," Tory said sympathetically.

A lump the size of Texas was stuck in Tracy's throat. She swallowed convulsively and sat up, looping her arms around her knees and blinking furiously.

"Hey." Tory twisted on the towel, then her hand was soothing the middle of Tracy's back. "You okay?" she asked after a moment.

Tracy sniffed and swallowed her unshed tears. "I'm fine. I do miss him, that's all. He's a great little guy. Really smart, you know? I keep thinking about how much I'm missing out on, being stuck out here." Her sweeping hand took in the perfect white beach, the crystal-clear waters, the buff, tanned bodies all around them.

Suddenly the absurdity of the situation tickled Tracy's funny bone. She was in paradise and she couldn't be more miserable. Did that make her hard to please or what?

She started to laugh. Tory looked at her worriedly, and Tracy tried to explain around fits of laughter.

"All this, and me sitting here *bitching*," she gasped. Tory smiled, then she started to laugh, too. Before long they were both doubled over, giggling like school girls.

Finally they sobered, staring out at the water.

"Thanks. I think I needed that," Tracy said, shooting a quick smile Tory's way.

"Same goes. Big-time," Tory said.

"You want to go in?" Tracy asked, nodding toward the sea.

"Sure."

They walked down to the water's edge, chatting easily. Even though Sal would go ballistic if he knew she'd passed up an opportunity to grab the necklace, Tracy couldn't bring herself to make an attempt straight after the conversation they'd just had. She liked Tory. It had been a long time since anyone was kind to her without wanting something in return.

Pretending that she and Tory really were friends, that they really did have nothing better to do than spend a few hours lazing in the sun, Tracy tucked her head down and dived into the surf.

THE MOMENT SHE GOT back to her stateroom after the afternoon lecture, Tory put the Do Not Disturb sign on her door and sat down on her bed to stare at the FedEx pouch that had been waiting at the port offices when she'd stopped by for the second time on her way back to the ship. Taking a deep breath, she tore open the pouch and tipped her brother's letters out onto her bed. She'd had a surprisingly good time at the beach with Tracy today and later at the spice markets, where she'd stocked up on fresh ingredients for her jerk-chicken recipe, but Michael's letters had never been far from her mind. Glad to have her official duties over for the day, she sat down and began sorting through the mass of envelopes.

She spent five minutes arranging the letters in chronological order, then she began to read. Almost immediately she teared up. She had forgotten how much fun her brother's letters were. Reading them was like having him sitting beside her. Even his big, loopy handwriting was full of personality. But she knew that if she was going to get through the stack of letters before they arrived in St. Maarten tomorrow, she couldn't afford to let sentimentality and grief get the better of her. Swallowing her tears, she forced herself to read on.

By the time she had to prepare for the jerk-chicken cook-off, she'd worked her way through the first two months of her brother's correspondence. He'd been moving around a lot, working with various local police groups, and she found it hard to get a handle on where he'd spent the bulk of his time. She jotted down any names or locations that he mentioned, but so far she'd found no hint that there had been a special woman in his life.

She was feeling distinctly frustrated as she donned her chef's uniform. She'd been hoping to unearth a name to help her in her search on St. Maarten. Going ashore with nothing but the boy's pho-tograph was truly going to be like looking for a needle in a haystack.

As she made her way to the cuisine arts center, her stomach per-formed a loop-the-loop and she acknowledged that she was also dreading seeing Ben again. Their afternoon session had been pure, unadulterated torture. Between fighting her stupid awareness of him and maintaining the jaded man-eater persona she'd adopted, she'd had sweat trickling between her breasts by the time the hour was over. She honestly didn't know if she could come up with a repeat performance while she was preparing her jerk-chicken recipe. But, of course, she didn't really have a choice if she wanted to maintain the pretense that last night had meant as little to her as it obviously had to him.

Pausing outside the center, she tucked a stray curl behind her ear, sucked in her belly and thrust out her chest. Composing her face into what she hoped was a devil-may-care smile, she swung through the door.

Ben glanced up when she came in, and her step faltered as she met his piercing regard. Just for an instant, she felt as though he could see clear through to her soul.

Man-eater, she reminded herself. *Think man-eater.*

"Hey, there," she said casually.

Ben grunted in response.

"Don't tell me you're nervous?" Tory drawled, slipping into her vamp routine and flashing him a flirty smile.

"I'm not nervous," he said flatly.

"Good. I hope you're a gracious loser, Ben," she said cockily. "I'm looking forward to the quote of yours in my next book."

"Don't count your jerk chickens yet," he said.

Crossing to the fridge, she began to assemble her ingredients. Ben had set himself up at one end of the prep bench, leaving her the other half. Carefully she arranged her spices and herbs, mortar and pestle and other tools. Ben, she noted, was already cutting up chicken pieces.

"You planning on cooking anytime soon?" Ben asked when she'd finished organizing her knives.

She shrugged lightly. "I like to be prepared."

"You're a pretty cool customer, aren't you?" There was a dark undercurrent in his voice, and his gaze was searching, almost challenging.

"When it comes to cooking, I know my strengths," she said.

His gaze flickered quickly down her body, and when he met her eyes again, she blinked at the anger she saw there. Then she blinked again and it was gone. Maybe she'd imagined it? She turned her attention to her chopping board, then shot another glance up at him from under her eyelashes. He was focused on his work, his expression neutral. She couldn't think of a single reason he would be angry with her; she must have imagined that burning look.

She shook off the odd moment and concentrated on the task at hand. Working methodically, she ground black pepper, allspice, nutmeg, cinnamon and sage leaf, inhaling the pungent aromas with pleasure. She'd searched all over the market for the hottest peppers she could find, and she removed the seeds of a bright red habanero pepper with brisk, economical movements. Occasionally she could feel Ben watching her as he assessed her mix and technique, and finally she spoke up.

"Trying to pick up a few tips?" she asked archly.

"Just curious."

She'd already noted that he was using far more nutmeg than her recipe demanded and that while she'd chosen to use smoked paprika, he was grinding up cayenne pepper. He also had four limes lined up beside his cutting board, while her mix only called for the juice of one lime.

It was only as she measured out olive oil and began to mix it into her assembled herbs and spices that Tory registered how tight the muscles of her back and belly were. She really wanted to win this battle of skills with Ben, she realized. Not to prove that her cookbook was authentic or that she was as good in the kitchen as Ben, but to win back some of the self-respect she'd lost last night. She'd offered herself to Ben in the most intimate, soul-baring way twice now, and both times she'd woken to disappointment and regret. Just once where Ben was concerned she wanted to come out on top.

It took another five minutes to finish preparing her marinade. Collecting her chicken fillets from the fridge, she pierced each piece several times with a skewer to allow the marinade to permeate all the way through the fillet.

"Interesting," Ben said, and she saw that he'd finished and already set aside his fillets to marinate. "Aren't you worried that they'll lose too much moisture during cooking?"

"No," she said simply.

He tilted his head and shrugged a shoulder as if to say she was digging her own grave. She nodded her head toward the bowl full of his chicken pieces.

"You're not worried that you won't get the full flavor through the meat?" she countered.

"No," Ben said, echoing her reply.

Just to show him she could play tit for tat as well as he could, she copied his shrugging gesture in return.

He moved away, and again she caught a flash of something belligerent behind his eyes. She stared at his back with a frown. If anyone had the right to feel belligerent, it was her. She was the one who'd scored Ben's morning-after debriefing talk, not him. She was the one who'd been left feeling exposed and foolish and vulnerable.

Reaching for a mango, she brought her knife down with a zealous swipe.

She *really* wanted to win this cook-off.

SHE WAS HUMMING. A jaunty little tune that set his teeth on edge. He shot her a narrow-eyed look, but she seemed oblivious as she sliced up chunks of mango for a salad.

He didn't get it. One minute she was keeping him at arm's length as though her life depended on it, then she was leading him back to her stateroom and—apparently—baring her soul to him. And now she was…what? Treating him like some gigolo she'd picked up in a bar for the night?

And he was feeling resentful again. He wasn't used to being dismissed. He wasn't looking for a commitment—God forbid— but he couldn't help feeling vaguely…used. She'd just taken what she wanted from him and left him gasping like a landed fish.

In the back of his mind a rational little voice reminded him that before Tory had signaled that she was more than comfortable with the transient nature of their relationship, he'd been feeling distinctly antsy about what she might expect from him. He'd had his little "I'm not a relationship kind of guy" speech all ready to trot out—she'd just beaten him to it.

But he wasn't in the mood to be rational. He couldn't stop thinking about touching her, tasting her, holding her, and he was thoroughly pissed that she seemed utterly oblivious to him now that he'd scratched her itch, so to speak. A trip down memory lane—that's what she'd called it. As if he was a tourist attraction, part of the whole island holiday experience.

Checking the time, Ben flung open the fridge and began assembling his own salad. Strictly speaking, jerk chicken was the only dish in contention, but presentation and accompaniment might influence Nikolas and Helena, and it was stupid to let Tory gain an edge, no matter how unlikely it was that her New Yorker's take on the dish would beat the real thing.

They worked in silence for twenty minutes, both concentrating on their own meals. When Nikolas and Helena were ten minutes away, Ben turned on the stove top and oiled a cast-iron griddle. In his restaurant, he'd char-grill any jerk-seasoned meat to really bring out the flavors. Traditionally the dish was cooked in a deep pit lined with stones and covered with green timber, the smoke from the timber adding extra flavor to the dish. Since he didn't have access to either method onboard *Alexandra's Dream,* the griddle would have to do. Tory would be at the same disadvantage, so he figured it was a level playing field.

"There's another griddle if you want it," he offered grudgingly as she placed her own marinated chicken on the counter.

"Thanks," she said.

He lifted the heavy plate onto the stove top next to his own, and she joined him to oil it and adjust the heat.

It was impossible not to brush up against one another, working so closely, and they proceeded to do so many times over the next ten minutes. Combined with the heat from the stove top and his own hormones, Ben was feeling more than a little steamy—and that was before Tory shrugged out of her chef's coat, revealing a formfitting black silk slip dress underneath.

"Too hot," she said, shooting him a sideways look as though she felt she owed him an explanation.

He wasn't about to argue. He was burning up—and not because of the slab of sizzling cast iron in front of him. The sun had given her skin a delicate golden hue today, and her neckline offered him an almost untrammeled view of her cleavage. After a few seconds of surreptitious appraisal, he confirmed his first instinct—she wasn't wearing a bra under the skimpy black silk bodice. He could see her nipples clearly through the fabric, and every nerve ending in his body went on hyperalert.

Even though he knew that a rematch with Tory could bring nothing but trouble, he couldn't help himself. She was hot, and last night had been too good to pass up an encore performance. That's what he told himself, anyway, as he deliberately brushed against her, holding the contact for a fraction longer than was natural. But maybe he also wanted to prove to both of them that what had happened between them hadn't been as forgettable and inconsequential as she'd made it out to be.

Her head shot up at the contact, and he saw her pupils dilate with desire before she gave a sharp little laugh.

"Careful, Ben, or you'll be giving me ideas," she said lightly.

He frowned as she moved away from him, the picture of unruffled calm. If he hadn't been looking into her eyes, he'd have bought it, he realized. *She still wants me.* He knew it, absolutely. He felt a ridiculous, absurd surge of triumph. She might have brushed him off this morning, but she wasn't immune to him. He wasn't completely without power in this equation. Very intent, he prepared to close the distance between them again.

CHAPTER NINE

"SOMETHING SMELLS wonderful," Nick said, and Ben looked up to see his friend escorting Helena into the center.

"That would be *my* jerk chicken," Tory said cheekily, flashing Ben a challenging smile.

He didn't return it. Instead he gave her a long, steady look, putting her on notice that there was unfinished business between them still. She gave absolutely no indication that she had received his message, but he noted that she stepped as far away from him as she could without abandoning the stove top altogether.

"I have been thinking about this all day," Helena said, eyeing with interest the two platters he and Tory had made up. "Is that *watermelon?*"

She was looking at the salad Ben had put together.

"Yep," Ben said. Quickly he explained that watermelon-and-tomato salad was a great accompaniment to any jerk-seasoned dish, as it cleared and cooled the palate.

"But you've chosen mangoes and bananas, Tory?" Helena asked.

"For the same reasons. More sweet, where Ben's is tart, but the same principle," Tory explained.

Nick produced a bottle of Semillon sauvignon he'd brought with him to accompany the meal and insisted they all have a glass. Ben took cool mouthfuls as he watched Tory presenting her meal.

Nick and Helena helped themselves to a portion each and ate with obvious relish.

"Very flavorsome," Helena said, rolling her eyes enthusiastically.

"Great mouth feel—very tangy," Nick said, slightly tongue in cheek. "Am I getting the lingo right?"

"Close enough," Ben said drily.

Tory gestured toward her platter. "You want to try some?" she offered him.

"Sure."

She cut off a bite-size piece of chicken and offered it to him on a fork. Instead of taking the fork, however, he captured her hand and raised it to his mouth so that she was forced to feed him.

"Next thing you know, I'll be spitting on a handkerchief and cleaning your face," she said flippantly as he at last released her hand.

He saw with satisfaction that her color was high, but the explosion of flavors in his mouth swiftly distracted him. Tory's chin lifted as she waited for his verdict.

"It's good," he said once he'd swallowed. "I like the smokiness from the paprika. It's a good option when there's no chargrill on hand."

"Come on, then, Ben, let's have yours," Nick said, waving a hand imperiously.

"Even you are not Captain in the kitchen," Helena said admonishingly, nudging him with her hip.

Ben presented his meal and slid the platter forward. Both judges took care to cleanse their palates with a mouthful of wine before sampling Ben's chicken.

Again Helena rolled her eyes as she swallowed. "Oh, that's wonderful," she said.

Nick nodded as he chewed and swallowed. Ben felt Tory tense beside him. He spared her a sideways glance. She looked as wound up as a thoroughbred before a big race.

"Very zesty. Lots of citrus flavors," Nick said thoughtfully.

Helena added, "Mmm. And nice fire. I like a bit of heat."

Tory shifted restlessly from one foot to the other. Ben almost felt sorry for her. She was a great chef, and her cookbook had been thoroughly researched. He knew it would kill her to be judged second, but there was no substitute for authenticity.

"Well, I have made up my mind," Helena said, turning to her fiancé. "Nick?"

He looked thoughtful for a beat before nodding. "Yes, I'm ready," he said.

"I am sorry, Tory, but I am voting for Ben's," Helena said with a charming grimace of apology. "As I said, I like it hot."

"Interesting, because I preferred Tory's," Nick said, black brows raised. "No offense, Ben, but the smokiness won me over."

Beside him, Tory let out a gust of air. "A draw," she said slowly. Ben frowned as she turned to him, blue eyes sparkling. "We're evenly matched, one vote each," she said.

"A fitting outcome, since they are both outstanding dishes. Would you mind very much if we ate the rest?" Nick asked hopefully.

"Are you kidding? Go for it!" Tory said gleefully. Settling back against the counter, arms crossed over her chest, she tilted her head to one side as though she was deep in thought. "I think a nice long quote would be good. Something about the authenticity of the recipes."

She was practically dancing with triumph, he noted. For the first time all day, he felt as though he was seeing the real Tory. Her eyes were sparkling, her cheeks were pink and the tension was gone from her shoulders.

Probably he should be more annoyed about being bested on his home turf, but he was too busy noting the change in her demeanor to care much.

"I'll contact my editor and let her know she can expect a quote from you for the jacket of my next book," Tory continued blithely. Ben held up a hand. Even he had his limits.

"I believe the word was *draw,* Tory. To the victor the spoils—and the way I see it, there is no victor."

"We're both winners," she countered. "I'm more than happy to give you my father's port-wine glaze recipe in return for what you laid on the table."

"I don't really want—" he said, but she cut him off.

"It's Dijon mustard," she said quickly. "Just stir a teaspoon in before basting."

Ben shut his mouth and she grinned unrepentantly.

"You can e-mail the quote in anytime before the end of March," she said.

The clatter of knives and forks being laid down drew his attention back to their guests. Nick was swallowing the last of his wine, while Helena was savoring the last mouthful of Ben's chicken.

"Fantastic. Don't tell Dominique, but it's the best meal I've had all cruise," Nick said.

Helena dabbed at her mouth with a napkin. "Now we're promised to some VIPs in the Emperor's Club for drinks, but we would love for both of you to join us," she said.

Ben spoke before Tory had a chance to decline or accept.

"Thanks, Helena, but we've got to clean up here and we've got prep work for tomorrow."

He felt Tory stiffen beside him, but he refused to meet her eye as Nick and Helena took their leave, thanking them both for their efforts.

"Just because we slept with each other once doesn't give you the right to speak for me," Tory said the moment they were alone.

"Twice," he corrected her, placing both griddles in the sink to soak.

"I beg your pardon?" she asked, blinking rapidly.

"Twice. We slept with each other twice." Undoing his apron, Ben wiped his wet hands dry and closed the distance between them.

Eyes wide, Tory backed away. "What are you doing?" she asked, her voice quavering.

"Making sure I'm not going mad," he said and then he reached for her.

She tasted hot and sweet and he couldn't get enough of her.

Backing her toward the counter, he drew her closer still and murmured his approval as her hands found his hips and slid around to grasp his butt. Angling her head back, he teased her lips before kissing a trail across to her elegantly extended neck. She gasped and ground her hips against him hungrily as he pressed wet open-mouthed kisses down into her cleavage.

His hands slid up to cup her breasts, and he brushed his thumbs over her nipples through the silk of her dress. She wriggled against him, and he shuddered as she smoothed a hand round to his fly and began working on his zipper.

Wanting to see her, needing to see her, he peeled the straps of her dress down, revealing her breasts, pink-tipped and aroused and so responsive that his hands curled possessively into her hips as he picked her up and placed her on top of the counter, the better to worship her, as instinct demanded.

"Oh!" she cried as he pulled a nipple into his mouth. His hands found her knees and slid up her bare thighs even as he spread them apart, his body sliding into place against hers.

"Ben…what if someone comes?" Tory murmured as he switched his attention to her other breast. She had him out of his pants by now, hard and hot in her hand.

He shot a glance toward the door. It was unlikely that anyone would come calling at this time of night, but the last thing he wanted was to be interrupted just when he had Tory where he wanted her.

In two steps he was at the door and it was locked, and when he turned back, his heart lurched in his chest as he took in the sight of her ready and waiting for him, arms braced behind her on the counter, head tilted to one side as her heavy-lidded gaze followed his progress.

Without another word he crossed the space between them, a savage feeling of triumph rising inside him. *This* was undeniable. There was no way she could dismiss *this* as a walk down memory lane.

TORY COULDN'T THINK. She knew there were things she should be doing or saying, smart, self-preserving things, but she was operating on pure instinct—and that instinct was to get as close to Ben as she possibly could. She wanted to feel his mouth on her, his strength inside her, his hands on her skin. Almost sobbing with need, she tore at his shirt and pulled him close so she could rub her breasts against his chest.

"Yes," she whispered as his fingers teased along the lacy edge of her underwear.

How could something that felt so right be wrong? How could she possibly deny what her body needed and only Ben could give her?

Only Ben.

The thought made her stiffen. It wasn't *only Ben. Only Ben* had a whole lot of connotations attached to it that she didn't like one little bit—especially given the way last night had turned out.

Thinking about the awkward speech Ben had tried to deliver that morning pretty much killed the last of her buzz. Suddenly she was supernaturally aware of where they were, what they were doing and how she was going to feel if she let herself get swept away again.

Abruptly she broke their kiss, tilting her head back from him and bringing her hands up to push his chest away. Ben's hand froze on her thigh, and she could feel the instinctive drive in him to see their encounter through to its natural conclusion.

"Ben, I can't do this," she said, reaching for the straps of her dress and pulling the bodice up to cover her breasts.

They were both panting, and a dark flush colored his cheekbones.

"We can go to my room," he said, obviously thinking she was objecting to the venue.

"No. This is not a good idea," she said.

"It was five seconds ago," he countered.

She forced a world-weary note into her voice. "Look, I didn't mean to lead you on. I guess I was just carried away with the whole competition thing."

He tensed and stepped away from her. "Right."

She slid off the counter as though she dealt with scenarios like this every day.

"Last night was great, but I have this rule about going back for seconds," she said nonchalantly, smoothing the skirt of her dress with an apparently unconcerned hand—except her hand was shaking so much she had to curl it into a fist to disguise her reaction.

"A rule," he repeated incredulously.

"Yes. About—about keeping things uncomplicated," Tory improvised wildly, way out of her depth. She could count the number of lovers she'd had in her lifetime on the fingers of one hand—including Ben. "I really prefer to keep these things to one night only. Saves anyone from getting the wrong idea."

"And we wouldn't want that happening," Ben said in a curiously flat tone.

"Exactly. I knew you'd understand," she said lightly.

He shot her a dark, unreadable look before turning away and raking a hand through his hair with frustration.

She knew exactly how he felt; her whole body was screaming for his touch. She'd never thought of herself as a particularly sensual person. She enjoyed sex, but only Ben could turn her on to the point where she forgot all her inhibitions.

Only Ben.

Her resolve hardened. She'd done the right thing. Definitely she'd done the right thing, no matter that her body was thrumming with need, no matter that Ben thought she was some kind of one-night-stand queen.

"I've got things to organize," she said briskly. "We've got the tour tomorrow, remember."

They were catching the ferry from St. Maarten to Anguilla tomorrow, Ben's home, and touring his restaurant in lieu of the day's lectures. The short ferry trip had been tacked on to the original shore schedule when Jacques St. Clair had been forced to pull out and Ben had stepped in.

"It's a tour. What is there to prepare?" he said.

Desperate to get out of there, she ignored him, scooping up her chef's coat and moving toward the door. Her neck prickled, and she knew Ben was following her with his eyes. She held her breath, expecting him to see through her facade with every passing second. But he didn't call her back. He didn't say a word as she unbolted the door and exited to the corridor. She let her shoulders sag and her breath sigh out once she was out from under his scrutiny.

Pressing a hand to her chest, she felt the heavy thump-thump of her heart against her palm. Even knowing how it would end, how she would feel afterward, she had it in her to regret walking away from him.

Which was exactly why she knew she'd made the right decision.

BEN CLEARED THE COUNTER and scrubbed the two griddles on autopilot. Even though there were kitchen crew on call to help out with this sort of thing, tonight he welcomed the familiar routine of cleanup.

He was still reeling from what had happened with Tory. Not her calling a halt—although there were parts of him that were none too happy with that. He was more shell-shocked about what had happened when he'd kissed her. He'd done it to prove a point, to himself as well as her—that last night had not been a figment of his imagination, that they really had been that good together.

Or maybe he'd been hoping to prove just the opposite. He was so screwed up right now he had no idea what he wanted or how he was feeling. All he knew was that the moment he'd had Tory in his arms again, he'd lost all sense of himself.

He frowned as he emptied the sink and put the griddles aside to dry. He'd never lost control with a woman in his life and he didn't like the feeling. He felt uncertain, off balance. Confused.

Hands on his hips, Ben stared out at the stadium seating with unseeing eyes. He'd come on this cruise looking for a distraction, but he felt as though his whole life had been turned upside down. She'd been on his mind almost constantly for the past three days. Even as a teenager he'd never mooned over girls. He figured that at thirty-one, he was a little too old to start—but apparently his psyche had other ideas.

Flicking off the lights in the cuisine center, he started to walk back to his suite, but the thought of sitting alone with his thoughts all evening held about as much appeal as a tax audit. Instead he gravitated toward the Emperor's Club in the hope of catching up with Nikolas and Helena. After a quick scan of the club, he concluded that they must have already moved on. Spotting a vacant stool at the bar, he shrugged. What the hell. At the moment, anything seemed better than going back to his empty suite.

He'd barely taken the first mouthful of his cognac when an attractive blonde at the other end of the bar gave him a come-hither smile. Automatically he checked her out. Slim, tanned, big brown eyes, built. Probably midtwenties, maybe a little older. And looking for some fun.

Six months ago, he'd have picked up his drink and sauntered over in response to the unspoken invitation in her eyes. But, for better or for worse, Eva had come along and revolutionized his life. And now Tory looked set to finish the job.

Not wanting to appear rude, he raised his glass in silent acknowledgment but didn't budge. After five minutes, the blonde exercised her equal-opportunity rights and slid onto the stool next to him.

"Hi. I'm Jenna," she said.

"Ben," he said easily.

"Can I buy you a drink, Ben?" she asked.

He'd gotten a really good look at what was on offer when she'd walked over—her tight red minidress didn't leave much to the imagination at all. And still his heart sank.

If it hadn't been so damned unsettling, it would be amusing. He knew guys who would crawl over broken glass to sit next to a hot woman like Jenna. Hell, he didn't even have to make the running—she was offering to buy *him* a drink, giving *him* the eye. If he wanted to, he could just go along for the ride and barely break a sweat.

And there was no reason why he couldn't—or shouldn't.

He simply didn't want to. The only woman that he wanted in his bed tonight was Tory. For good or for ill. As uncomfortable as that realization was, it was also undeniable.

"You know what, Jenna? I was thinking of turning in after this one drink, so thank you, but no."

Her smile became a little more wicked. "An early night sounds pretty good, actually," she said.

Ben groaned inwardly. He'd had a lot of practice picking up women but not in repelling them. A dozen gambits occurred to him, but he decided to opt for honesty.

"I'm sort of involved with someone," he said apologetically. "But thanks for the offer."

She shrugged gamely and slid off the stool. "If you don't ask, you never know," she said philosophically.

Ben watched her tight, gym-honed butt wiggle back to the other end of the bar.

Shaking his head at himself, he threw back the last of his drink and stood.

Maybe he really was losing his mind.

CHAPTER TEN

TORY FOUND THE NAME at midnight, just as she was rubbing her eyes with weariness. She hadn't had the best night's sleep last night—for obvious reasons—and she was wilting over the stack of her brother's correspondence when she read the woman's name.

Anneisha. She jerked upright and rescanned the letter. Michael was talking about a day tour he'd taken with a local tour guide. Her name was Anneisha. Michael wrote that for the first time in six months, he'd met someone who laughed at all his jokes. Anneisha, he'd concluded, got him. That was all, but it was enough. Apart from work colleagues, Michael hadn't mentioned another woman's name in all his letters. This had to mean something. She checked the date—May tenth. Michael's plane had crashed in October. More than enough time for him to start some kind of relationship with a tour guide who "got him."

There was a hopeful light in the blue eyes that stared out at her from the bathroom mirror as she brushed her teeth. She had a location, a name and a photograph of the boy. All she needed now was some luck….

Inevitably her thoughts slid across to Ben as she closed her eyes and burrowed into her pillow. If she let herself, she could relive the heat of his hands on her skin. If she let herself—which she wasn't about to do. She wasn't a stupid woman. And she certainly wasn't a glutton for punishment. She'd made the right decision when she'd pushed him away. Definitely.

A restless night's sleep was the thanks she received for her self-control, and she woke feeling distinctly edgy. A thought popped into her mind before she'd even rolled out of bed: she was going to see Ben's home turf today. She was going to tour his restaurant and kitchen garden, watch him interact with his staff and customers, get a sense of the man he'd become, the life he lived. She sat on the edge of her bed and ran her fingers through the knotted mess of her curls. She was nervous. Which was stupid and irrational and…stupid. Ben meant nothing to her. What did it matter to her where he worked, what kind of a restaurant he'd built up? But she could still remember the dreams he'd painted for her that one night they'd had together back in their student days. He'd described the beachfront shack his parents had run for the past twenty years on Rendezvous Bay and he'd talked about their love of local, traditional foods and how hard they worked. He'd imagined the restaurant he wanted to build in the shack's place—open and airy, with balconies to eat up the sea views. She'd lain beside him and imagined, too. And today she was going to see how he'd made his dream a reality. A Michelin-star-winning reality that drew the rich and famous like magnets to his door.

Shrugging off the butterflies line-dancing in her belly, she showered and did her hair and makeup in record time. She had to be back at the port by eleven to lead the tour onto the ferry and take the forty-minute trip across to Anguilla. There, a tour bus would pick them up and take them to Café Rendezvous. Before that, her time was her own. Time she was going to use to try to find the little boy.

The ship docked at nine, and two hours wasn't exactly overly generous to comb an island in search of one small person, but it was all she had. And, realistically, it was probably the end of her search. If she found no clue, no lead here, she had to let it go. As perhaps she should have that first night when she'd found the boy's photograph in the paper.

Rubbing in the last of her sunscreen, Tory was about to head out the door when she spotted the silver teardrop pendant on the vanity. She hesitated, remembering the conversation she'd had with Tracy the previous day. She'd told the other woman that she hadn't wanted the pendant and all it represented—but she'd still worn it every day of the cruise. Her hand hesitated over the silver chain. She'd grown used to the reassuring weight of it against her skin—that was the only reason she felt strange leaving for the day without it around her neck. Before she could second-guess herself, her fingers closed on the cool metal.

She was just settling the pendant around her neck as she opened the door, ready to head out. She pulled up short when she found Tracy standing there, hand raised as though she was about to knock.

"Hi," Tory said, pleased to see her. "You just caught me."

Tracy's gaze dropped to where Tory's hand was still on the necklace before returning to Tory's face. "Oh, hi. I was coming to ask if you wanted to come to a party me and some of the girls are throwing tonight in our cabins after the show. Kind of a pyjama party, with cake and face packs and manicures…?" Tracy asked hopefully.

Even though she never wore nail polish and had never used a face mask in her life, Tory was unable to say no to the woman. There was something sad and vulnerable in Tracy's eyes that touched Tory. After their talk the previous day, Tory suspected it was something to do with her son, Franco.

"Okay, sure. That sounds fun. What time and where do I go?"

They ironed out the details, after which Tory made her apologies.

"I've only got two hours before we head off on the tour of Ben's restaurant," she explained, "and I've got some errands to run."

"Sure. I'll catch you later," Tracy said easily.

After making her way to the access deck, Tory strode briskly across the gangway onto the dock, squinting against the bright Caribbean sunlight. Sliding her sunglasses on, she consulted her map. Confident she knew how to find the street where Matt Striker had snapped the little boy, she wove her way into the heart of Philipsburg.

TRACY SPENT THE MORNING congratulating herself on Tory's acceptance of her girls'-night-in invitation. The entertainment staff threw one every cruise as a relief valve for the inevitable tensions that built in a closed environment like a cruise ship, so Tracy knew exactly what it would be like: women doing each other's nails, talking about sex and relationships, offering each other foot and shoulder massages and eating chocolate. Getting the necklace off Tory under those kind of conditions would be child's play, and afterward it would be easy to claim it had simply been lost.

She was feeling deservedly smug when her supervisor, Janice, called her out of their morning rehearsal and over to the phone.

"It's for you, Tracy," she said, not bothering to hide her disapproval.

Immediately Tracy's stomach lurched with fear. Ever since having Franco she'd developed a dread of unexpected phone calls. In her experience, they almost never boded well for anyone.

Janice maintained her grip on the receiver when Tracy crossed to her side to take the call.

"Personal phone calls belong on personal time," Janice said snippily, not bothering to cover the mouthpiece and thus ensuring that Tracy's caller got the message, as well.

"Sorry," Tracy muttered, secretly wanting to shove Janice in her pneumatic chest. The woman was her supervisor, after all, not her mother or parish priest.

Reluctantly Janice released her grip and Tracy put the receiver to her ear.

"Yes, Tracy speaking," she said warily.

"It's me." She recognized Sal's voice immediately and her

disquiet grew. There was no reason for her to hear from him like this—unless something had happened to Franco.

"What's wrong? Is Franco okay?"

"Relax, don't get your thong in a knot. He's fine. I've got my guy ready to pick up the necklace again. You'll need to leave the ship this afternoon and find your way to a place called the Blue Lagoon in the old part of town."

Tracy spoke across him before he could get too far into his directions.

"I don't have it—I won't have it until tonight," she said, casting a nervous eye toward Janice to make sure her boss wasn't snooping. Janice was such a busybody Tracy wouldn't put it past the other woman to eavesdrop on the conversation. But Janice was busy telling one of the other dancers how sloppy her high kick was.

"You were supposed to grab it yesterday," Salvatore said coldly.

"I didn't get a chance," Tracy fibbed, remembering her swim with Tory. In hindsight, it had been foolish to let herself get carried away with the feeling of camaraderie that had built during their beach trip. She owed Tory no loyalty, nothing—and she owed Franco everything she had and everything she was.

Sal swore darkly. "You're friggin' useless, you know that?"

"I didn't apply for this job," she said hotly. "It's not like I wanted to be a damned thief."

Sal swore again and she waited while he had a conversation in Italian with someone on the other end of the line. Even though he'd been living in the States for a while now, most of his friends were still native Italian speakers. And most of them were connected to organized crime.

She held her breath, remembering his threats to take Franco away from her for good. She shouldn't have fought back. Sal was spiteful—he'd hurt her just for the fun of it, just to make her squirm.

"Forget it," he said when he came on the line again. "You're fired. We can't afford any more screw-ups."

Tracy's hopes soared, then immediately plummeted to her feet. "What do you mean? What about Franco?" she demanded, clutching at the phone.

"What do you mean, what about Franco? You welshed on the deal, you know the consequences."

Her breakfast threatened to come up again as she panicked. "Sal, no! I tried. I tried so hard. You don't know what it's like. I've never stolen anything in my life. It's not easy for me. Give me one more chance, I'll get it for you, I swear." She was begging, throwing any remaining dignity she had to the wind.

"I don't want your half-assed help. I've got some boys on St. Maarten who owe me a favor. Just give me a description of this broad who's got the necklace," Sal demanded.

A chill stole down Tracy's spine. "Why? What are you going to do?"

"None of your goddamned business," he said menacingly. "Now give me the description."

Tracy bit her lip and stared at a scuff mark on the wall. He was going to hurt Tory, she knew it. Sal didn't do anything subtly. On the one Christmas they'd shared with each other, he'd torn into his gifts, ripping his way carelessly through the paper and ribbon she'd painstakingly wrapped around her offering, eager to get to the good stuff inside. He was like that with everything—sex, gambling, conversation. He always wanted to cut to the chase, and in this case that meant taking Tory out to ensure his investment was safe.

"You want to see your kid again or not?" Sal asked when her silence stretched too long.

She felt sick as she pictured Tory in her mind's eye. But the other woman wasn't her responsibility—Franco was.

"She's tall and slim, late twenties. Blond curly hair, kind of sits up around her jaw. Blue eyes. Looks a bit like Meg Ryan, I guess.

But she'll be on tour all day, Sal, taking the passengers to some restaurant on Anguilla. Why don't you just let me do this my way? I guarantee you'll have the necklace by tomorrow morning."

"I sometimes wonder whose side you're on, Tracy," Sal said nastily. "Some people might think you didn't want to secure the financial future of your husband and family."

You're not my husband in anything but name, she wanted to yell at him. He'd been blackmailing her for weeks, forcing her to do things she hated. And she knew she and Franco would never see a cent from the sale of the diamond inside the pendant.

But, as always, he held the trump card: her son.

"I'll do whatever you want me to do, you know that," she said quietly, utterly defeated.

"I know that—I just wanted to make sure you remembered that was the case," Sal said smugly. Then she was listening to the dial tone.

"If you care to join us, Tracy, we'll go over the routine again," Janice called from the dance floor.

Tracy stared unseeingly at her boss. What was she going to do? She couldn't let Tory walk into a setup. Could she? But to interfere might mean she pushed Sal too far.

"Excuse me, Tracy? Hello? A little professionalism wouldn't go astray," Janice called, hands on her hips now.

Tracy pulled her focus back to the here and now. Ducking her head, she fell into line. It was what she always did, after all—kept her head down and let herself be pushed around. It was the price she paid for keeping Franco safe. Right now, however, it felt very steep indeed. She might survive this situation, she might even successfully rescue her son from the man she used to call husband, but she doubted she would ever be able to forget offering an innocent person up as sacrifice.

TORY KNEW WHAT THE woman would say even before she explained what she wanted and showed the newspaper photograph of the boy. She'd been walking the streets of Philipsburg for nearly two hours, trying to find places where locals might go rather than tourists, showing the photograph of the little boy and explaining she was looking for a woman called Anneisha who might be his mother. Nine times out of ten she got blank looks and head shakes, and every now and then she got a cold-eyed stare from someone who obviously doubted her motivation. It dawned on her eventually that in an age of custody disputes and broken families, her questions might lead people to jump to the wrong conclusions. There was precious little she could do about that, however, short of explaining her full story. Even if the busy shop assistants she spoke to had the time to listen, she was reluctant to expose herself so completely. The reality was that she was on a wild-goose chase. But she'd always known that, no matter what she'd told herself.

The woman behind the counter of the local council offices studied the photograph steadily for a few long seconds before shaking her head.

"Don't know him, sorry," she said, shrugging one shoulder.

"Is there some record of births and deaths that I could search through?" Tory asked, grasping at straws.

"Without a name?" the woman asked incredulously. "Are you crazy, lady?"

Tory flushed with embarrassment. It was a stupid question, and she nodded her acknowledgment of that fact. "Sorry. Thanks for your time."

She stepped out of the air-conditioned quiet of the offices and back into the hustle and bustle of the street. For a moment she just stood and let the tourists stream around her, her head down as she stared into the little boy's face one last time.

She'd been so sure. But she was wrong. She was chasing a fantasy, a memory. And that was all Michael would ever be. He was gone. She had to accept that, once and for all.

The photograph crumpled as she clenched her hand, screwing

it into a tight, hard little ball. Before she could think twice, she took the two steps required to reach the nearest trash can and dropped the hard paper ball inside.

There. It was over.

She kept her mind deliberately blank as she made her way back to the ship. After all, nothing had really happened. She'd toyed with an idea for a few days, that was all. It was stupid to feel as though she'd just lost something important.

She forced a smile for the group of passengers who had gathered on the docks, waiting for the ferry to Anguilla.

"Okay, everybody, the ferry leaves from down the end of the docks, so let's make our way over there," Tory said once she'd nodded a greeting to a couple of familiar faces from her lectures. "Ben has gone ahead to get things ready for us, so we'll be meeting him over there."

She saw a couple of disappointed faces among the women in the crowd. No doubt they'd been looking forward to trying to hustle a little one-on-one time with Ben during the forty-minute ferry trip.

She was surprised to see Tracy's face among the passengers, and she made her way to the woman's side. "You didn't tell me you were coming," she said.

"I, uh, wasn't sure I could swap duties, but it turned out they wanted to assign someone to help you with crowd control anyway," Tracy said.

She looked pale and nervous, and Tory cupped her elbow warmly.

"Are you okay?" she asked quietly, stepping closer so none of the passengers could overhear them.

"I'm fine. Just a bit tired, I guess." Tracy smiled thinly.

Tory was convinced it was more than that, but she couldn't force Tracy to confide in her. And, anyway, there must be other dancers or crew on board that Tracy was closer to. Tory was sure that if she needed it, Tracy had plenty of support on hand.

"Okay, well, I'm glad they thought to send someone and that it's you. Looks like we've recruited some extras for today's sessions."

It was true; clearly some husbands had decided to join their wives on the shore trip, and the group was half again as large as usual. With Tracy's help, Tory herded them down toward the ferry and on board the smaller vessel, answering any questions as best she could along the way.

The fresh sea breeze and chop-chop of the ferry on open water delighted most of her charges, although a small number were soon clutching brown paper bags and turning green about the gills. Tory could only imagine how much worse it would be on the return journey when they were full of food and wine.

The blur on the horizon that was Anguilla quickly came into focus and she found a place on the railing to savor the view. This was Ben's home. She might even be about to meet his parents, if they were around for the day. From the few times that Ben had spoken of them, she'd gathered they were both very social people, so she suspected they might be on hand to greet the passengers today. Another reason to feel off balance, although she was also aware of an odd sort of melancholy. Much of it could be put down to giving up on her search for the little boy, but she was also aware of feeling sad and dissatisfied about her relationship with Ben. She'd started this cruise with so many hopes and expectations, and now it felt as though her world was becoming increasingly narrow. She'd let go of her dream of finding Michael's son, if indeed he'd ever had one. And she'd resigned herself to the fact that Ben Cooper was never going to feel the same way about her as she felt about him. She remembered Tracy's joking comment from yesterday, about being in paradise but still finding reason to bitch and moan. She was guilty of the same crime, but somehow she couldn't find it in herself to snap out of it. She felt...defeated. As though some of the color had leached out of the world. Glancing along the guardrail, she noticed Tracy standing nearby, and the breath caught in the back of her throat when she saw the anguish on the other woman's face. As soon as Tracy registered her gaze, however, she mustered up a brief smile. Tory frowned, but Tracy had made it clear she didn't want to talk about whatever was wrong. What a pair they both were. No wonder they had gravitated to each other so naturally.

The sight of Ben standing sure and strong on the jetty when the ferry pulled into the harbor on Anguilla was the cherry on top of what was already a trying day. He looked like a pirate, with his faded jeans rolled up on his calves, his chest displayed to advantage in a dark navy singlet and his hair wind-raked and disheveled. Tory's pulse went wild, even as she heard a few heartfelt sighs from some of the middle-aged women passengers. She forced her own face into a neutral expression. Whatever happened, she did not want to be categorized with a gaggle of romantically inclined spinsters.

Ben nodded his head in greeting when she met him on the jetty.

"Tory."

"Ben."

His gaze flicked over her from head to toe before he turned his attention to the large crowd she'd brought with her.

"Is it just me or has our group grown overnight?" he asked.

"We've recruited the husbands, I think, with the promise of a meal."

"Of course. Well, I'm sure we can squeeze them all in."

They were both excruciatingly polite as they ushered their passengers onto the tour bus the cruise company had hired for the day. Tory kept her polite smile fixed to her face as Ben proceeded to flirt with the circle of women who elbowed their way to his side for the twenty-minute-long journey. He was very charming. But she'd always known that about him.

Her first sight of Café Rendezvous took her breath away. The bus turned a corner on the coast road they'd been following, and the bay spread out before them, the café perched on the lower slope of what could only be an extinct volcano, the front beams of the structure marking the highest point on the beach. The closest comparison Tory could come up with was an open-sided oriental pagoda, elevated to make the most of the sea view. She had seen similar architecture in Bali and other tropical destinations and she guessed that it was a style uniquely suited to the balmy environment. Built high on timber stilts, the restaurant boasted balconies on all sides, and as the bus drew closer she saw that what she'd taken to be open sides were in fact floor-to-ceiling windows, ensuring that even in less-than-perfect weather, diners would be part of the outside world.

"My goodness," a passenger said beside Tory.

Forgetting what lay between her and Ben for a few precious seconds, Tory shared a smile with the woman. It was beautiful.

Immediately she felt the weight of Ben's regard and she met his eye briefly.

"It's very lovely," she said.

Her gaze fell on a small silver-timbered shelter hidden in the shadows beneath the restaurant's support beams. A delighted smile curved her mouth as she turned impulsively to Ben.

"Is that your parents' beach stall, still standing?" she asked.

He frowned. "How did you know about that?"

"You told me about it, back at the Institute," she said, only realizing afterward how revealing it was that she remembered their conversation eight years later.

The look he gave her was oddly intent.

"It must have been hell to build around it like that," she said, racing back into speech to cover her gaffe.

"We had to move it during construction, but we put it back once we were done," Ben said, his gaze on the humble takeaway stand that had started it all.

Tory turned her face toward the view, letting one of Ben's groupies leap in to take over the conversation. He kept surprising her. Every time she thought she had him pegged, some new aspect of his personality revealed itself. Like the whimsy and sentimentality that would lead him to reconstruct his parents' old premises. It was a world away from the cool distance that reigned in her own family.

She hung back when the passengers exited the bus and raced up the wide stairs to the restaurant in an attempt to secure the best sea views for themselves. Tory could only smile at their rote response—after six days at sea, she'd have thought they would have spent enough time staring at the rippling, frothy stuff. Casting a quick look around to ensure no one was watching her— particularly Ben—she made her way beneath the restaurant's mighty support stilts and inspected the Cooper family's beach stand.

The wood was so old the grain was picked out in ridges and dips. Rusty nails bled red streaks down most of the boards, but the faded sign across the serving window was still legible. *Café Rendezvous, the best island fare in the Caribbean.* Placing her hands on the sill of the serving window, Tory stood on her tiptoes and peered inside. She was disappointed to see that it was just an empty shell—obviously Ben's whimsy had not carried as far as hanging on to the old interior fittings.

He'd spoken of this little stand so fondly, with such fierce pride that first night they were together. He'd talked about his mother's way with fresh caught shellfish and his father's secret dipping sauces and the queues that formed at the height of the tourist season because everyone knew that the best beach fare was to be found at the Café Rendezvous. His love for this place had dripped from every word, and the expression in his eyes had become far off and distant as he'd remembered his island home. Leaning her back against the stand, she stared out at the stretch of beach and ocean that had been part of Ben's indoctrination into the world of cooking. Again she couldn't help but contrast it with the gleaming stainless-steel benches, hulking industrial refrigerators and high-stakes tension that had characterized her own early experiences in the kitchen. Her father had run Le Plat as though the fate of the world depended on every morsel that left his kitchen, and his daughter had not been exempt from the scathing vitriol that poured forth if ever something was not to his liking.

Worlds apart, indeed.

Abruptly she realized that she had lingered too long. With one last glance at Ben's past, she made her way toward his present. As she'd suspected, the dining room of his restaurant was superb—high opens beams arched overhead, native timbers gleamed warmly from tables set just the right distance apart from one another to create a sense of intimacy without crowding and deeply padded wicker chairs gave the whole a light island feel. Huge vases of tropical flowers graced strategically placed tables throughout, creating privacy screens and bringing yet more of the beautiful island scenery inside.

Her heart lifted ridiculously as she surveyed it all, silently approving the crisp white shirts and simple khaki pants of the serving staff, the unpretentious crockery and glassware and the soothing ambient music. It was perfect, all of it, and she found herself running a proprietorial hand along the smooth linen of a table cloth. It was only when she heard Ben's voice echoing out from the as yet unseen kitchen that she snapped out of her moment of indulgence. She had no right to feel proud of this place; the very thought was insane. Shaking off her own foolishness, she strode briskly to join the rest of the group.

"TODAY OUR SPECIAL IS fresh local snapper, and we're not going to dress it up too much. If there is one rule at the Rendezvous, it's that we let nature do all the hard work. With fresh, in-season produce, all a chef has to do is step back and get out of the way of the ingredients," Ben said. "Try to remember that when you get home—less is more. You don't need fancy sauces and a million different flavors competing on your plate—keep your choices simple and fresh and you can't go wrong."

At the very back of the crowd crammed into his kitchen, Ben saw Tory rejoin the group. He'd realized she was missing the moment they'd hit the restaurant, but he'd been too busy corralling the passengers to go in search of her. He'd dearly wanted to see her face when she first walked in, to read the expression in her eyes. The look of delighted amazement when she'd first caught sight of the Café's unique silhouette would stay with him for a long time.

He wanted her to like his place, he realized. Better still, to admire it. Not because he was comparing himself with her father's famous Le Plat or because he still felt he had something to prove to her but because he simply wanted her to gain pleasure from a building and business that he'd poured so much of himself into. This place, more than anything in his life, represented who he was. The way he chose and trained his staff, the respectful, friendly relationship he had with them, the easy informality of his dining room—all of it reflected his personality. And it was becoming increasingly urgent and important to him that Tory see him as more than a hard, available body or a nostalgic walk down memory lane. He couldn't get her out of his head. He was beginning to wonder if he even wanted to.

Aware that his thoughts had wandered once again into scary territory, Ben brought his focus back to the eager faces staring at him.

"Philippe here is seasoning the snapper with garlic, olive oil, a fresh bay leaf inside and a pinch of our own secret pepper blend," he said, turning to watch his employee with the rest of the group. "And, no, I can't tell you what makes it a secret. Once he's through with that, we simply place the fillets on a baking tray in the oven for just seven minutes—that's all it takes with fresh fish, and we don't want to dry it out."

Ben drew Philippe into the conversation, deferring questions to him and encouraging the young chef to step in with his own comments. After ten minutes, Philippe was comfortably holding the floor as he walked the passengers through the syrup he was making for banana-infused rum. Confident the younger man was more than holding his own, Ben slipped out the back to his office to run his eye over any messages or invoices that may have come in during his absence.

He pulled up short when he saw Danique and Eva waiting in his guest chair.

"Hi. What's up?" he asked, regretting his sharp tone immediately. He hadn't meant to sound so defensive and angry. At least not consciously.

"Your mother was looking after Eva for me this morning, and we agreed I'd pick her up from here," Danique said. "Your parents just left—your mom had some appointment she couldn't miss."

"Right."

Ben knew his parents had been shattered by the revelation that Eva was not their grandchild, and his mother had made it clear to him that she planned on continuing the friendship she'd struck up with Danique. Like Ben himself, she'd been unable to just turn off the flow of love she felt for the bright-eyed bundle in Danique's arms.

"She misses you, you know," Danique said, following Ben's gaze to where it rested on Eva's cherubic face. "I had to buy some of your aftershave and put it on her blanket to help her sleep."

Ben stared at Danique. What did she want him to say? That he missed Eva so much that it was like losing a limb? That one tiny baby girl had left a hole in his life the size of the Grand Canyon?

Danique seemed to read his anger and confusion.

"I'm sorry. I didn't realize you'd be here today. I know Eva and I need to get used to not having you around."

He frowned. "What does that mean? Don't tell me Monty's already shirking his responsibilities?"

"No. He's fine. He's good. He just…he's got his businesses to run and a lot of other things on his mind."

Ben could imagine exactly the kind of father Monty would make. But Danique had made her choice. He caught himself up on this last thought. There was no point blaming Danique for the fact that Monty was biologically Eva's father. It wasn't as though Ben would have preferred never to have known the truth. He could have gone on for years in ignorance if Danique had not confessed all. He might never have known Eva was not his, and where would that have left him?

Something in his chest ached at the thought, and he understood suddenly that it wouldn't have mattered—the important thing was the love that had grown within him for the small person cradled in Danique's arms.

The ring of a cell phone interrupted further conversation, and Danique scrabbled one-handed in her bag, awkwardly trying to balance Eva at the same time. The decision to step forward and take Eva off her hands was completely instinctive, and Danique flashed him a small, grateful smile as he eased Eva into his arms.

"Monty!" Danique said once she'd located her phone.

Ben was too busy relishing the weight and feel and smell of having Eva in his arms again to pay any attention to the phone conversation. Eva's dark brown eyes seemed to sparkle up at him in recognition, and she worked her legs and reached out a hand to grasp the lapel of his shirt. Ben knew only too well what would happen next, and he watched with a sappy, indulgent smile as Eva tugged the triangle of fabric imperiously toward her mouth and proceeded to gum it into soggy submission.

He was so absorbed in the play of emotions across Eva's face that he was actually startled when Danique touched his arm and indicated she was going outside to continue what was obviously a heated conversation with Monty. Ben nodded his acquiescence, returning his attention to the baby.

"Did you really miss me, little one?" he asked quietly, swallowing the lump of emotion that formed in his throat. Lifting Eva in his arms, he pressed his face against the silky down of her hair and inhaled deeply. Frangipanis and talcum powder, the most powerful perfume in the world as far as he was concerned. It had certainly been enough to bring him to his knees.

"You know how to wrap Daddy 'round that little finger of yours, don't you?" he said as Eva broke into a delighted gurgle.

If he hadn't heard the scuff of a shoe on floorboards, he would never have turned and seen the shock written large on Tory's face as she retreated from his office doorway.

She stared at him, her face paler than pale, for a long, drawn-out moment.

"You said she wasn't yours! What kind of a man lies about something like that? My God, did you think I wouldn't sleep with you if I knew?" She asked the last as though it made her want to gag.

"Tory, it's not what you think," he said, starting forward.

But Tory was already moving, blundering past Danique, who had entered the corridor behind her.

CHAPTER ELEVEN

SWEARING, BEN PASSED Eva back to Danique.

"Is something wrong?" Danique asked, staring after Tory with concern. "I didn't interrupt anything, did I?"

Ben shook his head and took off after Tory. He didn't stop to ask himself why it was so important to him that she understand the truth about Eva. A week ago, he wouldn't have given two pinches if she jumped to the wrong conclusion about him. But a lot had shifted since he'd boarded *Alexandra's Dream*.

He was just in time to see the side door closing behind her and he followed her down the back stairs and onto the beach. She didn't realize he'd followed her for a few seconds, and he saw so much confusion and disappointment and anger on her face that he couldn't stop himself from striding to her side and grabbing her shoulders.

"She's not my daughter, Tory," he said firmly. "I know it looked bad, but it's true."

"You called yourself Daddy—I heard you," she said accusingly. "I know you think I'm a naive idiot, but I wasn't born yesterday."

Ben frowned at her self-description and shook her lightly. "I don't think you're anything of the sort. For six months I thought Eva was my daughter. Danique—Eva's mother—was having an affair with a married man. She told me Eva was mine when the real father wasn't prepared to face the music."

Tory's forehead pleated with confusion. "I don't understand.

Are you saying she *lied* to you?" she asked, the notion obviously so foreign to her that she could barely comprehend it.

"I guess. Yeah. She lied to me. And then Monty came good, and she fessed up and told me that Eva wasn't mine." He shrugged, aware that the casual movement hid a depth of emotion that he wasn't ready to face yet.

"Ben," Tory said, her expression stricken. "Oh, Ben—you had her for six months, and then you found out she wasn't yours?" Tears filled her eyes and she let them fall unhindered. "I can't imagine how that must have felt. You must be so angry. You must have wanted to tear the world down."

Ben snorted his amusement at her very apt description. "I think I just settled for being an asshole to you," he said self-deprecatingly.

Tory blanched further still. "You mean you only just found out about this? My God, no wonder you were such a…" She trailed off rather than kick him while he was down, waving her hands in the air to indicate how irritable and unforgiving and damning he'd been.

"*Asshole* is the word you're looking for," he prompted her helpfully.

"You had every right to be," she said.

"Not with you. The moment I walked into Brown's in New York City and they all stared at me like I'd grown an extra head when I announced I was there to work with them, I knew you'd found out about the bet. And I knew I was in the wrong—I just had to grow up a bit before I could admit that to you and myself."

She shook her head, rejecting his words. "I should have confronted you on the spot about the bet, screamed at you or something, but I have this stupid pride. I can't ever let anything go. Like with the jerk chicken. I'm always trying to prove myself…" She broke off, shaking her head again.

"You had a point about your jerk chicken, though," he said lightly.

A corner of her mouth quirked into a half smile.

"I'm sorry. About Eva, I mean. You obviously miss her." She placed a gentle hand on his forearm.

There was so much comfort and genuine compassion in the gesture that Ben felt hot emotion burn at the back of his eyes. He hadn't cried since the time he broke both his arms when he was six years old and fell out of a tree—and he wasn't about to damage his near-perfect record now. Squinting toward the horizon, he gave himself a few long moments to compose himself.

"Yeah, well," he finally said.

Tory just squeezed his forearm in mute understanding before relaxing her grip.

"Ben!"

They turned to see Danique standing near the entrance to the car park, Eva in a babysling across her chest and a baby bag over one shoulder.

"I'm going now, but could you give me a hand with the box of storybooks your mom is giving me?" Danique asked.

Ben felt Tory bristle beside him.

"Excuse me?" Tory muttered under her breath, obviously taking offense on his behalf at Danique's continuing proprietorial attitude toward him. For some reason, he found Tory's reaction very endearing.

Placing a calming hand on her shoulder, he responded to Danique. "Sure. Where is it?"

"Back in your office," Danique said.

Unconsciously echoing her earlier gesture of comfort toward him, Ben squeezed her shoulder gently before removing his hand.

"You should go grab a seat," he told her. "Lunch should be ready by now."

She nodded, but her narrowed gaze remained fixed on Danique. Oddly warmed by her defense of his position and feelings, Ben turned back toward the restaurant feeling better than he had for days.

TORY TURNED TO FOLLOW Ben, but she was halfway up the stairs when she heard Danique exclaim in annoyance. Unable to stop herself from glancing over her shoulder, she saw that the other woman had dropped her baby bag and the contents were now strewn across the ground. Hugging her child to her chest, Danique attempted to collect her scattered belongings, but it was clearly going to be a long, slow process.

Tory sighed. She wanted to slap this woman for treating Ben so cheaply, so cruelly, but she also couldn't walk away when Danique needed help.

"Wait," Tory called, descending the steps. "I'll help."

Danique shot her a curious look and a half smile. "If you don't mind. It's so awkward, Eva is getting so heavy now."

Tory avoided her eye and bent to collect the contents of the baby bag.

"You are Ben's friend, yes?" Danique asked after a few seconds.

"We went to school with each other," Tory said coolly.

"Oh. I was hoping you might be his new girlfriend. He needs someone in his life."

"And why is that?" Tory asked pointedly.

Danique could not hold her eye. "He told you about Eva?"

"Yes."

"And you are wondering what kind of a woman I am. I wondered that, too, but I did what I had to do to ensure Eva would be loved and cared for. It's not easy bringing up a child on your own. I have a friend who struggles with it every day, so I know how tough it can be. No one to step in if you get sick. No one to run errands or help carry the load. Maybe it makes me weak, but I knew I would not be giving Eva everything she deserved if I tried to cope on my own."

Tory held her ground. "Ben loves that little girl with all his heart." Tory had only to watch him as he held the baby to see that.

And before, on the beach, he'd been about as close to tears as he probably ever allowed himself to get.

"Yes. I know. He will make a wonderful father one day," Danique said sadly.

The sound of heavy footsteps drew a line under the rest of their conversation.

"What the hell did Mom put in this?" Ben said as he joined them. "It weighs a ton."

Tory didn't miss the speculative glance he shot between her and Danique. He was wondering what they'd been talking about while he'd been gone. As well he might.

"They are old books. They made them differently back then, your mother tells me," Danique said.

Since Tory still held the baby tote, she walked with them toward Danique's car, a sensible wagon with a baby seat strapped in the back. Ben stowed the books in the trunk, then stood back as Danique strapped Eva in securely. Tory could see he was itching to check the straps were secure and ensure the safety of the little girl. Her heart ached for him and she got mad at Danique all over again.

She was so distracted by her private outrage that she almost missed what Danique said as she started the car and prepared to drive away.

"I've spoken to Anneisha about babysitting Eva on Wednesdays while I'm at my training course, but if you still want her, she's all yours," Danique said through the open car window.

Ben shook his head. "No. You're better off making your own plans," he said firmly.

Danique bit her lip, then she ducked her head once in acknowledgment and slowly pulled away.

Tory stared after the car, her whole body as tense as piano wire. Without thinking, she grabbed Ben's forearm.

"Did she just say Anneisha? Does she know someone called Anneisha?" she demanded urgently.

"Her friend. An old school friend, I think," Ben said, staring at her with concern.

"Did she used to be a tour guide? And…and does she have a little boy?" Tory asked, her heart in her mouth.

"Tory, what's going on? Are you okay?"

She saw that her fingernails were digging into Ben's forearm, almost as though she was afraid that if she let him go, this new lead would fly away on the brisk breeze.

"Does she have a little boy?" Tory repeated, easing her grip on his arm.

"She's a single mom, yeah."

She released his arm and pressed both hands to her suddenly overheated face.

She'd found Anneisha. Which meant she might also have found Michael's son.

"I need to meet her. I have to meet her and her son," Tory said.

Ben's frown deepened. "She lives on St. Maarten. Tory, what's going on?"

Suddenly Tory felt light-headed and weak-kneed. She glanced around for somewhere to sit, but the only things on offer were the large rocks that bordered the pathway from the garden beds. Without second thought, she dropped down onto one and gripped her knees.

"Did I ever tell you I had a brother?" she asked once she had solid rock under her butt.

"Yeah, sure. Back at the Institute."

"Michael. We were twins. He died in a light-plane accident off Barbados eight years ago. He's one of the reasons I came on this trip. He thought the Caribbean was heaven on earth, and I wanted to see the places he loved so much."

"I didn't realize," he said awkwardly. "It must have been pretty hard on you."

Tory stared up at him, needing him to understand.

"Ben, this is going to sound crazy, but I found a local newspaper on board the ship, and it had this photograph of a little boy in the crowd watching a pre-Carnival parade. I took one look at him and I just knew…I can't explain. I felt this *connection*. He had these amazing blue eyes, and Michael's chin…but most importantly he had a birthmark on the back of his neck. Every male in my family has had that birthmark for as far back as we can trace."

"You think this kid is your brother's son?" He sounded so incredulous she flinched.

"He mentions a woman called Anneisha in his letters home. He sounded really taken with her, you know. Is it so impossible that she was pregnant when he died?" It was a plea as much as a question, and Ben held her gaze for a long time.

"Tory, it's a massively long shot. You must know that. And Anneisha isn't that uncommon a name on the islands. The odds of this being the right one are slim."

"I can't go home without at least trying to find that little boy. Because what if I'm right? What if my brother left a son behind?" Her voice broke, and Ben hunkered down so his face was on a level with hers.

"This means a lot to you," he stated.

Tory swallowed her tears and nodded fiercely. "He was my twin. If this is his child, it means we haven't lost all of him."

"This is what you've been worrying about all cruise, isn't it?"

"Yes."

Ben pushed himself to his feet and held out his hand. "Come on."

Tory slid her hand into his and allowed him to pull her to her feet. "Where are we going?" she asked hopefully.

"You're going inside to eat lunch with the rest of the passengers, and I'm going to ring Danique and get Anneisha's contact details for you."

A bolt of adrenaline shot through her at the prospect of finally knowing one way or the other. She frowned as another thought occurred.

"What do I say to her? I mean, I could have it all wrong. I don't want to stir things up for her if I've got the wrong end of the stick," she said worriedly.

"I'll ask Danique. She'll know what happened to Tarik's father, whether he's still around or not."

She relaxed a notch. The last thing she wanted to do was barge into a stranger's life and start throwing crazy suggestions around. She wanted to be as sure as she could be before she introduced herself and told her story.

Joining the passengers when all she wanted to do was jump the next boat back to St. Maarten required a real exercise of will. The superb meal that Ben's team put before them went some way to calming her jangled nerves, but she kept a constant eye on the door to Ben's office, waiting for him to come out and pass on what Danique's response to his questions were. After twenty minutes, she was going slowly crazy with impatience, but finally Ben reappeared. She rose from her chair and met him halfway.

"Okay. Tarik's father was an American who was down here on a working holiday, scuba diving or something. He made a lot of promises, but when she told him she was pregnant, he disappeared and never came back. She's never heard from him again."

Tory's mind was racing. "The American part fits. And Michael was with the DEA—I know he couldn't tell anyone what his real profession was down here, since it was an undercover operation. God, she probably doesn't even know his real name, so when the plane went down, there was no way she could have connected it with him. She just thinks he abandoned her." Tears filled her eyes and this time she didn't try to stop them. Even though most of what she'd said was conjecture, it had to be pretty close to the truth, and it was a horrible situation for everyone involved. "How awful for him. When the plane went down, to know that Anneisha was pregnant with his baby… And all this time she's been hating him, and he's been dead."

Ben pulled her into his arms, and she rested her head against

his chest for as long as it took for her to remember the very interested audience of passengers behind them. Sniffing inelegantly, she
disengaged from him. Ben tilted her chin up with his forefinger.

"Tory, you know that the chances are this woman has never
heard of your brother, don't you?" he said quietly.

She nodded. "I still want to meet her."

"I had a feeling you'd say that. I tried her place on St. Maarten,
but there was no answer, so I rang Danique back. She said
Anneisha does odd work here and there, trying to make ends meet.
She's found it pretty tough, I gather, coping on her own."

Tory remembered something Danique had said earlier.

"Danique mentioned a friend who was a single parent. She
said she knew how tough it could be coping on your own."

"Sounds like Anneisha, doesn't it? Danique said she always
picks up Tarik after school at three-thirty."

Tory checked her watch. "The ferry gets us back at three. Will
that be enough time to get there?"

"Philipsburg isn't that big. As long as the ferry is on time,
we'll make it."

It took her a moment to register the full meaning of his words.

"We?" she asked hesitantly.

He shrugged. "You don't know the way, right? Only a bastard
would send you off on a mission like this on your own."

She felt absurdly disappointed. For the last little while she'd felt
as if Ben was on her side, as if she wasn't alone. But he was only
helping her out of a sense of duty, not because he cared about her.

"Of course."

For the second time, Ben tilted her face up with his finger.

"And I want to be there with you, Tory," he said, his voice low
and gravelly with sincerity.

Her heart seemed to shimmy in her chest at the warmth she saw
in his eyes.

"Okay," she said stupidly.

TRACY WATCHED BEN AND TORY sitting close together on the ferry back to St. Maarten, their heads never more than a few inches apart as they talked quietly. Several times Ben reached out to touch Tory's knee or arm or thigh reassuringly. Something was going on between them—but Tracy had already guessed that from the way Tory had behaved at the beach in Grenada, refusing to watch Ben wade into the water.

A cynical smile twisted Tracy's lips. She felt a completely inappropriate desire to march over to both of them and warn them that this was the best it was ever going to get, that one day soon they would discover that the person they thought they were attracted to was just an illusion, a figment of their own imagination. Inevitably Ben would let Tory down, and Tory would become resentful—and it would all be downhill from there.

Registering her own thoughts, Tracy combed her fingers through her long, dark hair. Since when had she become such a hard-ass killjoy? She smirked self-deprecatingly as the answer popped into her mind: probably finding out her no-good husband was a criminal and then having him kidnap her son and use him as leverage gave her some excuse for feeling a little jaded.

She checked her watch again, glad that the day was almost over. Once Tory was back on the ship, she would relax. Tracy figured that as long as she stayed near the other woman and ensured she remained with the tour group, there was precious little Sal's cronies could do. So far, her theory had served her well. Once the group shuffled back onto the *Dream,* she was going to go have a long, stiff drink. Her nerves were officially shot. And then tonight she would grab the pendant her way—and Tory would never know a thing.

A change in the rhythm of the ferry's motor signaled their imminent arrival back into Philipsburg, and Tracy joined the queue to disembark, being careful to keep Tory in sight all the while. Panic fluttered behind her breastbone when she saw Ben and Tory angling sharply away from the rest of the passengers, all of whom were crossing the dock to where the *Dream* was berthed. Tracy's flip-flops slapped her heels as she hustled to catch up to Tory and Ben.

"Hey, guys. Wait up," she called.

She could see the impatience in Tory's face when the woman stopped to allow her to catch up.

"Where are you going?" Tracy asked. Probably she should have been more subtle about her inquiry, but she was nearing the end of her tether. The last thing she wanted was for Tory to wander off somewhere alone, where she'd be vulnerable to Sal's goons.

"I'm going to meet a friend of Ben's," Tory said. "Sorry, Trace, I'd ask you to come along, but it's kind of private."

Tracy eyed Ben's broad shoulders. "Ben's going with you?" she clarified.

If Tory stayed with Ben, surely she'd be safe? Ben didn't look as though he'd budge easily if someone tried to take him out of the game.

"Yes," Tory said, darting a glance toward the man in question.

Ben was looking at Tracy oddly, and she huffed out a laugh.

"Sorry. Before Christmas, one of the passengers got into some trouble when he went off on his own. Just…just be careful, okay?" It was as close as she could come to issuing a direct warning without giving herself away entirely.

"We'll be fine, Tracy. The crime rate's pretty low around here," Ben said lightly.

Tracy could see they wanted to be off, so she stepped back and shooed them on with her hand. "I guess I'll see you tonight then, Tory."

"No problem," Tory said.

Tracy watched as they hailed a cab from the rank out in front of the terminal, automatically scanning the area for anyone who looked out of place or too interested in a tall, slim, curly-haired blond woman. The place was thronging with tourists, and she'd never been good at judging people from appearances alone. Admitting defeat, she gave up her search after only a few fruitless minutes. Sighing heavily, she turned back to the ship. She'd done what she could to keep Tory safe. Hopefully it was enough.

TORY WAS SO NERVOUS she could barely sit still in the taxi on the way to Philipsburg Elementary. After she'd recrossed her legs and wriggled in her seat for the fifth time, Ben reached out a hand and patted her knee reassuringly.

"Relax. You don't even have to speak to her today. If the little boy is who you think he is, you could break the ice by sending her a letter. That way she can have time to adjust to the situation before anything further happens."

"That's a good idea. I feel as though if I can just see him, I'll have some idea. Which sounds really flaky, doesn't it?" she asked anxiously.

"The past few months have taught me that family ties are the most powerful bonds in the world. Why shouldn't you feel something for your twin's child?" he said.

She flashed him a grateful smile. He'd been so supportive, so solid. He'd done everything she could have wanted a friend to do and more.

Her gaze slid away from the strong muscles of Ben's thighs, outlined by well-washed denim. Okay, she didn't think of him as a friend and she probably never would. But he was behaving like one, and that was the important thing.

The taxi jerked to a stop in the street just before the school gate, and before she could fumble in her purse for the correct money, Ben slipped the driver some notes and urged her from the car.

"School should be out any minute, then we have half an hour to get back to the ship before it sails," Ben pointed out as they made their way to the corner of the cross street in front of the school.

Tory bobbed her head to signal her understanding, but her gaze was glued to the front door of the single-level prefabricated school building. Painted in a cheery mint-green with pastel-pink trim, the school's grounds were peppered with palms and frangipani shrubs. She could see hopscotch grids painted onto the concrete school-yard to one side, as well as a set of monkey bars.

"Michael used to love the monkey bars when we were kids," she said. "The things he used to do—he'd hang upside down and swing and try to do one-eighty-degree flips...." She shook her head, remembering how anxious she used to be, standing on the sidelines, urging him to be careful.

"You guys were obviously close," Ben said after a short silence.

"Yes. He was my best friend. It's hard to explain, but we were like two halves of a whole. He was crazy, reckless. I was anal, studious. When we were together, we balanced each other out."

She felt Ben watching her and she shrugged, wishing she could brush off all the memories and the grief as easily.

"It's stupid. He's been gone for a long time now."

"Some things you never get over," Ben said.

He sounded bleak, and she wondered if he was thinking about Eva.

The sound of chatter and laughter spilled out of the school as a stream of children began to emerge into the bright afternoon sunlight. Tory tensed and grasped her hands together nervously. Again Ben seemed aware of her anxiety, placing a reassuring hand in between her shoulder blades.

She only realized she was holding her breath when she started to feel light-headed. Eyes narrowed, she studied every little boy who exited the building, trying to find the connection she'd felt when she'd opened the newspaper.

Ten minutes passed and the stream had dwindled to the odd straggler or two when a small boy emerged from the building. Tory gasped at the resemblance to her brother. In that moment she knew in no uncertain terms that this boy was her brother's child. She could feel it in her bones, in her blood, in her heart.

"It's him," she said, eyes glued to the boy.

"That's Tarik," Ben confirmed slowly. "He's a little taller than when I last saw him, but that's him."

"I can't believe it—I can't believe I found him," she said, suddenly overwhelmed by what it might mean. If this boy was who she thought he was, her parents had a grandchild and she had a nephew—and a sister-in-law. Even if Michael had never actually married her, she believed down to her soul that he had cared for the Anneisha in his letters.

Tarik was making his way toward the school fence when he glanced up and saw Ben. His face split into an adorable smile, and Tory saw with a pang that he had a tooth missing.

"Hi, Ben," Tarik called.

Tory froze. What to do now? She hadn't meant to talk to the boy or even to Anneisha. Not today, when her head was still spinning. Ben solved the problem by moving forward easily, as though hanging around outside the school with a strange woman was the most usual thing in the world for him.

"Hey, there, Tarik, how you doing?" Ben asked lightly.

"I'm good. Are you here to ask my mom out?" Tarik asked boldly.

Ben laughed. "Why would you say that?"

"Mom and Danique said that Mom is the only woman on the island you haven't taken out," Tarik reported.

Tory hid a smile at Ben's obvious discomfort. There was a mischievous glint in Tarik's eye, and she suspected that even if the boy didn't know exactly what he was implying, he definitely knew that he was teasing Ben.

"Who's that?" Tarik asked, and Tory felt the full force of his blue-eyed regard as he stared at her.

He was so much like Michael that she wanted to laugh and cry at the same time. The dimpled chin, the nose, those eyes…

"This is my friend Tory," Ben said, drawing her forward.

"Ben, I don't know if this is a good idea," Tory said in an undertone.

She cast a look over her shoulder, wary about being caught talking to Tarik without his mother's permission, and saw an attractive, tall islander woman approaching. The woman's step faltered when she saw Tory. She blinked, and Tory knew in her gut that this was Anneisha and that the other woman had just registered Tory's uncanny resemblance to Michael.

"Get away from him!"

The beads in Anneisha's braided hair clacked together as she raced to her son's side.

"How dare you turn up out of the blue like this and try to inveigle your way into my child's good graces," she said, her eyes spitting fury.

"Anneisha," Ben said, stepping forward. "It's me. Tory is a friend of mine—"

"I know exactly who she is. You think I can't see the family resemblance? You tell that no-good brother of yours that I don't want anything to do with him, you hear me?"

Before Tory could gather her scattered thoughts together, Anneisha grabbed Tarik by the wrist and began to haul him after her as she strode toward a rusty sedan parked nearby.

"Anneisha, it's not what you think. Michael didn't send me down here to take Tarik away from you," Tory called after her, suddenly realizing how it must look, she and Ben hovering outside the gate, talking to Tarik without first squaring things with his mother. She'd handled this all wrong.

"You stay away from me and my family," Anneisha yelled as she slammed the car door.

In the passenger seat beside her, Tarik's face was creased with bewilderment and worry, and Tory's heart wrung as she saw Anneisha gesticulate vehemently, no doubt telling Tarik to never talk to strangers again.

Tory shot Ben a look.

"I don't know what to do," she said helplessly. "How do I make this right?"

Somewhere, some part of her brain was rejoicing in the fact that she'd been right—Tarik was her nephew, Michael's son. But she knew it was too soon to celebrate yet. Not after what had just happened.

The screech of aging tires on hot bitumen announced Anneisha's departure, and Tory took a couple of steps after the car before realizing how futile it was to even think about giving chase. Even if she and Ben weren't due back on the ship, there was no guarantee that Anneisha would calm down anytime soon. She'd had eight years to nurse her resentment and hurt over what she saw as Michael's lies, empty promises and betrayal.

"Come on. We need to head back," Ben said, tugging on her elbow as she stared helplessly after the car. "We'll work things out, I promise."

She was so shaken by the whole experience that she didn't question her instinctive faith in him or the fact that he'd once again included himself in the equation.

Numb, she allowed him to lead her away.

BEN CURSED HIMSELF FOR being ten different kinds of idiot. Michael and Tory had been twins, ergo it stood to reason that the family resemblance was strong. Of course Anneisha was going to recognize Tory the moment she saw her. And of course she was going to react badly—Michael had fathered her child and then to all intents and purposes abandoned her. Anneisha had every reason to feel scared and righteously angry, especially given the ham-fisted way he and Tory had bumbled into her life. He should have used more common sense and been less swayed by Tory's need to confirm her instincts. But he hadn't been thinking rationally. All he'd wanted to do was help ease the lost, lonely look in Tory's eyes. And now between the two of them they'd created a mess.

He knew from talking to Danique that Anneisha was a strong-willed, fiercely proud woman and he suspected that Tory was going to have her work cut out for her in getting the other woman to listen long enough to learn the truth.

"I have to tell her Michael's dead," Tory said quietly as they trudged toward town, keeping an eye out for a taxi. Ben had already used his cell phone to call ahead to the *Dream* to reassure them that he and Tory would be back by sailing time.

"Yes," he said. Telling Anneisha the truth was the first vital step toward building a relationship with the other woman.

"All these years she's imagined he's out in the world some-where, partying, having a great time, having forgotten about her and Tarik. And I have to tell her that he died and that she's been hating him for no good reason...."

Her shoulders were hunched as she wrestled with the difficul-ties of the situation, and he was powerless to stop the urge to comfort her. Sliding an arm around her shoulders, he pulled her tight against his side.

"It will be okay. She'll calm down, and then you'll tell her the truth and you can start from there," he said.

"I know. I believe that, I do. It's just... She must have loved him once. Or at least liked him a lot. Even though it's been eight years, it's still going to hurt. Perhaps worse than thinking he aban-doned her."

He looked down at the curls on the top of her head. They'd just been through a harrowing scene, but all of Tory's thoughts were for Anneisha and Tarik. He'd never consciously registered what an emotionally generous person she was. With a sudden flash of insight, he realized how much it must have hurt her when her father closed his restaurant. Tory would do anything for her family. Friends, too, he suspected—even Tracy, who she barely knew, merited concern and attention. He remembered how she'd bristled beside him today when Danique had called him into service to collect the box of books. She'd wanted to fight for him, protect him, he understood now. The thought made him tug her closer to his side.

"There's a cab," she said, and he forced himself to release her so he could hail the cruising taxi.

She stared out the window for the bulk of the ten-minute drive to the cruise terminal. He racked his mind in vain for something to say to reassure or ease her, but he'd said everything already. She had a right to feel sad. It was a sad situation.

It was five minutes from sailing time when the driver dropped them on the far side of the docks. Ben could see various crew members clustered around the steps of the gangway in the distance, waiting for the last stragglers to return to the ship.

"We made it," Tory said.

"Yep. Listen, if you don't feel up to our afternoon lecture, I can handle it on my own," he offered. "If you want to go have a sleep or whatever."

She flashed him a weary smile. "Thanks. But I'll be okay. I was thinking back in the cab—what about Danique? Do you think she might act as a sort of middleman for me? If I explained the situation?"

"That was my thought, too. And I don't see why not. Let's face it—she owes me a favor or two."

Tory snorted her wholehearted agreement, then her eyebrows shot toward her hairline and she stopped in her tracks. He'd been so busy watching her face, trying to read the expression in her eyes, that he'd barely noticed the three men leaning against the wall of a nearby warehouse.

Now, however, the three men had moved to stand in their path. Instantly adrenaline surged into his gut and all his senses went on hyperalert. He was more of a lover than a fighter, but he'd had his fair share of punch-ups in his time. These guys were not out for a Sunday stroll.

His fight-or-flight response kicked up another notch as the biggest guy, a bald islander with a bone plug in one earlobe, moved forward, his deep-set gaze intent on Tory. The two smaller guys zeroed in on Ben, obviously planning to keep him at bay while the bald thug bravely took on the woman. Ignoring them all, Ben reached for Tory's arm and jerked her behind him.

"You can have all our money, no problem," he said clearly, already reaching for his wallet.

He heard Tory fumbling in her handbag behind him. Never taking his eye off the menacing bald thug, he held his hand out behind him and Tory pressed her purse into his palm.

"There. Take it and go," he said, tossing his wallet and her purse in front of the men.

The bald man simply smiled. Ben's hands curled into fists and he automatically widened his stance to give himself more balance.

"Tory—run!" he ordered, just as the big islander lunged forward.

Ben had no time to check to see if she'd followed his shouted instruction or not. Rounding his left shoulder forward, he stepped into the big man's path and aimed for his solar plexus. The thud of solid abdominal muscles against his shoulder told him his aim was off, but it had always been a long shot.

The world dissolved into a blur of possibilities, pain and endurance as the thug engaged in earnest. Ben managed to duck a swinging roundhouse, but the big man deflected the straight kick Ben aimed at his knee, and Ben was too off balance to avoid the right uppercut that came whistling toward his jaw. He turned with the blow, dispersing some of the force, and brought his own fist up hard into the thug's kidneys.

It was only when he heard Tory cry out that he realized she hadn't escaped.

"Help! Help!" she cried, her voice echoing off the nearby buildings. She was struggling against the side of the warehouse with one of the smaller goons. Ben's distraction cost him; the islander grabbed him in a vicious bear hug and Ben almost lost his footing. But the sight of Tory being pawed by the other goon gave him the surge of power he needed to break free from the thug's hold and launch himself at Tory's attacker. Seeing him coming, the goon shoved her away, sending her sprawling. Then Ben was on him, pounding his fists into the other man's face and belly, driven by a fierce, primitive need to protect Tory.

The smaller man reeled backward under his onslaught, and Ben was vaguely aware of the sound of running feet as help finally came. But he was fixated on one thing and one thing only—keeping Tory safe. Rage filled him when he saw her on the ground still, kicking out at the remaining two attackers as they attempted to subdue her, her soft-soled shoes doing little damage as she fought to keep them off.

Then three of the *Dream*'s crew surged into the fray, able-bodied men who didn't hesitate to use their fists. Within seconds the thugs had decided to cut their losses and were sprinting along the docks and into the maze between the warehouses lining the waterfront.

"Call the cops?" Ben panted, shaking his grazed right fist to ease the pain in his knuckles.

"Someone went to raise the alert, but I don't like their chances of catching up with those guys," one of the crew members said, glaring after the escaping thugs.

Ben privately agreed, but there were far more important things to worry about. Two of the crew members where squatting beside Tory, and he elbowed them out of the way unceremoniously to reach her side.

She was breathing heavily, and one cheekbone was grazed from where she'd been thrown to the ground. Her T-shirt was ripped down the front, revealing the delicate lace of an ivory-colored bra, and her eyes were wide with shock and fear.

He captured her hands in his and held them tightly. His chest ached as he realized how close he'd come to losing her. Anything could have happened, anything.

Without saying a word, he hauled her into his arms. She clung to him, her face pressed into his neck.

"Ben," she whispered brokenly, her fingers curling into the soft fabric of his shirt.

"I know," he said, holding her as tightly as he dared. "Believe me, I know."

CHAPTER TWELVE

TORY COULDN'T REMEMBER the last time someone had raised a hand to her. Preschool? The playground at elementary school? And now three grown men had torn at her clothes and thrown her to the ground, and Ben had fought them off with his bare hands.

Every time she remembered the way he'd told her to run and then launched himself at the biggest, ugliest thug, she felt sick and dizzy. What if he'd been killed? That one thought reverberated around and around her mind as she allowed herself to be escorted to the ship's medical center to be checked over. Ben was in the next room, and she could hear the low rumble of his voice as he assured the nurses and doctor that he was fine. Just hearing his voice and knowing that he was nearby made her feel better, calmer.

"I can only offer my heartfelt apologies that this should happen to you on one of our cruises, Tory," a deep voice said, and she looked up to find Nick Pappas in the doorway, his brow furrowed with concern.

"I'm fine, really," she assured him. "Ben is the one who took the brunt of it. And it was on the docks, nothing to do with the ship."

"I still don't like it and I want you to know that we'll be taking steps to ensure the local police don't let this drop. Between yourselves and our crew members, we've got strong descriptions of your three attackers. I don't imagine the criminal underworld in Philipsburg is so heavily populated that they'll be too hard to find."

Tory had already met and talked to Sean Brady, the ship's security director. He'd taken her statement alongside the local police, and she'd gained the impression that he was also very concerned by what had happened.

"Come to check out our bruises, Nick?" Ben said from the doorway.

Tory's head came up and she took in the darkening bruise to the left of his forehead, the bandages around the knuckles on his right hand and the ugly red graze down his left forearm. No doubt he sported other bruises beneath his clothes, just as she did. They were already beginning to ache, and she suspected she was in for a painful couple of days.

"Come to see if you are both all right and to offer you anything that will make your remaining nights with us more comfortable. Patti has canceled your sessions for this afternoon and tomorrow morning and arranged for a standby video presentation we have on hand, so you can both have a rest overnight."

Ben attempted a carefree shrug but wound up wincing. "Thanks. I think we're both going to appreciate the extra shut-eye."

There was something in his tone that made her look at him sharply. He crossed to her side and looked down into her face.

"How are you feeling?" he asked quietly.

His hand landed warm and heavy on her shoulder, almost as though he couldn't quite stop himself from touching her.

"I'm fine. Bit shaky but fine." She eased to her feet, trying not to reveal how much the movement caused her bruised hip to ache.

Both Nick and Ben regarded her with deeply doubtful expressions. Tory couldn't help but smile.

"Really. I'm fine," she insisted.

Except for an alarming tendency to want to throw herself at Ben's chest and cling like a limpet, it was true.

"I want both of you to let me know if there's anything else you need," Nikolas said as he headed for the door.

The moment he was gone, Tory remembered the pendant.

"Damn it—I meant to give someone this," she said, pulling the silver chain and pendant from her pocket. It had fallen from her neck in the struggle; she'd found it wedged into a crack in the pavement when she'd calmed down enough to realize it was missing.

"You want to get it repaired?" Ben asked, eyeing the break in the chain. "I can take care of that locally for you, if you want."

"Oh, it's not mine. It's sort of a passenger promotion that Patti cooked up with the ship's librarian, according to Tracy. Each cruise someone 'finds' this pendant in their room. It's supposed to bring good luck," Tory said, fudging the legend of the teardrop pendant a little.

"We'll drop it in to Patti's office later. Right now we're going to my suite," Ben said decisively, taking her arm.

"I beg your pardon?" Tory squeaked. Had she just missed a vital part of the conversation or had he leapfrogged two steps ahead of their current status quo?

In answer, Ben stepped forward and slid his arms around her waist. She didn't resist the gentle pressure of his palms on the small of her back, drawing her against his body.

"I will not sleep a wink if I don't know where you are," he said rawly, staring down into her eyes.

Something big and warm expanded in Tory's chest at the expression on his face.

"Me, too," she confessed shyly. "I mean, I won't sleep if I don't know where you are, either."

Ben lifted a hand to tuck a stray curl behind her ear. "I never want to go through something like that again in my life. I was so scared of what those bastards were going to do to you."

Feeling as though she were walking on eggshells everything was so new and fragile, Tory reached up to slide her hands behind Ben's neck.

"You were the one throwing yourself at those creeps like a

lunatic. I was just waiting for one of them to pull a knife or some-thing." A shiver raced down her spine at the very thought.

"You should have run when I told you to," he said gruffly, his thumb caressing her cheek now.

His body felt warm and solid against hers, and for the first time since the assault, the shaky feeling inside her faded away.

"There was no way I was ever going to leave you on your own," she said, offended by the very idea. "What kind of a person would do that?"

"A smart one," he said with a wry smile. "But I should have known you'd be too stubborn to do as you were told."

He said it with so much affection, so much familiarity, that she couldn't take offense. She figured he could pretty much call her anything he liked as long as he kept looking at her the way he was looking at her.

"Tory, I know it hasn't always been plain sailing between us. I know I've been a jerk a lot of the time because I was so in-timidated by who your father was and how I felt about you, whether I wanted to admit it to myself or not. But today, when I realized what might happen, that I could lose you…I couldn't believe I'd been so stupid, that I'd held back so many times. Tory, I love you."

She could only blink. Even breathing was beyond her for the moment. Ben Cooper loved her? Ben Cooper, the man she'd lusted after for all of her training years, the only man who had ever in-furiated her to the point of insanity and coaxed her to such heights of passion?

"Ben," she finally breathed. "Ben, I've been in love with you since you made that croissant shaped like doggy poop in our pa-tisserie class."

He laughed loudly.

"You have no idea how scared I was that you didn't feel the same," he said, dragging her body closer to his and nuzzling the soft skin below her ear. "After that night, I was sure there was something between us, because of, well…you know."

"Because I cried?" she asked wryly, smoothing her hands down his back, reveling in the fact that she was allowed to hold Ben like this, that she didn't have to second-guess herself or him anymore.

"Stupid, I know. Talk about an ego." He pressed butterfly kisses to her neck.

Slow, liquid heat trickled through her veins, but she couldn't help smiling a smug little smile as she realized that Ben still believed her morning-after vamp routine.

Pulling back from him, she caught his face in her hands and looked him square in the eye. "Ben, I have never, ever cried with another man," she said boldly.

The flash of possessive triumph in his navy eyes was infinitely rewarding.

"Yeah? So all that stuff about rules about more than one night…?"

"A girl has to protect her pride."

Ben laughed. "I believed every word, you know."

"I wanted you to. I'd already humiliated myself enough all those years ago. I wasn't giving you another shot at it."

"And now?" he said, his voice dropping to a husky vibrato.

"Now I'm willing to give you as many shots as you want to take."

His mouth quirked into a wicked grin, and he leaned in to kiss her. For a second she allowed herself to be swept away on the tide of their mutual passion—then she heard the sound of a phone ringing in the cubicle next door.

"We *so* don't need to be in a hospital right now," Ben muttered as he broke their kiss.

Grabbing her hand, he tugged her toward the door. "Let's go."

Tory was filled with a sense of rightness and lightness as she followed him. After all this time, after all the misunderstandings and bad reactions and bad behavior, they'd finally gotten it right.

BEN'S HANDS WERE shaking as he swiped his key card to access the penthouse suite. Some of it was reaction to nearly having the living hell beaten out of him, he knew, but most of it was anticipation—mixed with a liberal dose of terror.

He loved Tory. He'd never felt this way about a woman before. He couldn't think of anything he wanted more in the world than to get as close to her as was humanly possible, claim her, worship her, adore her. But, given that they were sporting matching sets of his-and-hers bruises after the attack, he figured he'd have to settle for some serious spooning action for tonight. It wasn't perfect, but it would definitely go a long way to assuaging the ache that had settled around the region of his heart ever since he'd realized how much he loved her and how close he'd come to losing her.

"Wow. This is a little different from my room," Tory said, admiring the spaciousness of his living room.

They stood awkwardly in front of the butter-colored leather love seat and smiled nervously at each other.

"Would you like a drink?" Ben asked. Maybe some champagne would ease the tension a notch.

"Probably not a great idea with the pain killers they gave me," she said apologetically.

"Right. Of course. I'd forgotten about the painkillers." He'd taken some, too, which might explain how woolly-headed and dopey he was feeling.

Or perhaps that was all him, floundering in a situation that was unique in his experience.

"What about a hot drink, then? Coffee? Tea?" he asked in desperation. Dear Lord, he sounded like his mother, desperate to offer hospitality to a guest.

"Coffee would be great," she said.

Was it just him or did she sound as relieved as he felt? She certainly looked a bit dazed, as though she was still trying to come to terms with the things they'd told each other back in the medical center.

He crossed to the minibar and plugged the coffeemaker in. His hands were shaking so much he had trouble tearing the coffee sachets open.

"Ben."

He glanced up and saw that Tory had moved closer.

"You're exhausted. Maybe we should do this another time," she said, and he realized she'd seen his shaky hands.

"No. I mean, I'm not exhausted. But if you're tired, I'll show you the bedroom. For you, I mean," he hastily corrected himself. "I'll sleep on the sofa bed."

Her head cocked to one side as she tried to puzzle him out.

"Are you tired?" she asked.

"No."

"Me, neither," she said.

The look she gave him was loaded, and Ben felt all his good intentions melting away.

"I thought maybe you'd be too bruised to want to do anything except cuddle," he said slowly.

She smiled a gentle, delighted smile that stole his breath away.

"Come here," she said, beckoning him toward her.

Abandoning his coffee preparations, Ben stepped toward her. She caught his hands in hers and placed one on each of her hips. Then she reached up and looped her hands around his neck. With the slightest pressure, she tugged his head down for a kiss.

Her mouth opened beneath his, and he tasted her sweet desire as their tongues danced. Her hands slid around his back to draw him closer still, and she made a needy sound in the back of her throat as he glided his hands around her hips to cup her butt.

After a long, long time, she broke the kiss and looked straight into his eyes, their noses just an inch apart.

"I figure as long as we're gentle with each other, we should do whatever comes naturally."

"I so agree with your diagnosis, Dr. Fournier. In fact, I think the first thing we should do right now is lie down."

Hooking her forefinger through his, she towed him behind her as she headed for the bedroom. Once inside, she stopped in front of the bed and turned to face him again. Holding his gaze, she pressed her palms against his chest and smoothed them down his belly toward his waistband.

"You have the best chest," she said, clearly savoring the feel of his body beneath her hands.

Her desire fueled his own and he reached for her.

"The feeling is definitely mutual," he said, hands finding the perky curves of her breasts.

She smiled and slipped her hands under his T-shirt, sliding them up his torso while simultaneously caressing his chest. He did his best to help her undress him, rolling his shoulders obligingly as she tugged his top over his arms. Looking down at his chest, she splayed her fingers across his pecs, her mouth parting slightly as she licked her lips in the most unconsciously sexy gesture he'd ever seen.

The next ten minutes passed in torturous bliss as they slowly undressed one another, kissing and soothing bruises and grazes, hands cupping curves and gliding over muscles. Finally they were standing naked in front of one another, their clothes scattered to the four corners of the room. Tory had never looked so beautiful to him, her blue gaze vulnerable, one knee bent self-consciously as he ran an appreciative gaze up and down her body.

"You are my dream come true," he said as he at last allowed himself to press his naked body against hers. She sighed as flesh met flesh, and for a long moment they just held each other, feeling the rise and fall of each other's breaths and the thump-thump of each other's hearts. But desire soon wound itself around them and they began to move, slowly at first, their caresses long and languorous, their sighs appreciative, their kisses drugging. Soon it wasn't enough to just touch her and hold her and tease her with his mouth and hands. Soon he needed to be inside her, as close as he could be, and they sank to the bed as one, hearts racing now, breaths coming in short, hard bursts.

Somewhere in the back of his mind Ben remembered that he'd wanted to go slow, to be gentle and considerate, and he tried to bank the flames of their mutual desire, to slow things down and stretch the moment out.

Tory had other ideas. Her hands and mouth demanding, she set the pace until finally all he could do was give in and slide into her hot, tight embrace.

"Ben," she whispered as they found each other's rhythm.

"I love you," he whispered into her hair. "I love you, Tory."

"I love you, too, Ben," she said and then she dropped her head back and arched her spine and locked her ankles around his hips, riding the crest of her desire.

He followed not long after, crying her name into the soft skin of her neck, his hands clutching at her hips as he lost himself inside her.

Afterward, he pulled her tightly against him, tucking her head beneath his chin, his palms pressed flat against the silky skin of her back. He didn't ever want to let her go. He'd never felt like this before, and the unknown of it terrified him, but he suddenly knew that there had been a large portion of life that he'd been missing out on because he'd never been able to give himself in just this way before.

With the benefit of twenty-twenty hindsight, he thought back to their first night together, all those years ago when they were students. If he'd been older, more experienced, less desperate to prove himself, he might have recognized then what he saw so clearly now: he and Tory were made for each other. Their bodies meshed like two halves of a whole, and her sharp, analytical mind was a perfect complement for his own more laid-back take-it-or-leave-it attitude. Her skill in the kitchen, her gentle giving nature, her stubborn pride, her high standards—he admired and adored everything about her.

No wonder he'd freaked out when he'd woken in her cabin the other night. On some level he'd understood that he'd met his match—and the implications of that had scared the hell out of him. Falling in love with Tory had changed his life. He would never be the same man again, just as he would never be the same man after falling in love with Eva and understanding the joys of being a parent. His bachelor days were officially over—and he didn't feel even a tiny pang of regret.

Nuzzling the back of her neck, he squeezed her tight. "Thank God you weren't hurt," he said.

"Thank God *you* weren't hurt," she said.

He smiled. "At last, something we agree on."

"I can think of a few other areas where we do okay, too," she said, and he knew she was smiling.

Closing his eyes, he at last allowed his body to relax. Tory was safe, in his arms, and they had finally acknowledged what was happening between them. Life didn't get much better, in his opinion.

TRACY PACED THE SMALL cabin she shared with another dancer, her nails biting into her palms.

Tory and Ben had been attacked and hurt badly enough to warrant them being rushed to the medical center. She felt sick with responsibility—but most of all she hated herself for the thread of hope that kept wending its way through her mind. Now that Salvatore had the pendant he might give Franco back. He'd never been a particularly sentimental or involved parent. She knew for a fact that he'd have precious little time for bringing up a child on his own. Being an asshole criminal was a full-time job. Surely if he had what he wanted, he'd just hand Franco back, even if Tracy had not fulfilled her part of the bargain?

I'm a horrible person, Tracy thought as she remembered Tory and Ben again. They were the ones who'd paid the price for her bad decisions, ultimately. *Sal has turned me into a horrible, selfish person.*

Unable to stay away, Tracy made her way to the medical center to hear the latest news, only to learn that Tory and Ben had left over an hour ago with minor cuts and bruises. Armed with the information that Ben had left his cabin as the contact point for both of them, she visited the onboard gift shop before making her way to the Aphrodite deck.

She had to see for herself that they were both okay.

Tory answered the door in one of the ship's complimentary bathrobes, her hair ruffled and her cheeks flushed.

"Oh! I didn't mean to interrupt anything. I can come back later," Tracy said, hastily backtracking.

Tory laughed, the most carefree sound Tracy had ever heard come out of the woman's mouth. If it hadn't been for the graze on Tory's cheekbone, Tracy would have thought she'd gotten it all wrong.

"Relax. Ben's on the phone. Come in." She stood aside to usher Tracy into the suite.

Tracy had only seen the inside of a penthouse suite once and she took a quick glance around at the stylish olive-toned walls, white curtains and buttery leather sofas.

"I heard about what happened," Tracy said, quickly recalling her mission. "I wanted to make sure you were both okay."

"Apart from a few bruises, we're fine," Tory said, grimacing as she mentioned her bruises. "I have a doozy on my butt, let me tell you."

Guilt making her squirm, Tracy unceremoniously offered up her gift. "Here. For both of you. They're from Europe," she explained as Tory accepted the bumper-size box of fine Belgian chocolates.

"Oh, Tracy, that's so nice," Tory said, reaching out to rub Tracy's arm in gratitude. Tracy almost snatched her arm away. If Tory knew the truth, she'd be spitting on her, she was sure.

"So do the police have any clue who might have attacked you?" Tracy asked. That's what anyone else would ask under the circumstances, right?

"No clue at this stage, but Ben and I and some of the crew got a pretty good look at them. Hopefully they won't have too much trouble tracking them down."

Tracy hid a squelch of fear. Surely Sal wouldn't have been stupid enough to let his hired goons know who his contact was on board the ship?

In the background, she heard Ben winding up his phone call. Tory tensed, looking toward him expectantly as he put the receiver down.

"Well?" she asked. "Will she do it?"

"You write the letter, we'll e-mail it to Danique and she'll make sure Anneisha gets it. I've booked two return flights with Island Hoppers tomorrow morning from Tortola back to St. Maarten. The flight only takes forty-five minutes, so we should be back in plenty of time for the afternoon session," Ben said.

Tory let out the breath she'd obviously been holding. "Ben, thank you," she said, crossing to his side to grasp his hands.

Tracy had to turn away from the blazing adoration on Ben's face as he looked down at Tory.

"Don't be an idiot," he admonished gently.

Tory smiled. "Tracy bought us a jumbo box of chocolates. Although I feel like a bit of a fraud taking them since there's really nothing wrong with me."

"I think bumps and bruises qualify us for chocolate therapy," Ben said, inspecting the box. "Yum."

Lifting the lid, he helped himself to a shell-shaped chocolate, then proffered the box to Tracy and Tory. "Dig in, ladies. I guarantee they won't last long," he said with a boyish smile.

Tracy waved her hand in negation, sure that guilt would only make her gag. Apart from the bruise on Ben's forehead and the graze on Tory's cheekbone, they both seemed in remarkably good spirits, but it could have been so much worse if the crew hadn't been close at hand.

"I'm really glad you guys are okay," she said fervently.

"We were lucky," Tory said, then she held up a finger as though she'd just remembered something. "Speaking of which…"

Tracy watched as Tory disappeared into the bedroom, shooting a confused look at Ben. He just shrugged a shoulder and reached for another chocolate.

"I wasn't kidding about wolfing these down. Get in while you can," he encouraged her.

Because she thought it would look strange if she didn't oblige, Tracy selected the smallest chocolate from the box and was about to pop it into her mouth when Tory emerged from the bedroom.

"This broke during the attack, and I really want to get it back to Patti. Would you mind giving it back to her when you see her next?" Tory asked, and Tracy saw that she was holding out the tear drop pendant in her hand.

The chocolate slipped from between Tracy's fingers as she stared at the tarnished piece of jewelry.

She'd just assumed that Sal's men had won it back his way. She had no other reason to think otherwise. But they hadn't. And now Tory was offering it to her on a silver platter.

"Dust it off, it'll be as good as new," Ben said, and it took her a moment to realize that he was talking about the chocolate she'd just dropped, not the pendant.

"Right, yeah," Tracy said, stooping to collect the chocolate.

"You don't mind, do you?" Tory asked anxiously, the pendant still extended in her hand.

Tracy hesitated a moment, unable to believe that after all she'd been through, it was going to be this easy. "No way. Of course not," she said, at last reaching out to accept it.

The silver felt cool against her skin, and the chain slithered through her fingers to dangle from the pendant's loop.

"I feel better already," Tory said. " I know it's probably not worth much, but I would have hated to lose something that belonged to the ship."

"Sure, I understand," Tracy said vaguely.

Once she left the suite, she would have to contact Salvatore and tell him the good news. She frowned as she considered what his response might be. Perhaps the best game plan would be to insist on seeing Franco before handing over the pendant—that way she was in control for a change instead of Sal holding all the cards.

A knock at the door drew Ben's attention away. Tracy's head snapped round and her hand closed convulsively on the pendant as she recognized the voice of Ben and Tory's latest visitor.

"I just had to see for myself you were both unscathed, and we wanted to give you this," Patti Kennedy said, holding out a huge fruit-and-wine basket.

"Hell, I'm beginning to see the advantages of being mugged," Ben said. "Come on in."

"We were just talking about you," Tory said with a smile. "Weren't we, Tracy?"

Tracy stared blankly at Patti for a full five seconds. Her first impulse was to charge from the room with the pendant. She quickly discarded that as completely deranged, since the ship had already left port and was well and truly at sea. For a second she toyed with the idea of trying to hang on to the pendant—perhaps she could offer to take it to the jeweler's for Patti to have it repaired—but Tory was already speaking.

"I just handed over the moon pendant to Tracy so she could give it back to you, Patti," Tory explained. "It broke during the attack, but I was incredibly lucky and found it afterward."

"The important thing is that you two weren't badly hurt," Patti said, but both women were looking at Tracy expectantly.

Slowly, reluctantly, Tracy unclenched her hand and offered the necklace back to Patti.

The other woman cupped her hand to accept the broken chain and pendant into her palm.

"We'll get this repaired in plenty of time for the next cruise," Patti said. "It doesn't look like anything major is damaged—and I can't help thinking that it's done its good work here." She smiled knowingly at Tory and Ben.

Tory blushed, and Ben slid his arm around her shoulders.

Suddenly Tracy had to get out of there. She'd been so close, so close to having her nightmare over. "I have to get back to work, but I'll, um, see you guys later," she said, edging toward the door.

"I have to get back, too," Patti said.

Tracy watched with a sick feeling as the other woman slid the pendant into her hip pocket as she moved toward the door.

"You two rest up and look after each other, okay?" Patti said with a twinkle as she stepped out into the corridor.

Tracy just gave a halfhearted wave in response to Ben and Tory's thanks for their gifts. Patti gave her a curious look as they made their way toward the elevator bank.

"You and Tory have struck up a bit of a friendship?" she asked.

"Yes," Tracy nodded. "She's—she's a really nice lady."

"I think they make a lovely couple, don't you? I had a feeling there was something going on there the first time I saw them together," Patti said with satisfaction. "I know it probably makes me a sentimental idiot, but I do like a happy ending."

Tracy stared bleakly at the floor indicator as they waited for the elevator. Happy endings. Why did it feel as though everyone got one except for her? A single tear slid down the side of her nose, and she wiped it away discreetly before Patti could see it. She had to keep up appearances, after all. Especially since it looked as though Salvatore was still going to need her to get the pendant back. Next cruise, it would start all over again. And she still would not have held her son in her arms.

Stepping into the elevator with Patti, Tracy's shoulders slumped. Somehow she had to find the strength to keep going. Franco needed her.

SPENDING THE NIGHT IN Ben's arms was pure paradise. This time when Tory woke there was no doubt about whether he was still in bed with her—his arms were wrapped tightly around her torso, one hand spread possessively over a breast. When she attempted to ease herself from the bed to use the bathroom, he mumbled a protest and pulled her closer still. Smiling to herself, she wriggled free and shut herself into the en suite. Her graze had bruised around the edges overnight, and her hip sported a purple-and-black bruise the size of a side plate. She was achy and stiff, too—but not all of that could be attributed to the work of their attackers. Smiling a self-satisfied little smile, Tory went to the bathroom, then stepped into the shower.

She felt…effervescent. Buoyant. As though she could fly, like Peter Pan or Superman or any other mythical gravity-defying figure.

Ben loved her, and last night he'd shown her just how much with every inch of his body. Her knees went weak and her breasts peaked with desire just thinking about the things he'd done to her, with her. She'd never felt so precious, so adored, so needed and wanted.

She smiled as Ben entered the en suite, wasting no time in joining her in the shower. Predictably, it didn't take long for mutual back soaping and washing to turn into mutual caresses, and soon they were making steamy love against the cool tiles.

It was only as Ben was toweling her dry that Tory allowed herself to think of the visit they hoped to pay to Anneisha today. Last night, she'd written a from-the-heart request to Anneisha to talk to her about Michael and Tarik. She'd been loath to tell the woman that Michael was dead via a letter, and Ben had agreed that she should only do so as a last resort. Fortunately Danique had been able to persuade her friend to give Tory an hour of her time.

Tory was determined to use that time to clear up the misconceptions of the past and lay the foundations for her family's future relationship with Anneisha and Tarik. She had no doubt at all that her parents would want to meet their grandchild and the woman Michael had spent his last months with.

After a late supper with Ben, Tory had scoured the last of her brother's letters for any mention of Anneisha, hoping to find some proof to offer the other woman that her brother had been sincere in his feelings. What she'd found were subtle clues to her brother's mind-set. He'd talked about looking for a permanent post—tellingly, St. Maarten had been his first choice. And he'd encouraged Tory to join him once she'd graduated. There were people he'd wanted her to meet down here. Michael had even mentioned a house he'd seen that had great sea views and enough rooms to accommodate a family. She could remember scoffing out loud as she'd read that paragraph eight years ago, thinking her brother was just swept up in island fever. But now she suspected he had fallen in love with Anneisha and she was determined to prove as much to the other woman.

Reading her nervousness easily, Ben dropped his hands onto her shoulders and kneaded the tense muscles there gently.

"It's going to be okay," he said. It had become their mantra, and she threw a smile over her shoulder at him.

He'd been so wonderful. He'd cajoled Danique into acting as Tory's agent, he'd calmed Tory's nerves and made all their travel arrangements. She realized with a sudden flash of insight that the lost, lonely feeling she'd carried around with her since Michael's death was gone. She wasn't alone anymore. Ben loved her and she loved him. She belonged again.

"Come on, we need to hustle to get to the airfield," Ben said, halting his massage.

Tory followed orders, and within twenty minutes they were hailing a cab from the docks of Roadtown, Tortola, to take them to the local airfield.

The first crack in the fantasy she'd woven around herself came as Ben pointed out local landmarks as they flew high over Tortola on their way back to St. Maarten.

"The great thing is, there are direct flights out of New York now straight into Philipsburg," he said. "Your parents can shoot down anytime. Who knows, I might even let your old man into my kitchen one day."

Tory was glad she had her face turned toward the window as Ben's words sank in. In the midst of all their declarations and caresses and promises to one another, not once had she considered that they were floating on a cruise ship in the middle of the Caribbean and that she and Ben had lives that were literally thousands of miles apart. He had a restaurant—a thriving restaurant with loyal staff and a reputation that was only going to grow with time—and she had plans for her own place. Backers were awaiting her return to New York, former colleagues were poised to hand in their notices to come join her, her real-estate agent was scouring Manhattan looking for the perfect site.

Yet Ben was assuming she would be joining him in the Caribbean. She understood why he would do that—his world was here, after all. And she couldn't imagine him thriving in New York, not after seeing him in his element. He belonged with sun and sand and palm trees.

The question was, did she?

She thought of the feeling she'd had when she'd first seen Café Rendezvous as the bus had turned the corner. She remembered the sense of pride and approval she'd felt when she'd walked into the dining room. And she decided that she had enough on her plate for the day without borrowing trouble before it had presented itself.

There was no way she could untangle such a difficult problem on her own. If their love was to survive the significant hurdle offered by geography, it was something she and Ben were going to have to work through together.

Lacing her fingers with Ben's, she concentrated on the here and now. She was about to spend time with her brother's son. And she had just spent the night in the arms of an incredible man who loved her. It was more than enough to get her through the day.

IT DIDN'T ESCAPE BEN'S notice that Tory didn't respond to his comment about easy access to St. Maarten from New York. He could see her face reflected in the plane's window and he had no trouble reading the uncertainty and hesitation in her eyes.

For the first time he considered how much both their lives were bound to change now that they'd found each other. He would have to get used to living with someone and sharing his hilltop home. Hell, he'd have to get used to sharing his kitchen with Tory, but he was convinced that both were tiny asks in exchange for waking with her in his arms every day.

But Tory had to want those things, too, and it suddenly struck him that Tory had never once spoken about wanting a family or a husband or anything other than her work—her new restaurant and her new cookbooks. Ben frowned as the plane began its descent into Philipsburg. His experience with Eva had taught him that he desperately wanted a child. He wanted to love and nurture his and Tory's children, to guide their first steps and watch them become individuals with their own hopes and dreams. But Tory might not want kids. He'd been too busy falling head over heels in love with her to consider practicalities like common goals.

"I can't wait to talk to him—I wonder if he likes swimming, like Michael did," Tory said beside him, and something inside him relaxed as he saw the look on Tory's face when she talked about her brother's child. Suddenly he was confident that they could work things out, no matter what those "things" might be.

He recognized one of the taxi drivers on the rank, and soon they were winding their way up into the cool of the forest. He knew from things Danique had said over the years that Anneisha struggled to make ends meet. Her mother helped out with childcare when she could, and Anneisha worked a number of part-time jobs to pay the bills. The small timber house that the cab stopped in front of was certainly no mansion, but it was well kept and had recently been painted a cheery pale yellow. Shoes were lined up in a neat row outside the front door, and an old-fashioned ship's bell served as a doorbell.

Tory was nervous, and Ben gave her an inquiring look, asking silently if she needed more time to pull herself together. She shook her head, her chin coming up in the stubborn, proud gesture he knew so well. Resting a hand on her lower back, he rang the bell.

For a long beat there was nothing but silence, as though the house's occupant was having a good long think about answering the door. Then they heard footsteps moving about the interior, and at last the door swung open. Anneisha was a shadowy figure on the other side of the screen door, and they all three stared at one another for an awkward moment before she flicked the latch.

"I suppose you'd better come in," she said.

As welcomes went, it left a bit to be desired, but he figured Anneisha had good reason to be pissed with the Fournier family, given what she still believed regarding Michael. Holding the screen door open for Tory, he followed both women through to a small but scrupulously clean, brightly furnished living room.

Anneisha sank down onto the couch, leaving two wooden hard-backed chairs for her guests. Ben hid a rueful smile at the woman's tactics—it was possible Tory had just met her match in the pride department.

Tory took the chair closest to Anneisha and clasped her hands together on her lap. He could see the anxiety in every line of her body, but there was nothing he could do to make this moment any easier for her. He knew that the thing that had been weighing most on her mind was telling the other woman that Michael was dead. It would be a shock, that was for sure. But it had to be done.

"Thank you for seeing us," Tory said. "I know you must be very angry with Michael."

Anneisha's lips thinned. "And myself for being stupid enough to believe a word he said."

Tory took a deep breath and leaned forward.

"Anneisha, I'm really sorry to have to tell you this…but Michael died in a plane accident off the coast of Barbados on October seventeenth, eight years ago. That's why you never heard from him again."

Anneisha's pansy-brown eyes widened and she sat back on the couch, one hand pressed to her chest. "What? No, I would have heard. It would have been in the papers," she said, shaking her head.

"Michael was down here working with the DEA and your local police." Tory explained quietly. "His name was kept out of the newspaper reports because he was working undercover."

"But he said he was a scuba diver," Anneisha insisted, and Ben realized that the other woman would prefer to think that Michael was an alive-and-well rat rather than that he had truly loved her and died.

"I'm so sorry," Tory said. "I know this is a shock."

"I can't believe this. All these years I've hated him for lying to me…." Fat tears rolled down Anneisha's face, and Tory joined her on the couch, sliding a hand tentatively around her shoulders.

"It's okay. I'm so sorry to have to tell you this." There were tears in Tory's own eyes.

"It changes everything." Anneisha kept shaking her head, the tears plopping off her chin and into her lap unheeded as she stared sightlessly at the floor.

"I brought you some of Michael's letters to me. He talks about you, Anneisha. He wanted to settle here on St. Maarten, and I think that was because of you."

Tory reached for the letters that she'd selected from her

brother's collection. "When did you tell him you were pregnant?" she asked gently.

Anneisha frowned, absently wiping away her tears with the back of her hand. "The week before he disappeared."

Tory smiled. "In this letter here, dated the end of September, he talks about finding a house he wants to buy—how it would be great to bring up a family in," she explained, pressing the letter into Anneisha's hands. "He didn't even know about the pregnancy and he was already making plans for the two of you. He loved you, Anneisha. I know he did."

Anneisha's face crumpled at Tory's words, and Tory pulled her into her embrace. Aware that the two women had much ground to cover, memories to share, connections to make, Ben stood.

"I'm going to go make us some coffee," he said quietly.

Tory nodded her acknowledgment, flashing him a watery, grateful smile.

Easing from the room, he navigated his way to the kitchen at the back of the house and busied himself finding the makings for coffee. What had happened to Anneisha, Michael and Tarik was unfair and very sad. It made him realize afresh how lucky he was to have had a second chance to get things right with Tory. His fingers tightened on the coffee can. No matter what, they would find a way to make things work.

CHAPTER THIRTEEN

TORY'S NOSE WAS RED from too many tissues, and she suspected her eyes were puffy from crying. None of it mattered, however, because standing in the doorway was Tarik, her brother's son.

She and Anneisha had talked for an hour, filling in each other's blanks. Anneisha had wept on and off, heartbroken over Michael's death. Tory understood that, despite the protective wall of anger that Anneisha had built up around herself over the years, she'd never stopped loving Michael. Tory had shared childhood tales with the other woman, describing some of Michael's crazy exploits. Ben had moved in and out of the room, making coffee, serving up cookies, hunting out a fresh box of tissues. She'd exchanged smiles with him as he'd guffawed at some of Michael's worst stunts and for the first time registered that Michael and Ben shared many personality traits—the easygoing attitude, the devil-may-care risk taking, the mischievous bent. She wondered if that was why she'd been drawn to Ben. Like Michael, he balanced out her own seriousness and tendency to worry.

When Tory had explained that she and Ben needed to be at the Philipsburg airport by one, Anneisha had called her mother and asked her to collect Tarik from school and bring him home. Now Tarik stood uncertainly in the doorway, frowning at his mother's reddened eyes and the pile of soggy tissues on the coffee table.

"What's going on?" he asked, fiercely protective of his mother.

"I want you to meet someone, Tarik," Anneisha said. "This is Tory. She's your aunt."

The other woman's voice had choked up, and Tory had to swallow fresh tears of her own.

"Hi, Tarik," she said. "I can't tell you how pleased I am to meet you."

"Hi," he said uncertainly, still wary.

"Tarik, come here, baby—I have something to tell you," Anneisha said.

Tarik stepped forward to join his mother on the couch. Picking up one of his hands, Anneisha held it between both of her own and pressed it tightly.

"You know how I told you about how your dad had to go back to the U.S. because he had important stuff to do there?" Anneisha said.

"Yeah. That's why he doesn't want to be with us," Tarik said.

Tory's heart wrung for him. She didn't blame Anneisha for telling her son a version of what she'd believed the truth was. Tarik was clearly a smart, perceptive little boy. No doubt he would have seen through anything but the truth.

"Well, it seems I made a mistake. Your aunt Tory just told me that instead of leaving us all those years ago to go back to America, your dad had an accident in his plane."

"You mean he's dead?" Tarik asked, frowning. Tory could see him trying to work out what he should feel for a man he'd never met and who he'd always thought had abandoned him and his mother.

"Yeah, baby, I'm sorry. But the thing I want you to know, the really, really important thing, is that he wanted to be with us. Aunt Tory has just been showing me all his letters. He was going to buy us a little house, set us up real nice. He loved us. He didn't mean to leave us. All these years Mommy had it wrong because she didn't know about the plane accident."

Tarik nodded, taking it all in. Tory very badly wanted to comfort him, but she wasn't sure what to say or even if he wanted to hear kind words from a virtual stranger.

He surprised her by lifting his head and looking her in the eye.

"When I saw you yesterday, I thought you were someone special," he said. "Is that because you knew my dad?"

Tory's heart squeezed in her chest. "Yes. I think so," she said. She met Ben's eyes across the room. She was so glad he was here with her, experiencing this moment. She honestly didn't think she could have done it without his silent, supportive strength.

"Aunt Tory and your dad were twins, Tarik," Anneisha explained. She'd pulled herself together again.

"But she's a girl," Tarik asked, confused.

"Not twins like Billy and Jackson at school," Anneisha said. "They're identical twins. Sometimes there are other kinds of twins, too."

Tarik was frowning with concentration. He stared, wide-eyed, at Tory. "So you shared your mummy's tummy with my dad?" he asked, amazed by the concept.

"Yep. And we shared a room when we were kids and toys and a bunch of other stuff. Your dad taught me how to ride a bike and how to swim and how to skip a rock six times on the top of a lake."

For the first time since entering the room, Tarik smiled. Tory reached out and touched the dark port-wine-colored mark on the back of Tarik's neck.

"Your daddy had one of those, too. And my dad has one and his dad and all the other dads for ages back in my family. When I saw it, I knew exactly who you were."

Anneisha reached across and squeezed Tory's knee, and Tarik reached up a hand to rub his birthmark.

"I never liked it much before," he said. "But maybe it's not so bad."

"I think it's pretty damned fine," Anneisha said with verve, and they all broke into laughter.

Again Tory caught Ben's eye. Everything was coming together.

Remembering the disquiet she'd felt on the plane, she shifted uneasily for a moment. Then she pushed the thought away again. They could work things out. There had to be a solution, somewhere, when they were both so willing.

They stayed with Anneisha and Tarik as long as they dared, meeting Anneisha's mother, shedding yet more tears and finally accepting a ride from her newfound family back to the airport. Tory gave Anneisha all of her parents' and her own contact details. For obvious reasons, Tory preferred to break the news to her parents in person, and Anneisha gave her a stack of photographs of herself and Tarik to take home with her.

Lastly, before she hugged Tarik and Anneisha goodbye, Tory explained about Michael's estate. He'd drawn up a very sketchy will when he'd joined the DEA and he'd left everything he had to his sister, in lieu of having any progeny or a spouse. Tory explained to a wide-eyed Anneisha that Michael's life insurance money had been invested for the past eight years and was still untouched. Tory would take steps to sign it all over to Anneisha and Tarik the moment she returned to New York.

Predictably Anneisha's stiff-necked pride led to a tussle of wills, but Tory was insistent. Once she pointed out that Michael would have done anything in the world to avoid his fate and be there for Anneisha and Tarik in person and that giving Anneisha the means to ease some of her financial burdens would be the very least that her brother would have wanted to do, Anneisha piped down.

The flight back to Tortola seemed both faster and slower as she and Ben talked over the small moments of the day.

"He's so much like Michael I can't believe it. Did you see the way he held his fork when we had cake? That's exactly how Michael used to do it. And he loves the water, just like Michael did. I can't believe I found him. And I can't believe how close I came to not finding him," she said as they left the airfield in Roadtown and made their way back to the ship.

"He's a nice little kid, too. Anneisha's done a great job with him."

Ben was frowning and rubbing his forehead just below the dark bruise that discolored his tanned skin. Now that the excitement of the day had worn off a little, she was much more aware of her own injuries and she soothingly cupped her palm around his jaw.

"You've got a headache, haven't you? We've got time for a nap before our afternoon session, so you should take some more pain-killers and try to sleep it off."

"Only if you promise to join me," Ben said, eyebrows wiggling suggestively.

He wasn't feeling too bad, then. She gave him a saucy smile.

"Since you asked so nicely."

But any thought of sleep went out the window when they entered Ben's suite to find the phone ringing. Tory was surprised when Ben beckoned her to take the receiver after he'd answered the call.

"It's your father," Ben said quietly.

Tory stared at him openmouthed for a beat before lifting the phone to her ear.

"Andre. Is everything all right?" Her father never called except on birthdays and Christmases—and even then she suspected her mother did the dialing and simply stuck the receiver in his hand.

"Momento has gone belly-up!" her father reported gleefully. "Apparently they had a bad review last year and the numbers have been down and the backers have decided to go elsewhere."

Tory actually took the receiver away from her ear and stared at it. Her father had called her to tell her that a restaurant had failed?

"Okaaaaay," she said slowly. "Um, how's Mom?"

"Tory, are you listening to me? The site is free. Midtown Manhattan, surrounded by cashed-up yuppies. It's perfect for you," Andre said.

Tory felt a thrill of excitement as she realized that he was right. She'd often envied Momento its location. In fact, she'd even told her real-estate guy that she wanted a site that rivaled it.

But most of the thrill wasn't generated by her father's news, it was driven by the exuberant enthusiasm in his voice. She'd been talking to him about starting up her own place for more than three years, but he'd never been anything but disapproving. Now he was scouting locations for her. She would never have thought such a turnaround was possible.

"I'll call my real-estate agent," she said.

"I've done that already. He's speaking to the landlord tomorrow."

Tory blinked and shook her head. "Wow. Thanks for looking out for me, Andre."

"I tried that coconut prawn recipe from your book the other night," Andre revealed, apropos of nothing.

She reached for a seat. Finding locations for her *and* cooking from her book?

"You liked it?" she asked, aware that her voice came out sounding high and childish.

"It's very interesting," he said. "The spices and herbs are strong, but I'm intrigued by the possibilities with this island cooking. There is a lot of potential, and New York does not have a restaurant of the caliber you are planning. I guess what I am trying to say is that you have my approval."

He said it like the Pope handing down a benediction, and it brought a wry smile even as she registered the warm feeling in her chest. All her life she'd been waiting for her father to show this much interest in her dreams.

"That means a lot to me," she said quietly, deeply touched.

"When you get back, we'll go over there and take a look around," Andre said, and she listened to his ideas for the next ten minutes, getting more and more excited about what his involvement in her start-up would mean. She could look to him for advice on everything from kitchen design to dining room decor, and with his wholehearted endorsement she'd be guaranteed reviews in all the important newspapers.

Several times during their conversation she was tempted to blurt out the news about Tarik and Anneisha, but she knew that it was a story best delivered face-to-face. She could hand over the photographs and reassure her parents. Over the phone, it could easily escalate into an unnecessary drama.

When she hung up the phone, she was feeling buoyed by her father's enthusiasm. She'd taken two pages of notes while they'd talked, her pen dashing across the page, and more than anything she wanted to share them with Ben. Then she caught the expression on his face and everything in her went still.

All day she'd been aware of the potential roadblock that stood in the way of their relationship turning into something more than an intense holiday fling. They lived in different countries, for Pete's sake. How had that tiny geographical impossibility slipped both of their attentions while they'd been falling madly in love?

And now they were about to slam head-first into reality, thanks to her father's phone call.

"Sounds like good news," Ben said neutrally, the words the first salvo in what was going to be a long and difficult conversation, she guessed.

"Yes. I don't know if you're familiar with Momento? It's a family bistro in midtown. My father has just gotten word that they're going out of business."

"So the site's open?" he asked.

"Yes."

They stared at each other.

"So where does that leave us?" His expression was unreadable, like his voice.

She knew it was a hard question for him to ask, that he'd probably never asked anything like it in his life before. Equally, she'd never been in this situation either. All her dreams—both the secret, unacknowledged ones about having a husband and family, as well as her more public ones—were on the verge of coming true. Except now it seemed she was faced with a choice.

"I don't know. I don't want to lose you, Ben."

"Ditto. We've already wasted eight years."

They met in the middle of the room, hands meshing. Tory pressed her cheek to his chest and listened to the steady rhythm of his heart.

"Opening up your own restaurant is important to you," Ben said after a long silence.

She thought of all the time and energy she'd put into finding backers, the informal meetings she'd had with former colleagues to secure their interest, the huge file of ideas she'd accumulated over the past three years. She thought of her father's excited voice on the phone, of how it would be to work together on something, to build something between them.

"Yes," she said.

Ben took a deep breath. "I'm about to lose Philippe. He's going home to Normandy, and I'll need six months to recruit and train a replacement. But after that, if you want me, I can probably join you in New York."

Tory pressed her face hard against his chest, unable to believe what she was hearing, what he was prepared to sacrifice to be with her.

"Ben, I don't know what to say."

"I want children. I should probably say that up front," he added. "After Eva, I know I want a family of my own."

"Yes," she said, thinking of the look she'd seen on his face when he'd been holding Eva yesterday and of the burgeoning love she already felt for her brother's son. "Yes, I want children, too."

She frowned as she thought about the logistics of setting up and running a new restaurant. It would be grueling, grueling work, she knew. And it would be at least twelve months before all the creases were ironed out. Only then could she even consider taking time out to have a baby. She chewed her lip, aware once again of the competing urgencies in her life. She wanted the restaurant so much, but she also wanted Ben and the life they could have together. Was she being greedy, reckless, trying to have them both?

"We'll work it out," she said out loud. Hadn't they just proven to each other that they both had the will to make sacrifices to ensure their relationship got off the ground?

"Yes," Ben said.

They kissed then, and kissing quickly turned into making love, and Tory was painfully aware of every precious moment, every touch, every breath or sigh or caress. Ben would fly home to Anguilla tomorrow. And the day after that they docked in Fort Lauderdale, and she would fly home.

She told herself it was stupid to feel a sense of desperation, even mourning. They were going to make this work. Ben had already spoken of direct flights from St. Maarten to New York. They could fly back and forth as many times as they liked before Ben joined her more permanently.

Nothing she told herself could silence the cynical voice in the back of her head, however. Long-distance romances never lasted. Everyone knew that. Was she really prepared to risk the feeling that burned between her and Ben for the sake of ambition? Because wasn't that what it boiled down to in the end—her ambition versus the life they could have *now* if she walked away from the restaurant start-up?

It was a question that was still ricocheting its way around her mind the following morning when she stood in the airport in Freeport, the Bahamas, and watched Ben stride toward the plane that would take him home. They'd spent the night in his suite, curled together, alternating between making plans and making love. Despite their decision, a weight hung over them, and Tory knew it was because they were both still uncertain about how their newly burnished love would survive the pressures of separation and demanding work schedules.

She pressed her hands flat against the glass separating her from the tarmac as Ben disappeared inside the plane. She had no idea if she was making the right decision. So much was at stake, at both ends of the equation.

There was a message from her father when she returned to the ship, and she spent over an hour with him on an insanely expensive phone call going over his ideas. It was impossible to remain uncertain in the face of his enormous, enthusiastic confidence. That night, before she fell asleep, she told herself that Ben was coming to New York in six months, that he loved her now and he would still love her then. It *was* going to work out.

Her heart made a liar of her the moment she stepped out of the terminal building in Fort Lauderdale. A tall, dark-haired man stood waiting, his back to her, and her stomach dipped and her mouth curved into a delighted, astonished smile as she raced toward him.

"Ben!" she said, grabbing his arm.

But it wasn't Ben. She blushed and offered her apologies and retreated back to her luggage.

Ben was in Anguilla, looking for Philippe's replacement. If she closed her eyes, she could picture him in his beautiful restaurant, looking out at the ocean view. It was stupid to think—hope—that he'd flown to Florida to...do what? Talk her into staying in Anguilla with him? Or did she imagine he was going to abandon his restaurant altogether and throw his lot in with her dreams and fly home to New York with her?

She spent the flight home writing a long letter to Anneisha and Tarik and a shorter one to Tracy. She'd felt oddly as if she was abandoning the other woman when they'd said their goodbyes on the ship. She'd expected Tracy to be happier about being back in port—surely she would be seeing her son?—but once again she hadn't pushed. Hopefully the other woman would stay in touch, but Tory would understand, also, if their friendship had merely been a shipboard thing.

She was astonished to exit the luggage collection area at JFK to find her parents waiting. Her mother hugged her warmly and her father began bombarding her with yet more suggestions for the restaurant. The news about Anneisha and Tarik was on the tip of her tongue, but Tory waited until they were in her parents' Long Island home before broaching the subject.

"But I don't understand how this could happen," her mother kept saying as Tory passed her the photographs of Anneisha and Tarik.

"In the usual way—Michael and this Anneisha woman took their clothes off, and a baby came along like magic nine months later," Andre said.

Her mother touched a baby photo of Tarik, tears shining in her eyes.

"He looks so much like Michael," she said.

Tory nodded. "Yes. He walks like him, even holds his fork like him—remember how Michael used to do that weird thing with his thumb? It drove Andre crazy."

"I just can't believe this," her mother said, but she was smiling now, flicking through the photographs eagerly, hungry for anything that Tory could tell her about her new grandson and almost-daughter-in-law.

"And it's an easy flight down there, yes?" Andre asked.

"Not too bad, and well worth it," Tory assured them both. "I told Anneisha you'd probably be down as soon as possible."

"We'll have to wait till we've signed the lease for the restaurant and got the renovations under way, but we should be able to spare a few days next month," Andre said.

His wife shot him a horrified look. "Next *month*? Are you kidding? I want to get on a plane right now. I can't wait until next month."

Tory frowned at her father's words. He'd never been the most passionate of fathers, it was true—haute cuisine had always been his first love—but she'd expected him to be more invested in his grandson.

Andre made a noncommittal noise, and Tory saw the familiar look of resignation settle over her mother's face. Her mother always allowed him to dictate the running of their life. Kendra was her husband's number one fan, a role which automatically demoted her role to support crew and not equal partner. For her mother's sake, as well as Tarik and Anneisha's, Tory hoped that Kendra stood up for what she wanted this time.

"Tory? Pay attention. We'll never get anything done if you're going to drift off cloud-gathering like that." Andre tapped her forearm with an imperative finger. "I have been thinking about the staff you have proposed. I think we should go over their credentials. I don't think it would hurt to have someone with Cordon bleu training on board, hmm? And I have scheduled an appointment first thing tomorrow to go over the restaurant site. If you are satisfied, you can sign on the spot and we can get this ball rolling."

Her father's eyes sparkled, and for the first time in ages—since he'd retired, in fact—there was color in his cheeks.

"Okay," she said. "If you think we need to."

"I do. Trust me on this," Andre said.

Later that afternoon, Tory put a call through to Anneisha and handed the phone over to her mother, sitting beside her throughout and soothing a hand up and down her back as Kendra tried to contain her tears and conduct a sensible conversation with the mother of her grandson. Tory knew the moment Anneisha put Tarik on the line, because her mother's face split into a big, watery smile.

Tory waited until she was in the privacy of her apartment later that evening before calling Ben. She lay in bed talking to him for over an hour, going over the small, insignificant details of her trip, discussing her plans for the following day, filling him in on her parents' reaction to her news about Anneisha and Tarik. Really, she just wanted to hear his voice, his laugh, to close her eyes and imagine he was lying on the pillow next to her and that they weren't separated by thousands of miles of land and ocean.

"I know it sounds crazy, but I miss you already," Ben said.

"It's not crazy," Tory said. "It's exactly how I feel."

"I'll book a flight tomorrow, try to get up next week sometime," Ben promised.

After they wound up their call, Tory spent a long time staring at the ceiling, her chest aching. It was stupid to feel so lonely when she'd spent her entire life *not* having Ben around, but that was exactly how she felt.

She dressed up in her hardiest winter wear before meeting her father at Momento the following day. Her few days in the Caribbean made the bitter cold seem ten times more bone-chilling than before, and she was shivering as she followed her father and the real-estate agent into the restaurant.

"Oh, yes, this is perfect," her father said as he inspected the dining room. He gestured toward the far wall, his body radiating suppressed excitement. "We can put in booths along the wall for family groups, and this central area can be given over to modular tables that we can group together for larger parties," he said. "We need to up the lighting, get someone in to give us golden tones so it always feels like a summer sunset. And I have a contact who could paint a mural for us on this wall here."

Her father strode around the dining room, pointing out features, pacing out the floor space, becoming more and more excited as his vision grew.

Tory watched him, a small smile on her face, pleased to see him so vibrant and energized. He hadn't been this happy for so long, she realized. Not since he'd retired, really. He thrived on the buzz of restaurant life, always had. And now he would be part of that world again, via her.

"Now, if only the kitchen is not a complete disaster, we are in heaven," Andre said, striding off to explore further.

The real-estate agent followed him, and Tory stood for a moment on her own in the dining room, ready to relish the triumph of the moment. Her dream was about to come true. This was it, where it all began.

She turned in a circle, trying to envisage the space as it would look when they had finished their revamp. But try as she might, she couldn't get a clear mental snapshot, and the only feeling she could muster was a general sense of anticipation and satisfaction.

She frowned. This was not how she'd imagined feeling all those times she'd lain awake at night building castles in the air. Why wasn't she feeling more fulfilled?

Her father swept back into the room, a broad grin on his face. "It is fantastic. We will hardly have to change a thing. I am very impressed with this setup."

Tory stared at her beaming father and slowly understanding crept up on her.

All these years that she'd been striving to open her own restaurant had been a gross exercise in self-delusion. She didn't want her own place—what she wanted was her father's approval. She wanted what she was getting from him right now—she wanted him to listen to her and pay attention to her. She wanted him to at last understand that she was of value and that shutting her out of his kitchen and closing Le Plat rather than entrusting it to her had been a mistake. She wanted to prove to him that she was worthy of him, the great Andre Fournier.

"I'm so stupid," she said under her breath, dropping into the nearest chair with a thump.

"Sorry?" her father said, frowning.

She opened her mouth to try to explain, then shut it again without saying a word. There was no point trying to articulate her sudden understanding to him. She remembered the way he'd reacted to the news of Tarik last night, how he'd instantly relegated his new grandson to second priority behind Tory's new restaurant. For the first time, she allowed herself to truly register the anger that had welled up inside her at his selfish response. Nothing was

more important than family and being with loved ones. Nothing—
certainly not the excitement and challenge of starting up a new restaurant—could compare to the feeling of completion and
belonging of loving and knowing you were loved in return.

A fierce surge of determination raced through Tory as she
thought about the children she would have with Ben. Their home
would be filled with love and laughter, and their children would
always know they were cherished and adored. She would never
keep them at arms length or let them doubt her approval or acceptance. She would do everything in her power to ensure they never
knew what it was like to be uncertain of a parent's love.

Her father had never seen beyond his own ambitions and he never
would. The only reason he was standing here with her today was that
she had subconsciously offered him the one thing she'd known he
truly wanted—a return to his old life, to being king of the kitchen.

She'd wanted his approval so badly that she'd manufactured the
one scenario where she'd been sure of gaining it. It hurt to admit
it to herself, but it was the truth—Andre wasn't standing here
today getting excited for her. He was excited for *himself,* for what
it meant in *his* life.

Talk about a hollow victory.

She shook her head, thinking of all that she'd thrown in the
balance against the need for her father's unconditional love: Ben's
love, their future together, the life they could lead on the sun-
soaked beaches of Anguilla. She'd risked all of that because her
father had called up from New York and at last given her what she
craved—his attention.

"Wow," she said under her breath.

"So all we must do now is sign up," her father said, ushering
the real-estate agent forward.

Tory stared at the contract she was being offered. She could sign
the lease and perpetuate the fantasy that she'd gotten what she
wanted. She could pretend that the excitement Andre felt right now

was for her and not for himself. She could place her relationship
with Ben second to her perpetual desire to please her father and
risk her future happiness.

Or she could at last accept that the fault in her relationship with
her father lay with him and not with her. And she could start to
live her own life.

She took a deep breath.

"Dad, we need to talk," she said.

BEN HEFTED THE LAST of the fresh produce into the walk-in fridge
and nodded his thanks to the delivery man as the other man
returned to his van. So far today he'd personally cleaned all three
of the enormous ovens that serviced the restaurant, ordered a
stocktaking on glassware and linen and set Philippe to reviewing
the menu. For the last half hour he'd been heaving sacks of produce
around, working up a sweat, but none of it had done a damned
thing to help reconcile him to the fact that Tory was thousands of
miles away.

Why had he let her go? He should have insisted she stay. Or he
should have come up with some solution to his own staffing
problems so he could go with her. But even if Philippe could be
bribed into staying on or a worthy replacement found readily
enough, he couldn't just walk away from Café Rendezvous. It was
a family business, his children's legacy, in the same way that his
parents' business had been his. He owed a duty of care to ensure
its success and survival, not just for his own family but for the
hundreds of people that the restaurant supported both directly and
indirectly.

As for insisting that Tory stay—who was he to tell her to give
up on her dreams? She was who she was, and he loved her that
way, dreams and ambitions included. He would never ask her to
turn her back on something she wanted. And so they were stuck
in limbo land until he could get himself organized and fly to her.

He would be lying to himself if he pretended he was keen to swap the laid-back island life on Anguilla for the stress and pollution of NYC. It was a great city, and he'd enjoyed his time working there, but Anguilla was in his blood, just as island food was in his blood. This would always be his home, and, he realized with a frown, he wanted it to be his children's home, too. Yet another thing he and Tory needed to discuss.

He rubbed his forehead in frustration, abruptly abandoning his self-appointed heavy labor and striding out through the kitchen, into the dining room and out the open French doors onto the balcony. The cool sea breeze hit him with its salty tang, and he braced his hands on the rail and squinted out to sea. It had been hell ending the phone call to her last night, knowing that she was miles away, that it would be at least a week before he could hold her skin to skin again.

He laughed mirthlessly. It figured that after all these years of being a bachelor, when he finally fell in love it was fraught with difficulty. He had no choice but to suck it up, however. He loved her. Heart and soul, body and breath. There was no way he'd change that for the world.

"See anything good out there?"

Ben's fingers tightened convulsively on the railing before he let go and slowly turned around.

Tory was wearing one of her summery holiday dresses, her curls dancing in the breeze. Her blue eyes were hopeful, but he could see the faint hesitation in their depths.

"So there I was, standing in the space that was going to be my new restaurant," she said as though she was taking up a conversation they'd started some time ago, "and I suddenly realized that I was chasing a mirage and that I was risking the best thing that had ever happened to me. Ben, I am so, so sorry for putting you through all that rubbish—"

The remainder of her words were swallowed in his kiss as he

swooped down on her and pulled her into his arms. Only the need to breathe made them break contact, and he caught her face in his hands as he stared down into her beautiful face.

"Tell me you're here to stay," he said.

"I'm here to stay. I'm here to have babies with you. I'm here to elbow my way into your kitchen. I'm here to be a part of Tarik and Anneisha's lives. I'm here to live *my* life," she said.

"What about your restaurant?" he asked before he allowed his heart to soar.

"I don't need to start a restaurant, Ben. The only reason I flew home in the first place was because it was my father who called with the news about the site. Andre has never been the most attentive dad, and I've spent so much of my life trying to please him it was hard to break the habit."

She looked sad, and he guessed she was remembering something.

"When I told my parents about Tarik, I expected them both to jump on the next flight down here. I mean, it's Michael's son, right? They've missed out on eight years already. Mom was ready to start packing, but do you know what Andre said? He wanted to wait until the restaurant was well on its way. A month, maybe two."

Ben could only imagine how she must have felt; he'd seen how driven she was to build bonds with Tarik.

"He's never going to change," she said. "His career, his reputation will always come first. I think I could only see that when it was Tarik he was slighting and shortchanging, not me."

"But what about the restaurant? It was still your dream." Ben wanted her to be sure.

"No. It was what I allowed myself to have because I was too scared that I would never find what I've found with you. When I first walked into this restaurant, I felt so…I can't describe it. *Proprietorial* is probably the best word. I felt as though I had come home, in the same way that I knew Tarik when I looked into his face, in the same way that I knew you were the one when we made love. I love you, Ben. You are my future. This is my future. I'm done with trying to please a man who will never be pleased by anything except a Michelin ranking or a five-star review."

"You have no idea how happy I am right now," he said, dropping kisses onto her face. "I was just standing here wondering how I was going to survive living apart from you for six months."

She wove her fingers through his hair and captured his mouth with hers.

"I don't even have to go home to pack. My mom's going to organize for my stuff to be boxed up and shipped down here. I hope you've got room for more cookbooks. And I'm going to need a room to write in," she added with a mischievous twinkle in her eye.

"Stop trying to terrorize an old bachelor," he said gruffly.

"A reformed bachelor," she countered.

"A soon-to-be happily married man," he said.

She smiled, the purest, happiest smile he'd ever seen.

"I thought you'd never ask."

* * * * *

MEDITERRANEAN NIGHTS

Join the glamorous world of cruising with the guests and crew of Alexandra's Dream. *The voyage continues with*

Starstruck
by Michelle Celmer.

Claire Mackenzie left behind her life as a Hollywood wild child years ago, so she finds it almost impossible to let loose and have fun while on a cruise aboard Alexandra's Dream *with her grandfather, screen legend Frederick Miles. And it doesn't help that she is convinced Liam Bates, the ship's assistant cruise director, is using her grandfather to further his own showbiz career. She doesn't trust his charms…but neither can she resist them.*

Here's a preview!

Starstruck

by

Michelle Celmer

CLAIRE STARED AT LIAM with assessing, slightly narrowed eyes, as though she was attempting to read his thoughts. To figure out if he was sincere.

"You know," he said. "I was wrong."

"Wrong about what?"

"Your eyes. They're not moldy at all."

She blinked in confusion. "Moldy?"

Brilliant Liam, call the woman moldy. "Sorry. I only meant that at first sight they looked more of a mold green. I realize now they're actually closer to the color of moss. Brighter, I think. A bit more yellow than blue."

For a moment she only stared. Silent. Then she said, "If that's a pickup line, you need to work on your material."

He grinned. It would seem the Claire he'd read about was still lurking around inside there somewhere. "I didn't mean to offend. I just have this annoying habit of saying what's on my mind."

One brow, a shade darker then her hair, arched slightly higher than the other. "They're in the same family, you know."

"Your eyes?"

"Mold and moss. They're in the fungus family."

"I didn't realize that," he said. "I'm afraid I don't know much about plants."

"Fungi aren't plants. They're heterotrophs."

He nodded, even though he didn't have the slightest clue what she was talking about. "I didn't realize that."

"Do know what a heterotroph is?" There was a playfulness to her tone, a hint of amusement in her eyes. She was calling his bluff.

He shrugged. "I haven't the foggiest."

"Unlike a plant, heterotrophs don't fix their own carbon through photosynthesis. They use carbon fixed by other organisms for metabolism." She paused for a second, then asked, "Do you know what that means?"

Not a clue, but he found her fascination nonetheless. He shook his head.

"Fungi are thought to be more closely related to animals than plants."

He folded his arms across his chest. "You're different than I expected."

She took a sip of her latte, eyes never leaving his face, and said bluntly, "I take it to mean you've heard things about me."

The woman was a puzzle. Awkward and demure one moment, sharp and direct the next.

"Here and there," he admitted.

"That girl doesn't exist anymore."

In his experience, people could change all they liked on the outside, but the inside part was much harder to renovate. Whoever she was, he found her absolutely fascinating.

He glanced at his watch, disappointed to see that he had to leave if he planned to get to work on time. He would very much like to continue this conversation. He liked Claire Mackenzie, and he had the sense the feeling was mutual. "On that note, I'm afraid I have to get to work."

He downed the last of his coffee and pulled himself to his feet, offering a hand for her to shake. As she clasped it, the warmth of her hand curling around his own, he felt it again. That zap of awareness. The eerie feeling of familiarity.

And he could tell, by the way she hesitated a second before tugging her hand free, by the perplexed look in her eyes, that she felt it, too.

"It was a pleasure talking to you, Ms. Mackenzie."

"Call me Claire," she said. "And if you really don't mind, I think I will sit in on rehearsal."

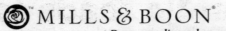

Romantic reads to
Need, Want

...International affairs, seduction and passion guaranteed
10 brand-new books available every month

Pure romance, pure emotion
6 brand-new books available every month

Pulse-raising romance – heart-racing medical drama
6 brand-new books available every month

From Regency England to Ancient Rome, rich, vivid and passionate romance...
6 brand-new books available every month

Scorching hot sexy reads...
4 brand-new books available every month

MILLS & BOON
Pure reading pleasure

M&B/GENERIC RS2 a

LOOK OUT...

...for this month's special product offer.
It can be found in the envelope containing
your invoice.

**Special offers are exclusively for
Reader Service™ members.**

You will benefit from:

- Free books & discounts
- Free gifts
- Free delivery to your door
- No purchase obligation – 14 day trial
- Free prize draws

THE LIST IS ENDLESS!!

***So what are you waiting for —
take a look NOW!***

DM/OFFER